LISA

LIPMAN

THE
TENTH
MONTH

A Novel by

LAURA Z. HOBSON

SIMON AND SCHUSTER

New York

Again
to Mike and Chris
and now to Sarah

THE TENTH MONTH

CHAPTER ONE

The moment was to stand out forever in her memory. There she stood, alone and naked, thinking of nothing except the minutiae of the bath, toweling herself dry, gazing idly about the warm steamy room, then at her image in the long panel of mirror in the closed door.

Her breasts looked fuller. She had gained no weight, but her breasts, always small, looked fuller. Below her navel, there was the faintest globe of fullness too.

She stood motionless, staring. Had the years of longing fused into some betraying lens of illusion? Or could it be at last the moment she had imagined so many thousand times?

She stepped closer to the mirror, looking away for an instant, then suddenly back to her image as if to trap something before it could escape. The same impression, of a most hesitant distension, tentative, a curving outward thrice over.

Oh God let it be true.

She stood, searching the glass. She saw the tight-muscled body of a girl, but she was forty. She saw the lifting spheres of a virgin's breasts but she had been married and divorced. She had never remarried and if this were true—oh let it be true.

She moved a step closer to the mirror but this time she looked only at her face, her eyes, too eager now to be her ordinary brown eyes, at her mouth, compressed now as if to clamp down on any word of pleading, and therefore not her ordinary mouth either. Then swiftly she looked again at her body and suddenly laughed aloud, as a child laughs.

She flung her arms wide and the towel billowed out behind her like a sail caught by a gusty wind.

Don't. It'll probably be all over by morning.

She let the towel drop and went to her telephone. It was late afternoon and Dr. Jesskin would not be there, but his two nurses knew her and when she said, "This is Theodora Gray, could I possibly see the doctor tomorrow morning?" she was given an appointment at nine thirty.

"I'm working you in," Miss Mack said, "so if you could get here a few minutes ahead?"

"Of course I will. And thanks."

She held on to the crossbar of the telephone after she had put it into its cradle, gripping it as if at a lever to propel herself into action. What she wanted to do was lie still, silent, commanding her mind not to leap ahead, yet yielding to her mind's rebellion, and for a while go on regarding this possibility as if it were already fact.

But it was nearly six and she was being called for in half an hour, for dinner and then a concert. She had been looking forward to the evening with eagerness, that special insistent eagerness that came from extended periods of loneliness. Loneliness came only at long intervals, but then it lasted a long interval too, like the changing of the seasons, never sudden, never over in a day or a week. There was a foreboding first, of the advent of another spell, like the lowering of a sky as the barometer drops and the winds gather, and then when the sun went, there was the knowledge that the bleak darkness would remain and remain and remain.

She hid these bad times, with success now, unlike the first year after her divorce when she could not possibly have fooled anybody, but the effort was still depleting and destructive and she always emerged as if from an illness, unsure of herself, except for her work, wary, yet eager for new people, for all people. Friendships that she had let lapse were picked up again, and new friendships welcomed with a readiness she for one knew was excessive.

She had accepted a date for the concert from a man she scarcely knew—had that alacrity seemed excessive? She had met him only the week before, at Celia's, and because it was there, it was easy to get talking about music; she had thought he might be involved professionally with music as Celia and Marshall Duke were, but he turned out to be a lawyer. His name was Matthew Poole; he called himself Matthew, not Matt. She liked the name that way, uncondensed. Her own name uncondensed was pretentious; Dori made it usable.

She still signed her pieces *Theodora V. Gray*, and though she was not one of the big names in the newspaper world, there was enough value in her by-line to make it foolish to consider changing it. *Dori Gray* in print would look cozy or cute or chic like *Suzy Knickerbocker* and her special pieces were not even remotely related to the cute or chic nonsense so many editors parceled off as the special province of their women writers. She had never considered going back to her maiden name ("I'll decide what to do about my name when I marry again") and by the time she began to see that she wasn't one of those women who remarry easily after a divorce, so much equity had been put into the name Gray by her own effort that she felt she had earned her own title to it.

"Haven't I just read something of yours?" Matthew Poole had asked when Celia introduced them. "In a magazine?"

"The Spock piece. I don't often do anything political."

"That's the one." Suddenly he added, "'Dr. Spock Brings Us Up Short.'"

"You remembered the title."

"Half my cases right now are conscientious objectors."

"Oh good."

She always felt drawn to, and safer with, people who were what was so scornfully called "liberal" these days by

3

the extreme left. She was used to the scorn of the extreme right, but this new scorn was harsher. She had never been very good at talking politics; she got furious at the camouflaged racists who were such devotees of law and order, and at the black-power toughs who talked so glibly about shooting whitey, and at the doctrinaire Communists who went livid over free speech in New York or Washington but remained sublimely untroubled by jailing or shooting of dissenters in Havana or Moscow or Peking.

Matthew Poole had shown himself more controlled when they had talked of these things. It was odd that she could remember this part of their talk that day at Celia's but not how they had got around to the concert. She was glad he was a lawyer and not a writer or editor or newspaperman. She always liked meeting people not connected, however tangentially, with deadlines and early editions and news-breaks. The Press—capital T, capital P—was an ingrown world where you were too close too often to the same people, covering the same stories, eating in the same restaurants near the paper, falling in love with the same men in a kind of inky incestuous turn and turn-about. She had from the first made it a point never to get involved with any of them; not once until last year, during the endless newspaper strike that had finally killed off her paper and made her for months, as Dick had said, "a press orphan"—

For the first time since the mirror she thought of Dick. Dick Towson. If this were true, what would Dick do? How would he take it, what would he say, what would he feel? They had been drifting apart, without rebuke and without misery, amiable toward each other as they had been before he left on his assignment in Vietnam, and though she had felt the same apprehension anybody would feel about his going into the danger of battle-reporting, she had almost welcomed the trip, as he probably also had, as a most tactful *Finis* to their dwindling affair.

"By Dick Towson." It was a by-line known in dozens of newspapers the country over, the by-line of a first-rate

4

reporter with a brisk, vivid style. If it was by Dick Towson, it would never be dull.

She glanced toward the open door of the bathroom, the blank mirror now reflecting only the edge of the tub and a strip of flowered wallpaper above it.

Unexpectedly she laughed again. If it were true, it would be "by Dick Towson."

On her dresser a small clock chinked six times and she jumped up, reaching for her underthings. As she drew her thin girdle up over her knees she suddenly stopped and, hobbled as she was, crossed the room to her low dresser. The beveled glass cut her off at mid-thigh, but above, embedded within the jut of her hipbones, was again that tentative orbing.

*   *   *

The concert turned into background music for her thinking, which meant that as a concert it was a failure. Usually she listened to music as she read a book, note for note, as it was word for word on a page, skipping nothing, her mind never wandering. But tonight there was no stillness in her for listening, nothing passive and receiving, though it was good to be there and good to be there with Matthew Poole.

At dinner he had talked of himself and his family for the first time, of his two teen-age children, Hildy and Johnny, whom he spoke of with a pleased satisfaction as if they were good children to have, and of his wife Joan, elliptically and briefly as if there were some disaster there that had best go untold. And then he had turned the talk to her, putting the inevitable questions, not trying to sound casual as he did so, not trying to disguise them as small talk.

"I know you're divorced," he had said. "But I didn't want to ask around about whether you're tied up emotionally as of now, or reasonably uninvolved."

She was glad he hadn't tried to make it sound offhand. This sort of question never was. But what a time for it! What a time for her to get interested in somebody new. Sitting here, watching the baton, focusing on it as if its tip

5

were the one solid point in a light swarm of fever and un-reality, she half wished he hadn't been at Celia's last week. What a time! Tomorrow morning would be only the first step, a quick examination and then waiting for the lab reports. But she would be saying the words aloud to Dr. Jesskin, not just hearing them in her own mind, but really saying them out into the air: I think I am pregnant.

"Reasonably uninvolved," she had answered Matthew at the table, and had gone on to say too much about herself, about how she seemed to go through awfully long stretches of *uninvolved*, like some vexing stubborn anemia, how irritated she was at times to be making so little use of her so-called freedom, how she sometimes swore she was going to turn promiscuous and have affair after affair after affair.

"But?"

She could still hear his amused "but." Now she glanced at him quickly and then back to the orchestra. He was absorbed in his listening, eyelids half lowered though not music-lover shut, his whole look one of repose and pleasure. She understood that; but tonight, for her, was something new. She tried again to listen as she always listened but the phrase "I think I am pregnant" went on repeating itself, a soft pedal-point against which the flow of sound went streaming by, rhythmic, mobile and somehow kind.

* * *

In the morning she was ten minutes early and the first patient had not yet arrived. "Then I might as well sneak you in ahead," Miss Mack said, as if she understood very well that this was no routine visit, no dutiful checkup. She opened the office door, said to the doctor, "Since Mrs. Reeves is late again," and withdrew instantly. She always remained in the examining room, with an obviousness that had always amused Dori. As if without this starchy and omnipresent chaperon no female patient could feel safe in the presence of Dr. Cornelius Jesskin. He was already preoccupied as she entered his office, reading his own notations in the folder opened and spread before him on his desk. She recognized it without looking at its slightly worn tab that would say Mrs. A. Gray, with the A crossed out and a T written in above it. Its last entries were over two years old; she had even been neglecting the annual Pap test.

The doctor had motioned her to the chair beside him and she waited until he looked up at last from his notes. Then in a rush she said, "Oh, Dr. Jesskin, it seems to me, yesterday I was having a bath and I—I think I may be pregnant. I think my breasts are a little different, and I began to think —I realized I might have skipped a period again. Do you remember when I began to be irregular about my periods? And then—"

"Just a moment," he said. "Suppose you start at the beginning, and tell me." He was looking at her carefully and she thought, He has to stay neutral, and then, making herself speak slowly, sounding almost docile, she began her recital once more.

He fingered the pen in his hand as he listened, not using it to jot down any note of what she said. His face wore no expression except his usual one of concerned interest, an intentness that shut out every other importance in the world except the one importance brought in by his patient. When Dori ended, he said, "I'll have a look at you soon, but tell me again when your skipped period, if you did skip, when it should have started."

He began to write and she gave him dates but again broke off and spoke in a rush. "Don't you remember the first time I skipped? You said it wasn't usual at that age, but that it did happen, and might again."

He searched his notes. "That would have been about when?"

"Two years ago. I was thirty-eight. In the spring, April."

He was nodding now, reading his minute, perfectly legible writing. She had gone to him then only because she was trained to go to doctors when the inexplicable showed itself, and it was inexplicable enough at thirty-eight to have no period for five weeks. "Early menopause," she had

7

joked to herself, but might it not be some symptom of—of what? A tumor, a cyst, the first fearful sign of malignancy. You didn't ignore it; you went to your doctor and faced it fast. That time there had been not even a stir of hope that it might be this; it had been one of the interminable stretches of total aloneness.

"Yes," Dr. Jesskin said, looking up from the folder. "You then returned to being regular. 'More or less' is the way you put it. You reported in by phone for four periods, then stopped calling in."

Suddenly tense she said, "You aren't going to tell me this may be just another skipped period?"

"I am not going to tell you anything as yet, Mrs. Gray. After I examine you, we will arrange for laboratory reports. But even before that, I think I should remind you of something you already know—we must remember it now—the possibility of pseudopregnancy. We see it, not very often, but enough to have to consider it. The menstrual break, the swelling of the breasts, even engorgement of the uterus. You know of such cases, do you not?"

Like a thin coating of sleet, his speech constricted and chilled her. "You told me, that other time."

He tapped the old-fashioned buzzer beside the phone and at once Miss Mack appeared.

"Mrs. Reeves is here now," she said.

"I'll see Mrs. Gray first."

Miss Mack ushered Dori into the examining room and indicated the curtained alcove where she was to undress. "He never likes it when patients are late," Miss Mack said fussily, "and this one always is. He wants to teach her a lesson."

That's not why, Dori thought. He also wonders if it could be true. She stripped quickly, not hearing Miss Mack's friendly babble, and then stepped back into the examining room. Again the table, she thought, again the stirrups, again the sheets draped so carefully over your raised knees as if it were immodest to let a gynecologist see your knees or thighs but sobriety itself to open the core of your body

8

to him. The idiocy of the rules. Miss Mack always staying right through, just to *be* there.

Her heart began to pound. It was a new sensation, disagreeable and heavy. I'm afraid, she thought. Through the closed door she could hear the doctor speaking, on the telephone probably, leisurely, contained, the same Dr. Jesskin he always was. Suddenly she remembered her very first visit to a gynecologist, long before she had heard of Dr. Jesskin. She was afraid then too, but in a different way, the orthodox way. She was twenty-two, then, and she and Tony had just been married. Less than two months later, she missed her period. She was stupefied with unwillingness, with unreadiness. They hadn't even talked of children except as a vague possibility in the future; she was not ready to stop being a girl, to stop being the young bride, the girl reporter on the paper. When she was certain she was pregnant, she told Tony. He was unwilling too. "We could stop it," he said. Filled with relief, she cried, "Oh, let's, till next year."

And next year had flown, and another and another and by the time she had sought out Dr. Jesskin, a specialist in sterility problems, had told him her history, she had faltered, "So you see I'm not sterile, Doctor, I'm not barren, I mean I wasn't, but this is the sixth year of our marriage and we've begun to be terribly afraid we can't ever have children."

She was not sterile. She was not barren. She had been injured by the abortion, Dr. Jesskin's examinations and tests had finally revealed, the slow tests, the careful tests, some painful, like insufflation to see if the Fallopian tubes were blocked or still open, others routine. She had been too harshly curetted; now she could not sustain a pregnancy. "I might be getting pregnant every month," she had explained to Tony, "but the ovum can't get embedded—it's like clinging to a wall of paper."

But this was reparable, the doctor had said, this damage that need never have happened, though the repairing would be slow, and progress for a long time indiscernible and unprovable. "You will bear a child someday, I think," Dr. Jess-

9

kin had said, and she had trusted him and had been faithful with her visits, never missing one for two full years, sharing in his patience, sharing in his confidence when he said at last, "Don't count on this, Mrs. Gray, but this might be your year, it might be. The uterine lining is getting back to normal."

But before another week of that year was out, Tony was gone and everything they had tried for was gone too. Later —she couldn't remember how much later—she had gone to Dr. Jesskin once again, and told him of her divorce. She promised to resume her treatments soon, knowing that if she stopped for good there would be retrogression, a loss of everything gained these two full years, a defeat forever. But even as she spoke, she wept uncontrollably, and Dr. Jesskin had counseled her not to commit herself as yet to any program, that shock and grief in themselves were often enough to upset all the body's chemistries and powers.

"But if I stop, I'll have lost my last chance."

She had made one appointment but when the day came she could not bear the going, could not stand the continuing of a purpose which now was off in the distance of "when you marry again." To marry at thirty was not as easy as it had been at twenty-two; her needs had taken on shape and firmness; she could no longer live in a vague happy cloud of girlish responses to a man because he danced well or because he took you to all the smart places. And by thirty-five, by forty—

Suddenly Dr. Jesskin opened his office door behind her. She lay inert; unafraid; simply waiting. Miss Mack reappeared, offered him a small tray with instruments and the examination began. It proceeded in complete silence, as always in the past, and as always, Dr. Jesskin's expression was one of total absorption. When the examination was over, he asked Dori to sit up at the side of the table, her legs dangling, and Miss Mack quickly rearranged her drapings, over her shoulders, scooped low over her navel, revealing only her breasts. As the doctor began the careful palping and prodding, Dori thought wildly, It's like the annual check for cancer—he never says anything then either.

"Would you please stand now?"

She slid off the table, with Miss Mack swiftly redraping her once more, this time leaving her torso bare, but gathering the white folds tightly around her hips into a bunched rosette for Dori to clutch to herself, an elaborate and coiled fig leaf.

It's so stupid, she thought; why can't I just be naked? The words were angry, but she could not have said them aloud. Dr. Jesskin was looking at her in profile, below her navel, up to her breasts, below again, and then he moved around to see her full on.

On his face was that familiar expression, absorption, nothing else. "When you are dressed," he finally said, "I will see you again in the office." He nodded, almost formally, and she hurried to the alcove and into her clothes. As she knocked and opened his office door a few minutes later, he dropped his pen on the page before him—it was still her folder—and said, "Well, my dear girl," and before she could interpret the words or the half-permissive tone of them, he added, "there is no way to be sure, as I said, until the tests are complete." She sat down, silent. "But it does seem, there is some slight evidence of change." Before she could speak, he raised his index finger an inch or two, a polite, cautionary inch or two, in renewal of what he had asked her to remember. "Some slight change, not only the apparent enlargement which you reported, but also perhaps a change in the cervix. It is out of the question to be certain, so early, but a change suggests itself, I must say."

"There is at least a possibility that I'm pregnant?"

"I must not answer in any way until the reports are in. I'll have the Drav Index done, which is faster, but also the A-Z test, totally conclusive."

"How long do they take? Could you tell them to hurry?"

"They always hurry, on pregnancy tests." He stood up and she did too. "But the A-Z won't be in until the day after tomorrow."

11

"Two whole days? Till Thursday?"

Suddenly he lost his look of absorption and controlled care; he put his hand on her arm and said, "You must try not to think about it."

She laughed, at him, at his suggestion, and said, "Oh, thank you, Dr. Jesskin."

*   *   *

Try not to think about it indeed. She stopped at a drugstore counter for toast and coffee and thought, Thank God for Martha Litton, and glanced at her watch. She was to be at Miss Litton's at eleven for the interview that had been so difficult to set up, now that Miss Litton's third comedy, *Time and a Half*, was a greater smash than her first two, and though she never worked at deadline heat for these special pieces, she could plunge along on this one for the entire day, and into the evening. She often did her best work in the evening.

Don't think about it. She walked to Miss Litton's apartment quickly, and was again too early, and walked around the block several times before going up. From Miss Litton's testy greeting—"I tried to reach you this morning but you were out. It's turned into the worst sort of time for an interview"—she knew she was in for a difficult session. Thank God for that too.

She rarely took notes beyond particularities of spellings and dates, but today she did, using not a notebook but copy paper folded and propped against her purse. Twice in the first minutes she had to say, "Sorry, could you tell me that again?" and twice Miss Litton repeated what she had said, showing an impatience that it should be necessary.

It was all useless stuff, the official gabble of publicity releases, but Dori hid that estimate of it. At the first chance she said, "Could we go back *before* your first play? You were born in Philadelphia, I know—"

"*Ab ovo?*" Miss Litton said primly, but began nevertheless to talk of her childhood, and for the first time Dori listened without bothering with her folded copy paper. Here it is, she thought, the only kind of thing that ever explains anybody, if you can ever get at it.

The interview went on for an hour and when Dori left she had the first paragraph of her piece clear in her mind. She would go straight to the typewriter and stay with it and not let herself think, and though she rather thoroughly disliked the current Martha Litton for her self-love and self-praise, she ought to be able to use that dislike judiciously and write something that had insight and some feeling.

"Anything by Dori Gray will have warmth," her editor at the paper had once said in her presence, "sometimes enough to singe your eyebrows."

It must be true; enough people had said so by now, enough letters had told her so. It wasn't a trick; it must come through her effort always to see into, to look for character instead of characteristic. She was never facile and easy with a phrase anyhow; that was what had ruined her the one time she had tried out for a panel show on television, that and the fact that she had gone stiff with self-consciousness, what with the whole production staff and the other panelists, experienced charmers all, waiting hopefully for some clever little mot.

Yet the light turn of phrase came readily when she was with one congenial person. Dick Towson always laughed when they were together, and had even asked why she didn't try writing light pieces or a humor column in some women's magazine. He was the one with the light touch, really; perhaps that was why he brought it out in her when they were together. If he were here right now she would probably burst out with her news; she was always apt to tell things to anybody close to her, close in the special closeness that came only with making love over a long period of time. D. H. Lawrence had talked in Lady Chatterley of the deep peace that came from steady lovemaking, only he had used the word, the lovely thick Anglo-Saxon word which she liked and approved of in theory but could not easily say, despite the uninhibited language of 1967.

But Lawrence was right; there was a peacefulness and

13

closeness from a continuing sexuality, if it was satisfying and solid for both, and she and Dick had known that closeness and knew it still, even though they also knew, each of them and without verbalizing it, that they were coming to the end. Paradox, paradox. She had never ended anything with hatred and blame, except after Tony, and she still felt warm toward Dick and linked with him.

Linked. A surge of feeling surprised her, for his share in what had happened—*it has happened, the reports will say yes*—a leap of grateful love, the best sort, for it asked nothing. Suddenly he seemed newly appealing; she remembered how exciting it had been, almost a year and a half ago, how flattering, that he should be demanding her time, her emotion, her body, when he could have chosen almost any younger or prettier girl. That first time they were in the apartment alone, she had said something about those possible other girls, and he had suddenly and roughly taken her hand and held it against himself and said, "But you're the one does this," and watched her as she felt the bulk of him rising to her palm, arrogant and sure.

They had gone to bed that night and it had been right and good and equal for them both, and there were none of the insufferable little coynesses and uncertainties and she had known she would see him whenever he was in New York and not off on an assignment. "Is it all right, about your family?" she had asked once, and he had shut her off, not brusquely, but with a decisiveness that removed all responsibility from her, and any need for guilt. "I've got a damn good marriage in all the usual twenty-five-years-of-it ways, steady, and no surprises, and all the kids know Dad's a newspaperman who's away half the time but won't ever go for good, and nobody's got any kick coming, so it's okay all around and you and I don't ever have to worry about it."

They had never worried about it. At the beginning he would telephone her late at night when he was covering some story in London or Washington or Tel Aviv, but though he never labored the point, she knew that he also called his

14

wife from those same places and that overseas phone calls were almost matter-of-fact to his four children.

At the beginning he would come straight to her from Kennedy Airport when he returned; for the past few months, though, he often went home instead and came to her the next day or perhaps the day after. It was one of the small signals of the passing of time, the passing of the first heat and press and gluttony of a new affair, and she saw it for what it was with a strange willingness, a wisdom she did not know she possessed but which she welcomed with a faint pleasure as if she were awarding herself the mildest of accolades for avoiding that most dreaded feminine failing, being too demanding.

Yet at this moment, if he were to phone and say he was just in from his assignment, impossible since he was off in that fierce part of the world, if he were by some fluke to phone and say, "Towson here, I'm at Kennedy, can I come over?"—

She glanced at the telephone as if it actually had rung and suddenly rose from the typewriter. She hadn't gone beyond the first paragraph of the piece on Martha Litton; she had let her mind wander, undisciplined and wanton, because the first major problem she would have when all the reports were in would be centered in Dick Towson and his right to know or her decent obligation not to let him know.

Suddenly another one of Dick's pronouncements popped into her mind, this also spoken with that brusque decisiveness that lifted all responsibility from her. "Either of us can want out and all holds by the other barred—yes?" She had laughed at the adroitness and thought how exactly his mood had suited hers. As for this kind of hold, it was not only barred but unthinkable.

She began to prowl restlessly around the room. Anyway, she thought, I don't have to decide now. He may be there for months. I'm going to take this just as it happens, one day at a time.

She went back to the typewriter and wrote hard for another paragraph and then once again pushed back from her

15

desk and began to move about. It was a pretty room, her bedroom and study combined, a room she felt easy in when she was alone, and a little proud of when she was not alone.

Suddenly she wished she were not alone. Remembering that first night with Dick had made her remember how marvelous it was to be made love to, how normal and sweet and good she always felt. She wished she were newly in love, newly in bed, for the first time with somebody new, caught in that fresh wild passion of beginnings, where you could never stop to think of any future—

The wrong moment for ruling out futures, she thought wryly. Again she went to her typewriter; another paragraph spurted from the keys and then the telephone rang. It was a shrill loud bell which she had often resolved to ask the phone company to mute or diminish and the sound of it scarred her mood. She lifted the receiver and heard Matthew Poole say "Hello?" and her heart lifted too.

"I thought you were going to Boston," she greeted him.

"I'm in Boston."

"Calling me from Boston?"

He laughed. "Long distance—it's a new invention."

"I've heard."

"I'm taking the five o'clock shuttle back," he said, "and I wondered if you'd have dinner with me."

"Tonight?"

"That's why I'm using the new invention."

"I'm not being too bright, am I?" She hesitated. "I was going to finish writing an interview I'm doing."

"That sounds disciplined and worthwhile. Don't be. Say you will have dinner with me."

"I'd love to. I'm in no mood to be disciplined and worthwhile."

"Good. Can I come by at about six thirty? And you tell me where to take you for dinner?"

"I'll give you a drink while I decide."

As she hung up she thought, I oughtn't to. Until I know for sure, I ought not to see him even once more. Suppose he—but he won't. He's not the sudden lover like Dick. And

16

if he is, I'm not. But my God, there I go. If it's not hindsight-thinking, devious and destructive, it's forward-projection, equally dangerous.

She moved toward her desk and boredom invaded her. Who cared about Martha Litton and her self-importance and vanity and mannerisms? There were days for working and days for restlessness and God knew this was a restless one. She went to the kitchen to ask Nellie to put out ice cubes and a few things to have with their drinks.

"I could stay on if you want," Nellie offered in a dubious tone. She always sounded dubious, a rather surly Swedish girl who arrived daily at three and left at five except by special arrangement.

"Never mind, thanks. We're going out."

The kitchen window suddenly streaked across with rain and Dori was dismayed. The afternoon sky had gone purple-gray and wind was whistling around the corner of the building. His plane would be stormbound or detoured to Washington or Richmond and the whole thing would be off. The telephone would ring again and he would explain and ask if they could make it another time.

They could but it would be different. Right now was the time, right now when she should be saying no; this mood was the mood, this restlessness the yeast that was rising—all part of the wild impossible present, with those technicians off in an unknown laboratory, starting their tests to find an answer they didn't care about one way or another.

She went back to her own room and stared out at the storm. The sky darkened further; streetlights came on and people raced along the edges of buildings, tenting sopping newspaper over their heads. She watched them minutely as if they were terribly important to her, as if they were her dearest friends suddenly attacked and hurrying toward her for safety. What made Matthew Poole so important, so suddenly important? Last night's dinner and concert added little to what she actually knew about him, but he somehow had revealed himself more freely; there had been about him a pleased and contented air that compelled attention, as

17

if he were not often happy. She hadn't seen it except during the music, but now she realized that it had been there through all of the evening. He had taken her home and come up for a nightcap and talked again about the boy he was going to defend as a conscientious objector; he talked with the calm tone of a man who knew she agreed with him, and an inordinate pride had ballooned in her for the Spock piece that had told him so. And then, with no word of whether they were to see each other even once more, he had said good-night and left, without so much as an extra pressure of her hand.

Now this. She turned abruptly from the window and went to work. This time she wrote without pause, telling herself it was only first draft anyway and better than hanging around waiting for time to get itself spent. When she wrote this way, without pause or question, she slid the spacing lever to position 3, so that she was doing triple-spaced pages, and they flew by. Time enough to improve them tomorrow. Or, if the storm went furiously on, this evening, when there would be nothing else. A fine lonely evening in the home.

Finally she bathed and dressed, and thought the rain and wind had abated, and could not be sure, and then a bell rang and it was not the shrill telephone but the front door.

She opened it and stood aside, letting him pass by her into the square little hallway, each saying hello as if they were constrained.

"Was it a rough flight?"

"Not to speak of."

"I thought—I always think everything is grounded if it rains. What can I give you for a drink?"

She started for the living room and he followed but he did not answer. At the small chest that served as a bar she turned to him questioningly. He was watching her with what looked like sternness; his mouth was drawn as if in disapproval, his eyebrows drawn as if in anger. Suddenly he put both his hands on her shoulders and said, "I cannot stop thinking of you," and drew her toward him, his face

18

seeking hers, but his mouth not. "It's been years since any-body's mattered this much."

She heard her breath as it was sharply drawn inward at his words, felt the weaving churning move of passion roiling, and thought, But I mustn't, not now, not now of all times. He turned his head to kiss her, and her breath sucked inward again and something wavered and fell within her and she was invaded all at once by the lovely helplessness of acquiescence.

Suddenly she pushed hard away from him, wheeling away, saying lightly, "Something to drink," lightly, falsely, the social tone she hated in others. "Martini? Or Scotch on the?"

"Scotch, please." He watched her put two cubes into a glass and then pour the Scotch, accepting the drink in silence when she offered it, waiting until she prepared one for herself. Then he said, without emphasis, "Why did you suddenly decide no?"

"I didn't decide. I just had to *not* go on."

"There was one moment when you suddenly stopped. Up to then you were as moved as I was."

"I was," she said, "oh, I was."

He waited but she did not continue. She sat down on the sofa and in a moment he sat down too, well away from her. "Last night you said you were reasonably uninvolved," he said finally. "Does it turn out you're not as uninvolved as you thought?"

She shook her head in denial.

"But if that *is* it, I'll wait around until you are."

"It's not being in love with somebody. It's something else. I don't think I can talk about it. For now anyway."

"Then don't. You needn't ever."

She turned quickly away and set her drink on the coffee table. Even his voice stirred her, the negation in it now. Just this once, she thought. Give in; don't make up rules about what you should do, what you shouldn't, when you should, when you shouldn't. Without knowing she was going to, she put her hand out behind her, reaching toward him. In another moment she was in his arms and there on the sofa, like two fumbling adolescents, they made love.

* * *

They stayed together for all of the next day, and through a second night, in the discovery and rediscovery of passion each felt was deeper and more meaningful than all the one-time passion of first youth. They talked, they told each other as much of autobiography and truth as they could tell, and they withheld far more than either knew, the censors at their lips unsuspected by either one.

"I'll be more expansive about this someday," Matthew said once when he was talking of his marriage and of his wife. "I'm difficult to live with, I guess."

"Who isn't?"

"Marriage is difficult, is what you're saying."

"It also has its good things."

He nodded and seemed to be deciding what those were but he did not speak. They could sit silent and remain at ease; already they had discovered this about each other. The truncated form of their self-revelation was, they each understood, only for the present, for this newness which was still so enveloping that though they were not inhibited in seeking each other's bodies, they still were restrained, as strangers might be restrained, from too ready an outpouring of revelation involving others.

It's one difference between being a girl and being older, Dori thought in the middle of a silence after she had swiftly told him of the sudden ending of her life with Tony. When you're older you summarize, you don't lavish detail on every scene, even the huge ones; there's been too much piled up by the time you're forty. She could remember the readiness with which she would tell everything there was to tell about herself when she had gone out with her first dates, tell about herself as a girl at school, at college, tell of her first experiences with boys. When she met Tony, they had sat for hours in some booth or at some table in one of his favorite restaurants, each telling the other "everything" in the first generosities and trusts of new love, a new love that was going to last forever. Tony had been equally ready to tell everything about himself, details of his first dates, his first discovery of sleeping with a girl—a woman, twenty years older and kind and gentle, with a healthy attitude toward sex so that he was at his best with sex, never furtive, never ashamed, and had in turn doubtless trained her to be the same, brought her up to be the same, as it were, since he had been her first lover.

But now with Matthew, narrative was synopsized as she went along. It was almost as if she were gliding rapidly over most of her marriage to tell of its abrupt ending, and even that she told in a hurried way as if she were recapitulating something he already knew, as if she were fearful lest she sound the stereotypic whining woman, the hurt and injured woman she would hate to be, and hate to be thought to be.

She fell silent then, remembering its ending and the aftermath with disbelief that it could have been so terrible. Through month after month she had been a creature in the positive and cunning control of a thing stronger and more skillful than she, an almost animate savage that could spring at her, direct her thoughts, her sleep, her instincts. For all those months, twenty, thirty, nearly forty months, her own will could beat back that savage only when she was actually working; in the first minute after she whirled the last page out of her typewriter, the other took over, the boss other, the controlling other, reminding her not of pain but of the happy hours they had had before he had left her for Hazel, reminding her of sweet and good evenings, of lovemaking that had gratified each of them and both of them.

Twenty, thirty, nearly forty months, and then somehow she had realized that she was what people called "over it," as if one ever were truly over one's first great wound, as if the fading scar tissue were not permanently part of one, livid no longer but toughly existing forever.

Sex had begun to be possible again, not love but sex. Quite suddenly she had stayed overnight with a man who made fun of her refusal—"You're afraid you might feel happy again"—and it had been a night of violent sexuality that she had violently responded to, suddenly restored to life and appetite.

She had seen the man a few times more, aware that for her it was loveless as it was for him, mindless, no memories or hopes or past or future, nothing but the throbbing wet wonderful rise and fall again and again.

Soon enough she had refused to see him and he had not believed that she meant it. "Why not? Who's going to get sore at you?" Nobody, she had agreed, and admitted that she ought to make better use of her free status, but she had gone on refusing, sinking again into the old unwanted and arid continence.

Why didn't she get married again, her friends had asked again and again. "You're so attractive and you can't really like living alone."

Nobody had understood that either and she had had no easy explanation. Hidden within her, doubtless, was the real answer; she had assured herself that she could reach down, find it, uproot it if she tried hard enough, if she needed to enough. But later, when searching for answers would no longer cause upheaval all over again.

But as time passed, her private creed had become, Let it be, leave it, don't touch, fragile. And now suddenly with Matthew, now in these two days and nights those wise admonitions no longer were necessary.

Now with Matthew—as she thought it, she touched his hair and closed her eyes in deepening intensity—she was finding again for the first time in all the lost long years the indescribable interweaving of sexual love and romantic love, both threaded through now with the gigantic new *perhaps* which those impersonal technicians off in some aseptic laboratory had already put their official negative or positive to, in some report that was surely in the mails at this very moment.

"No, we never had children," she had said in her swift account of her marriage. She did not say it airily as if it had never mattered but neither did she permit the tone or in-flection of some major sadness that would flag his attention. Later, if it were pronounced true tomorrow by Dr. Jesskin, she would decide whether to tell him and how to tell him. Already she wanted him to know that she was no benighted barren woman; already she found herself wondering whether this might change her in his mind from the desirable unattached woman he thought her into a—into a what? A problem? A shock? An untouchable?

Just for now, she kept telling herself. Just this couple of beautiful days. During the first evening he had telephoned his house, talked to his daughter, and the clear young voice of Hildy had sounded out to her across the room. "Are you still in Boston, Dad?" He had answered only "I won't be home until Thursday," and they had talked of other things. Her own telephone calls had been as free of explicit falsehood because nobody existed to whom she need tell or explain or alibi or dissemble. And she had thought, in extenuation she had not dreamed she needed, Otherwise I'd never never get through until Thursday morning with Dr. Jesskin. Now if something *is* wrong Thursday morning, now I could bear it.

To be hit by two such beginnings at one time! Almost it seemed that fate had sent Matthew to her now as a shield against the wildness of disappointment that might await her in the morning. And equally it seemed that this same fate was slyly asking her whether now she would still be over-joyed if the reports said yes, you are pregnant.

CHAPTER TWO

The telephone rang and her hand whipped toward it. Matthew had left at eight and she must have fallen asleep again. Asleep when this was Thursday?

"Good morning, Mrs. Gray." It was Dr. Jesskin. It was the first time he had ever called her himself.

"It's positive!" Her words seemed to jump at the telephone.

"Let's not talk by phone. Can you come in at eleven?"

"Of course I can. But you have to tell me—it *is* positive, isn't it?"

"Yes."

"Oh God."

Instantly everything else receded into the background, even Matthew. She was electrified by the core knowledge of that *positive* and yet was quieted by it too. A quiet seemed to flow through her veins and along her nerves, like the quiet shared after making love, completed, willing to put aside whatever required attention, saying "not now" to would-be interrupters: questions of work undone, of infidelity, of what weight and value their sudden lovemaking would prove to have in the days ahead.

Nothing else matters, she thought, her hands flying to her

hips, the fingers splaying out, their tips touching over her navel. Nothing else. Suddenly she doubted herself about Matthew. Had it been as real as it had seemed? Was it so irresistible because it would help get her through all the deliberate hours until Thursday morning?

She fled from that idea, but it was possible. She could not know now; now was dressing and getting over to Dr. Jesskin.

She thought of all the past years of Dr. Jesskin, all the visits, all the tests and treatments, the biopsies of uterine tissue to check on progress, the familiar steel speculum still warm from the gleaming sterilizer—it was curiously pleasant to remember, even, as she entered the waiting room this bright Thursday morning, suddenly new again, vivid, present, and yet strangely remote from her nerve centers where pain and envy could twinge, peaceful now as she glanced around at the other women waiting too.

All those years ago when she sat in this same waiting room, she had looked at the girls and women in their various stages of pregnancy, not with envy, but with a mute amazement that each of them could so easily accomplish what was so impossible for her.

Then, she used to avoid looking at Miss Mack or Miss Stein, the doctor's appointment secretary, both of whom knew all too well that she was one of his "other patients," who were there not because he was the obstetrician who would guide them through pregnancy and one happy day deliver them, but because he was also a "sterility specialist," a phrase he always quietly amended to "a specialist in so-called sterility."

I'm not sterile, I'm not barren. Dori could still hear her too earnest assurance to him on that first visit, as she had faltered through her recital, see him writing in her folder; it had held only a first page then.

Had he already added a notation this morning after the report had come in? Had he already written down the gist of what he was going to say to her today? And the questions he planned to ask? But she had no answers yet—except one.

Miss Mack signaled her, and ushered her directly into his office, closing the door with a soft snap behind her. Dr. Jesskin rose, silent, studying her as if she were a new patient whom he had never seen before.

"Oh, Dr. Jesskin, will you help me?"

She had rehearsed what she would say, but these were not the words she had ready. She had meant to thank him first for persistence and the rightness of his beliefs, and then only to speak of the present.

"Sit down," he said slowly, sitting down himself. "This is no time to hurry. That's why I said not to talk on the telephone." Before him was her folder, closed, but atop it was a single sheet of heavy stationery. He glanced at it and handed it to her.

She scarcely saw the letterhead of the laboratory or the half-dozen notations typed in at intervals, but the word *positive* leaped at her. Just seeing it there on the page added stature to it, made it more true, no longer a guess or a possibility, but a fact.

"May I keep this?" she asked, her voice shaking.

Unexpectedly he smiled, and she put the report into her purse. "So," he said slowly, "you are pregnant."

"Will you help me?"

"Are you sure what you will do?"

"Of course I'm sure."

He nodded but his face was expressionless—a routine look, one of interest and attention that he would give to any patient. Neutral, Dori thought, he's being neutral again, and an undefined disappointment invaded her. "Are you able to take me as a patient even though I haven't married again?" She was neutral too, determined to keep pleading or apology out of her voice.

"Let us see these dates again," he said as if he had not heard her, and opened the folder. He seemed to be preparing his thoughts, laying them out neatly, as his instruments were laid out neatly on the tray by Miss Mack.

"You had intercourse only once since your last period," he said simply, "and that was on October sixteenth. The first period you missed was due about November third. You may have missed a second, since today is December seventh."

"A date that will live in infamy," she said, smiling, but he only nodded.

"Usually we are uncertain about the precise date of intercourse and thus of conception, so to arrive at the most probable date of confinement we calculate backward three months from the onset of the last menstrual period, and then add seven days. But since you are sure of October sixteenth—"

"Quite sure. It was the date he was leaving for—"

He waved this aside as if he did not invite so personal a revelation. "In that case we can reckon forward two hundred and eighty days, which takes us to July twenty-third, nineteen sixty-eight. A few days earlier or later, but July twenty-third is our theoretical date." He was obviously reading from the page.

She drew in her breath. He had already put down the probable date: that simple act, that new notation in her twelve-year-old folder of struggle and frustration, suddenly was more convincing than a dozen laboratory reports.

"Are you able to take me, Dr. Jesskin, even though this will be what they call an illegitimate birth? It's not only that I am not married now but that I won't be. I don't want to fool you about that."

He closed the folder once more. "Why are you so sure? I do not wish to interrogate you, please understand."

"I do understand. I myself want to tell you. He—the man with whom I was having an affair—it was an affair, nothing more—we both knew all along that it was that, and we both knew it was ending."

"Now that you are pregnant, though?"

"I haven't told him. I don't know whether I should tell him. He's an awfully decent man, no scoundrel betraying me, and he assumed I was on the pill like everybody else until I told him once I wasn't because I couldn't get pregnant anyway."

His expression changed slightly; for an instant he looked gratified. "Has he, perhaps, the right to know?"

"I suppose it is a right, yes. But he's married and has four children, and we never talked of marriage, never. Anyway he's away now, abroad, so I can take enough time to think that out."

"Time, yes." He leaned toward her earnestly. "This is why I asked you to come in so we might talk, the way it is impossible to talk on a telephone. You haven't yet taken enough time to think of all the other matters you must think about."

"But I have. I've thought about everything."

"About everything as it is now, yes. But have you thought of six months from now when you will be big? Or a year from now when you will have a four-month-old baby? An adopted baby? A friend's baby? A relative's baby, after some fatal accident to the parents? You have to think through all these things, talk and discuss them, with whoever is the right person to discuss such matters with."

"Why, Doctor, I already know—"

"We think sometimes with our minds, at other times with our emotions, at other times only with our instincts. It is important now to give you enough time for all three thinkings, and I am going to ask you to go off and come back in two weeks for another visit." He saw her face change and added mildly, "Did you imagine I would then refer you to another doctor?" He touched the buzzer and as Miss Mack appeared, he said formally, "Please set up an appointment for Mrs. Gray for week after next." He nodded goodbye, and again Dori felt strangely disappointed.

*   *   *

All three thinkings. Only at rarest intervals did he slip into a foreignism that revealed his Scandinavian childhood, Danish, Swedish, whatever it was, but there always was a pleasing measured way he used language and occasionally a phrase that stayed with her.

All three thinkings. The mind, the emotions, the instincts.

But she had already engaged them all, she thought, and the results were final. I can't possibly conceive of changing my mind, even if I were to think for months instead of weeks.

I can't possibly conceive. That word—mysterious, powerful, ordinary, gigantic. I have conceived. I could never conceive, I did not conceive, but now I have conceived. What a conjugation for a woman of forty.

Think and discuss and consider. If Cele were in, she could go right over and, perhaps tonight, she would tell her brother Gene.

In the pale winter sunlight a glass telephone booth glinted at her from the corner of Madison and she opened her purse for a dime. Suddenly she felt an irrational impulse to call Tony and tell him. To telephone him this minute, though she had not spoken to him for ten years, call him right at his office and say, I told you I could, I always knew that someday it would be all right again as Dr. Jesskin said; it might have happened years ago but you ended that chance when you ended everything else. As quickly as the idea had come it fled. Tony? Why Tony at this late date? She stood contemplating the glass booth and remembered Tony's voice that last night, telling her he had been having an affair with Hazel for nearly a year.

"And letting me go right on with Dr. Jesskin?" she had cried out. "How could you, oh why didn't you make me stop trying? Letting me watch my ovulation dates? Making love to me on our special schedule? Oh God, how horrible, that you let me go right on."

She turned quickly away from the booth. Dignity, the straitjacket. She would no more make such a call than fling a rock through the nearest shopwindow. Yet she had been lost for a minute in a reverie of revenge that she had long thought done with forever.

Another booth beckoned to her from the next corner. What she really wanted to do was to tell everybody in the whole damn world. She wanted to phone the paper and tell them, she wanted to call all her friends who had always been so polite about her being childless, she wanted to wire Alan and Lucia in San Francisco and cable Ron in London.

Matthew. Matthew Poole.

Memory filled her: the sound of his voice, his touch, the feel of his hands, his body, the way he took charge, solicitous yet taking charge—that male authority that made it so wonderful to be female. The morning had falsified something; from the moment Dr. Jesskin phoned the word *positive*, she had pushed Matthew aside, and distrusted their two nights as an episode to speed time along. An episode? For her who had never been able to go in for a two-day episode, never in all the years?

It's more, she thought, and for the first time an unwillingness dragged at her. A few weeks was the longest they had. How many weeks? Two, three? At home, alone, naked? She saw again the way he had looked at her when she was at last naked before him, when they had left the sofa and the living room and gone decently to her bedroom, undressing, standing revealed to each other. She knew about her body, her one vanity perhaps, certainly her least wavering vanity.

He saw nothing of her "tentative orbing," knew nothing of its newness, its meaning. But in two or three weeks—how soon would she be too changed to let him see her?

Don't, she thought, don't think ahead. She went into the telephone booth and called Cele. "The most incredible thing has happened—can I come over?"

"Sure. The plumber's here. Give me twenty minutes."

"I'll walk."

*   *   *

She walked along trying to decide how to tell Cele—spring it at her? lead her slowly along and let her guess?—and she found herself thinking of a thousand other things instead. *Ab ovo*, Martha Litton had said so archly in the interview and she had put aside her notes, knowing that here it was at last, the only kind of thing that ever explained anybody. But did her own childhood explain her?

If so it eluded her, for when she tried to think back about

her own beginnings she found herself skipping from the story they always told—"I was born the night Lindy flew to Paris"—a story that struck her as sickening in its little-girl cuteness, skipping all the way to that line on the application blank for Wellesley when she had so hurt her mother and infuriated her father. "Episcopalian and/or Jewish," she had written, thinking herself so witty. What a row had ensued, what a frightful fracas with her father, one of the many and one of the worst. Though she was the youngest and the only girl and thus the supposed easy favorite with her father over her three brothers, she was in actuality a constant irritant to him from the moment she was turned New Dealer almost overnight by the simple act of going to a fine rich college where virtually the entire student body worshiped Franklin Delano Roosevelt and all his works. She who would tell anybody anything could barely admit to her new friends that her father hated labor, that he was part owner of a factory which fought unions, that he was rich and Republican and revolting about the poor.

She did admit it to her freshman roommate, and the sterling advice she received about "how to handle reactionary parents" was the first political solidarity she had ever experienced. That was Celia Kahn and that solidarity had never wavered thereafter. Perhaps that was why she felt that her real history began not with childhood but with Cele, although college too was like a prelude history, a preface, with the real Chapter One beginning four years later in the little furnished apartment Tony had on East Tenth, the first time she went there with him and knew that at last she was not going to pull back and say no. In 1948, three years after the end of war, she was still not only a virgin but a girl who had never much wanted to stop being a virgin. At twenty-one she had never really been in love. All through college, whenever she and Cele had one of their all-night talking bouts about boys and sex and how far you could go, she had never really had the kind of wild juicy episode that Cele so often told her about. "You're a slow starter, Dorr," Cele had once told her with great authority. "When it finally hits you, glory hallelujah."

It hadn't been glory hallelujah until Tony. Cele, then, was already married to Marshall Duke who was just starting out with a recording company and they quickly drifted into a related but quite different status. They were two married couples, whose separate, past loyalties confused and complicated the new demands of marriage. But soon enough she and Cele had rediscovered their older closeness and it had never again lost its private vitality. When Tony left, Cele saw her through those first empty weekends, the first summer and, the first Christmas. Later, when her life had become normal again, it was Cele who played matchmaker, a role she had always avoided. Whenever she or Marshall met an interesting new person, young or old, married or single, she had asked Dori over for drinks or dinner to meet him.

It was Cele who had first urged Dori to quit the newspaper grind for good, particularly since the journalistic debacle that had robbed her of the daily paper she had been with for fifteen years and put her on a rather amateurish, though well-meaning, weekly. "You've got some cash stashed away," Cele had said, "and you're rent-controlled, so you could ride out even a bad break in free-lancing."

"Thank God for that." Her fervent tone had sprung out of her proprietary sense about her four-room apartment, not inexpensive since it was two hundred a month, but protected from the wildly rising prices all about because it was in an old building, still under rent control. She cherished its large square rooms, its thick walls and doors, its windows looking down on a sunny quiet street, even its slightly worn look that told of ten years of her life in it.

But she was glad too that she did have some money, about thirteen thousand dollars, from money left by her father, minus death taxes, which had come in equal shares to her brothers and herself on their mother's death three years ago, minus further death taxes. And she had, more importantly perhaps, the equally solid fact that her special pieces had appeared in many magazines, little ones, big ones, occasionally in political ones and in the more literate women's magazines, though never in the ones that prided themselves on being "service magazines" as if they were roadside service stations for offering the most humdrum of provisions to keep you going. Nor did she write for the fashion magazines, with their satiny vocabularies, or for the one magazine most young writers looked upon as their one particular goal, *The New Yorker*. She had sold one piece to it when she had just begun to write, a caustic tale about a smart hostess, and when they bought it she had been as elated as she was supposed to be. But then she had tried other pieces in her more natural vein, with some feeling, with some emotion, even indignation, and these had been turned down—with kindly notes instead of printed rejection slips, telling her the editors still remembered the nice irony of "The Party" and hoped to see more of her work soon. She gave up submitting to *The New Yorker;* nice irony was not what gave her pleasure in writing, though she made a mental note to check that for sour grapes when enough time had elapsed for perspective's sake. She did so several times and each time decided it was true. "Keep your cool" was not her life slogan.

"You're too intense, Dori," her mother had once told her during the first year of her divorce. Then, before she could reply, her mother had added, "And thank God you are. It's the best, on balance."

"You blow your cool about this damn war," Dick Towson had said more recently.

"I have no cool. I hope I never do have."

Cool, coolth, cool it—the great desideratum of so many people in today's world. It was a living-in-ice, a living away from, never impassioned about right or wrong, never hot under the collar, never half sick with pain or pity. Keep your cool—a whole generation was chanting the slogan and they thought it was just an *in* phrase of the young, never seeing the paucity within their own lives that led them to this revealing admiration.

34

Not a *whole* generation. Not the young protesters on the marches and picket lines, not the boys refusing to kill, not the fathers and mothers who supported them, not the lawyers who defended them in court. Matthew—

She wouldn't tell Cele about Matthew. Not now. Not until she knew what it meant, what it would mean. Never had they confided to each other in the small tattling ways about men or marriage or sex, never since the half-bragging talk of college days. Cele did know about Dick Towson, vaguely, in large outline, and also knew that it was over or virtually over.

Poor Cele, she suddenly thought, she's so sure it will be at least a year before anything new starts up for me. She's probably all set for another one of my celibate years where she worries her head off about me.

"Mrs. Gray." It was Cele's maid, standing in the open kitchen door of the house to accept delivery of a parcel. "You going right past me like that?"

"Why, Minnie, I didn't know I was already here."

* * *

As she listened, Celia Duke's face went bright with pleasure. "Then what?" she would prompt if Dori paused in her recital. "What did Dr. Jesskin mean by that?" At the end she said, "So you have two weeks to think and discuss. Think and discuss what?" She looked around the room, searching, and they both laughed. Then she suddenly went over to Dori and hugged her. "It's so great, Dorr. Congratulations."

"Oh Cele. Dr. Jesskin was so professional and neutral, it's lovely to have somebody happy about it."

"He wanted to stay tentative so you could still change your mind in the next two weeks. It would still be safe two weeks from now—"

"To go back and say, 'After all I think I'll have an abortion'? He knows I'd never—God, it's nearly thirteen years since I first went to his office. No, it must have been something else; maybe he wondered if now I'd be getting married. Maybe he was thinking about his own position. What

35

do I really know about him? He might be the most church-going moralist alive."

"Want to bet?"

Dori apparently did not hear her. "Cele, when will I begin to show?"

"Let's see, this is the seventh week? Three more to New Year's, four in January—not till February at the earliest. He'll order you to watch your weight and stay thin anyway. They all do now."

"Can you remember when you began to look big?"

"Well, me." She looked down at herself. "I look a leetle bit, right now." She was wearing her usual stretch pants despite the ten pounds she had gained in the last few years. "But you're not weak-minded like me and you'll stay thin for ages."

"You mean I can keep on seeing people for another month, month and half?"

She said this so eagerly that Cele laughed. "What's wrong with you? Do you think you get pregnant one minute and start bulging the next? What about all the nineteenth-century novels where the dear servant girl goes unsuspected right up to the time she bears the child?"

"Hoopskirts. Crinolines."

"So now we've got tent dresses and shifts. Nobody will suspect for ages unless you tell them. Are you going to tell them at the paper?"

"Of course *not*."

"I didn't know. You didn't say."

"You mean—" She examined Cele's expression with sudden interest. "You mean, be the emancipated female and not keep it secret at all?"

"I didn't mean anything."

"Do you think I *should*?"

There was a pause and then Cele said slowly, "Look, Dorr, that's maybe the biggest of the three thinkings Dr. Jesskin meant. And it's got to be all yours. I would be ghastly to try to influence you."

"I guess I just took it for granted this wasn't something

36

you announced on a loudspeaker." She hesitated. "I was already thinking of where to go until it was over, what name I'd go under, how I'd get mail, all sorts of cloak-and-dagger stuff like that."

"Did you decide on a place?"

"Remember how crazy we were about the Grand Tetons? Not right in Jackson Hole where I'd run into people from the ranch, but some small town around in there."

"Wyoming? With your doctor in Manhattan?"

"I guess I overlooked that small matter of mileage. How often do I see Dr. Jesskin? Once a month?"

"About." She looked perplexed. "Isn't it weird, the things you forget that you were sure you never would forget? Me with three kids and I can't be sure. I guess once a month, to start with anyway."

"Apart from Dr. Jesskin, I wouldn't go that far because then I'd be cut off from the only people who know about it." She hesitated. "How will Marshall take it?"

"The way you and I take it." She spoke with vigor, but she looked uncertain. "Well, I don't know, at that. He can be pretty square at times. He didn't use to be, but he does seem to be changing."

"Lizzie starting to date. That would do it."

"The damn pill. He assumes Liz has a prescription on her own."

They exchanged looks that said, Men. "Maybe it would be better not to tell him for a while."

"I'd blow my top," Celia said, "if I couldn't tell somebody." As the words were spoken, as they became entities, alive, she drew back from them, disowning them. "There's the rub, isn't it?"

"I suppose."

"Who else is going to know?"

"Only Gene and Ellen."

"Oh."

"What does 'Oh' mean?"

"Nothing." *Oh* meant, Too bad Ellen has to be in on it, and

Dori knew that it meant that, so there was no point in elaborating. "What about Ron and Alan?"

"I hadn't even thought of them. Isn't that family love for you? If my mother were alive she would have worried but been happy and I think my brother Gene will be, but Ron and Alan?" She made a face.

Gene was the only one of her brothers whom she admired completely and for whom she felt a family warmth that was not briefly assumed at Christmas. He was older than the others, being fifty, and the only one who had always lived in New York, but her separateness from the other two was due to far more than geographical distance.

Ron, three years younger than Gene, had long ago settled in London where he was a partner in some fine neocolonial oil company operating in the Middle East, and Alan, who was only about a year older than she, was farthest away in everything that mattered to her. He lived in San Francisco with his wealthy wife Lucia, who seemed another species, come from another world, the world of the Social Register, of the D.A.R. and genealogy, and he seemed to enjoy that world with her, enjoy their status as Important People, going to the right dinner parties, belonging to the right clubs, sending their children to the right schools and camps. When it came to books and ideas, Lucia was close to being an ignoramus, and Alan didn't even seem to mind, which made him incomprehensible to Dori.

Alan was the only one of the four who had opted for the answer "Episcopalian" when the question "Religion?" turned up on a printed form; the other three wrote "None," meaning it. Even that had not really satisfied her father, though he had merely grumbled with the others, reserving his explosion for her and her inspiration of "Episcopalian and/or Jewish." Her mother who was Jewish by birth had only said, "You're making it seem like a joke," but her father had shouted, "if you're ashamed to write 'atheist,'" shouting it with a huger wrath than one indiscretion could have earned, even so monstrous an indiscretion. She had thought then that he was taking out on her all the rage he had suppressed over the boys, and had been infuriated at the injustice. Actually the one area of life where she could and did admire her father was religion: the amazing fact that he, Eugene Arling Varley, son of an Episcopal minister, had had the independence to declare himself not an agnostic but an atheist, to declare it as a youth and maintain it throughout a long life among traditionalists and conformists of every kind.

Suddenly Dori smiled. How predictable, that she thought of her mother and father now, in these first hours of discovery about herself. She looked at Cele as if she too must be smiling, but Cele was not looking at her at all. Her face had changed; it was somber.

"Look, Dori, here's something I probably ought not say, but I have to."

"What?"

"It's none of my business."

"I've made it your business. Say it."

"It's something that's been bothering me a lot, but I might—"

"Cele, stop fussing."

"Okay, you don't want to say who the man is, I'm not going to guess. But if it's somebody who's married and has lots of children and can't get free, then how about finding somebody else?"

"Somebody else?"

"Lots of women in the history of the world have told somebody who wasn't the father that he was."

"But who? Just pick somebody off the street?"

"You could start an affair now, and then a month or so from now, tell him and get married."

"Celia!"

"I don't mean some stranger, but I thought just now, What if there's somebody she likes, somebody she's drawn to, who isn't all tied up with a family?" She saw Dori's look and drew back from it. "Oh, skip it. It's a rotten idea. I'm the one could go in for finagling, not you, so forget it."

Dori said nothing. The right words would not come. She

39

could not say, That's such a cheap trick; but she could not stop the words from forming in her own mind. There was a sudden sweetness pulling at her too, a sudden longing to try it, to do what millions of other women had done in the history of the world, the traditional silence to a husband when a child came from an adultery, the traditional means of snaring an unwilling boy into wedlock. In her mind's imagery there suddenly appeared, tiny, floating as if they were suspended in a golden bubble, herself and Matthew, their hands extended toward each other as if to hold a sudden happiness, unexpected, unsought, all at once theirs. "If I thought I could carry it off," she said at last. "But I'm such a rotten liar, I'd be sure to blurt it out sooner or later, and then what?"

"Forget it. It's an n.g. idea. What about some small town around Washington? You could fly here on a shuttle to see Jesskin, I could meet you at the airport and drive you. How many people do you know down there that you'd run into?"

"Apart from Lyndon and such? Not anybody, and with Lyndon it's not reciprocal." She laughed. "If we're talking of an hour by plane, then how about Boston somewhere? Or the Cape?"

"It would be all right in February or March, but what about hot weather when it's mobbed?"

Dori was already rejecting the Cape. "It ought to be some place you get to by car; you always run into people you know at airports."

"Oh let's skip all that for now. We'll hit on the perfect hideout when we're not so jazzed up. Oh, Dorr, it keeps coming at me: it happened. After all this time, it finally happened."

CHAPTER THREE

He tried again, and again there was no answer. Off and on all morning Matthew Poole had tried to reach her to say whatever there might be to say, what he did not know. She was out. Each time he tried to call her, he had left his office and phoned from the row of booths in the lobby, though his secretary would never lift the receiver once the bulb on her desk glowed red. Knowing that was not enough. It was not security he needed but a sense of unrupturable privacy which he could not have in the realm of his busy office with the door opened at precisely the wrong moment by one of his partners.

Dori was asleep when he left at eight, not really asleep rather, for she was still smiling—smiling and happy, her eyes closed and sleep drifting into her again, or was it she who was drifting into sleep? He liked the first phrasing. She had begun to wake while he was dressing and he had told her not to let herself really wake—it had been nearly five when they had gone to sleep, a loss of rest he might have deplored or resented at some other time but which now was one more token of success and fulfillment. She had drowsily nodded at his words and her eyes had closed and she had smiled.

Why should he be so touched by this one small point, this small embellishment? Finding no answer, he at once felt impatient and desirous, a loutish need to go straight back to her and, almost without greeting, put her down on that sofa, or the bed, or the floor, and fall upon her as if he had not been near a woman for a year. There was something in her own passion that roused him beyond restraint; it was not merely that she was new, nor that they were ten thousand miles removed from the fatigue of familiarity—

He dismissed the thought, as a treachery, a lie, a tawdry falsehood. Not everybody experienced the lessening of desire in marriage, at least not to the extent he knew. Jack and Alma were still good together; Jack Henning was his closest friend and he had said so, unequivocally with a thumping robust lewdness that he, Matthew, had called a boast, a brag, all the while knowing that it was exactly the truth. Jack Henning was his age and had been married as long as he, and would not bother to say they were good together if they had long since lost the impulse toward one another that sought and was satisfied, sought and was satisfied, even at lengthening intervals as was inevitable with the passing of time. No man in his forties was fool enough to hope that after years of marriage and familiarity there would be the initial frenzy of need, the same insistence and insatiability. But if one could sustain that in marriage, how fortunate that man would be.

Man or woman. He thought of Joan. Perhaps she also had found that sexual delight—not merely sexual satisfaction striven for and achieved, sometimes arduously achieved, but spontaneous sexual delight—was to be had now only with another man. Had she anybody else? He had asked himself that several times in the past few years, for she was as tactful as he about not going near any situation between them that would normally lead them to bed together, and each time he asked it with less need to know the answer.

Once again he left his desk, this time for a luncheon appointment with two clients, about a contract that had been abrogated, not a case that caught at his deepest interests.

His years of self-discipline in the practice of his profession, however, marshaled his full abilities to their discussion, but interrupting his concentrated attention there was the knowledge that there was a girl in the world he was suddenly entwined with, a girl he would soon be talking to again, seeing again, taking to bed again. He had gone home in the morning for breakfast with the kids, letting them assume he was coming from the airport; then he had changed and shaved and left for the office. That night the Hennings were due for dinner; he considered calling it off and seeing Dori again but it was so rare that they had people in for an evening that he had let it alone.

After luncheon he tried her number again; she was still out. Suddenly he was vexed and angry. She had mentioned some morning appointment; she must have gone straight to the paper after it. She had talked about her job, not very fully, as if she had only partial interest in the new arrangement on the new paper, compared to the years of attachment to the troubled *Trib* which had finally gone under. He called the paper. She was out, perhaps on assignment. "She doesn't keep staff hours," a voice said, and he replied with a brisk "I know, thanks."

Persistent—he had always been called a persistent devil by people who did not like him and he supposed it was true enough. He had been called self-centered too, and that was doubtless equally true. Even in love that seemed the most outgoing and generous, the love for one's children, was there not in fact an enormity of self-interest? Was there any joy he had ever known comparable to the joy he felt in Hildy and in Johnny?

His father must have felt that about him, but he was ten when his father died and he had virtually no memory of him. His mother, a lawyer like his father, most certainly had felt— He stopped quickly; he did not want to think of his mother just then.

He tried the telephone again and gave up. He would send some flowers and try to put Dori out of his mind. Each hour made her more vivid, made their two days more important

43

in retrospect. This was no simple affair; he had had affairs ranging all the way from a quick easy encounter to a complicated convoluted entanglement from which he soon had need only to escape; he knew affairs and needed them and valued them for the part they played in keeping a none too happy life going.

The Hennings made the evening easier. He marveled again at how pleasant it was to have good friends in one's own house, at one's own table, with one's children there, scrubbed and sweet and clever; in a year Hildy would be off to college, and God knows what rebellious young Johnny would take it into his head to be doing. But it was good.

Usually the people Matthew valued he saw away from the house. In the office, over luncheon, over drinks, during the summer months when Joan and the kids were away at Truro—his own personal friendships, except for the Hennings, were normally carried on in the world outside. He no longer struggled to change that, and no longer struggled to remake Joan. How could a man be angry at a wife because she was shy? He could, at the beginning, try to get her past it, try to help her overcome it, try to coax, urge, wheedle, give her moral support, but if finally he saw that there was some incurable, some neurotic cut to her character that made her half sick with apprehension about meeting people, welcoming them, entertaining them at home, why, then, finally he had to accept her as she was and change his own expectations and his own ways of behaving.

Long ago he had learned that it was too difficult to have friends come to the house for dinner or the evening. Inevitably they felt so chilled that sooner or later they remained away, as one remains indoors in inclement weather. Not that it was Joan's purpose to freeze them out. At the beginning, in the first year of their marriage, she had tried to make all his friends welcome, and with the Hennings she had succeeded. Jack was so easygoing himself, with such equability and good nature, that he was easily able to ignore Joan's manner, able indeed to admire Matthew for handling it so adroitly. Alma Henning was not so equable;

44

for a long time she had been confused by her own inability to get through to Joan but she had finally seen that there was no point in pushing for a level of easy camaraderie that wasn't within Joan's grasp, and she had let it go at that. Matthew was interesting enough by himself, she had once told her husband, and he and Matthew together took over the evenings anyway, so that she could relax into a low output of effort and get by. While they were young, with no maid in either household, she would help Joan with dinner and washing up, and since they had their first babies in the same year, a surface kind of talk was easy. Later it was harder but Alma kept on managing and Matthew had been grateful. With lesser friends than the Hennings it had always been the same depressing cycle: the hearty first visit, the less hearty second, a straining and striving, and sooner or later an excuse offered and an invitation turned down.

"She's shy," he had said in those early days when he loved Joan with a young man's fervor. He had said it to his own mother again and again, his mother who had been so happy when he married, so quick to praise Joan's looks, to approve their apartment, admire Joan's cooking, Joan's taste. "It's only that she's shy." For a while it had been enough, though long afterwards, after his mother's death when it was too late, he had seen it could never have been enough, that his mother had been far too intelligent not to see the small wounds Joan gave her for exactly what they were, Joan's nonappearance the first time they were asked up to meet some of her friends, Joan's last-minute backing out as they were about to go to a funny movie; Joan's withholding of any sign of warmth.

But at the time he had seen only the week-to-week particularity, never the total that was putting itself together. Gradually—who could trace back these minor sadnesses?— every visit from or to his mother had become a tension, with the span between arrival and departure growing shorter and shorter, with a sort of gelid determination keeping the talk going. Once when he had chided Joan for never calling his mother week in and week out, she had wept, and

45

in the first year of marriage a bride's tears could outlaw any other consideration. "Darling, nothing could be worth your being so unhappy."

He would do the phoning himself, he had decided, but somehow he did not. As time piled itself on time, he had begun to think that when they had children, all would be well; Joan would not be so shy, there would be the natural talk and shared love that everybody could partake of. But Hildy's birth had deepened the chasm. Joan by then had yielded totally to her own aversion for her mother-in-law, still denying the aversion but no longer making even one phone call a year to her.

He should have put his foot down hard—now he saw it— should have turned on Joan and said, Damn it, suppose I treated your mother this way? Make do, put on an act at least with mine; she is getting old and she loves me and she has never hurt you and this damn cliché of daughter-in-law antipathy is not going to be our cliché anymore. Millions of families the world over have the mother-in-law– daughter-in-law problem, and somehow they cope, so damn it, you cope.

But he had never said it. When Hildy was born, his mother had come up once or twice; each time had been stiffly formal, like a state visit, with everybody knowing it would last no more than half an hour.

"Would you like to hold the baby?" He could still hear Joan saying it, politely, distantly, could still see his mother sitting alone on their sofa, holding her first grandchild, looking mostly down at the baby, sitting there as if she were a stranger in her son's house, which of course she was.

The last such visit had ended with Joan saying at the closing door, "Thank you for coming," in the tone one would have used to a visiting teacher from the neighborhood school. He had seen his mother's face change, but his one emotion was relief that the door was closing and the miserable visit ending.

Again months passed and again he determined to institute some communication between them. But the sight of the telephone would make him wonder what to say; the pen in his hand would pause after "Dear Mother." She did not call him either; only occasionally did he let himself know that her silence was a dignity. Then he would wonder if he were being callous with his own silences, perhaps even cruel, but the very idea of having it out with her made him uneasy. Reproof, the rebuke of women—he had always hated it and instinctively turned away from it.

Hildy began to talk, Hildy began to walk, Hildy was one year old and then two, enchanting as all two-year-olds are enchanting, and never once did he decide, It is too much, whatever is wrong between Joan and her, she doesn't deserve this from me. Only during the last weeks before Johnny's birth did he finally tell Joan he was going to start seeing his mother alone, taking Hildy along too, but before he actually did it, there was a phone call from her office that she had had a severe coronary and had died. The unknown voice had added tonelessly that of course it was the third attack in little over a year.

"Yes," he had said as tonelessly.

He resented her death. His mother had never told him of any of these attacks, had robbed him of the chance to set things right between them, had left him with words unsaid that would now stay unspoken forever. But he had sobbed that night when he was alone and forced himself to put names to his actions and his non-actions, still rejecting "cruel" or "callous," but seeking on, as if he were in a courtroom, himself both the accuser and the accused.

Only later, a long time later, could he accept the first fringe of truth in his unwilling fingers. He was not cruel or callous, but he couldn't handle emotional problems close to the nerve. He reacted badly, he could think only of how to end them, deaden them, escape them, nullify them. It was a weakness; he did not like it in himself. In any marriage it could become a major danger. In any love affair it was a danger too.

He had been married for eight years when he had his first affair. It released him from a thousand docilities and a thousand blindnesses; he felt a man renewed, his own man. Joan knew instinctively that he was no longer the same Matthew, and he agreed that she was right. "You're having an affair," she had said. "Am I?" he had answered, and she had accepted it for the statement he had meant it to be.

The idea of divorce must have occurred to Joan in the next nine years, as it had occurred to him; in the most banal of all phrases, they had stayed together because of the children. They had each stayed married because neither could consider giving up the one true pleasure left. The children were, to him, the full source of happiness and pride; to leave them, to see them only at preordained intervals, to drop out of their daily living, was not to be contemplated. The children and his work—that was enough.

And then he went to Marshall Duke's house and met Dori Gray. How could one know so surely that here was haven, here was a readiness for warmth, to receive it and to give it, here was eagerness and need? He had known it and had felt himself respond to it and had known that his life was going to change.

Now sitting silent over coffee with the Hennings, he thought of her again as she had been when he left her that morning, saw again the faint curving of a smile on her sleepy lips. Something had stirred in him at the sight, had touched him, and he had been unable to catch it. He had wanted to waken her, to tell her again how he felt, but he had kept silent, staring down at her, saying nothing. Was it that silence that had brought him twelve hours later to remembering his mother and the words unspoken forever to her? How strange, how harsh and unbidden, the associative freaks of memory, and how helpless one was against them. Yet this harshness now did not repel him; it seemed to speak to him with an urgency he did not yet understand, in a code he could not yet decipher.

* * *

Eugene Bradford Varley, named after his grandfather, was well aware that he was Dori's favorite brother and equally aware, he asserted, that he deserved to be. "If I were a low-minded oil tycoon like Ron," he had once said, "I wouldn't expect anybody but oil wells to like me, and if I were a high-minded snob like Alan, I'd not even expect that."

This amiable self-esteem was one of the characteristics Dori found so likable in him and one she wished she shared. Gene never needed reassurance from anybody about anything. He never needed to explain himself, justify himself, defend himself. If you disapproved of something he said or did, you disapproved; it was your right. If you tried to persuade him to change, he might try in turn to persuade you that he need not change, that you might have over-looked this or that aspect of the matter, but his attempt at persuasion would be mild, low-keyed and brief. If you opposed him outright, and showed scorn or anger or, worst of all, indifference, he drew down a windowshade in his eyes and closed you out, and you knew that you would not have the chance again to show scorn or anger or indifference because you would not be likely to see Gene Varley even one more time.

Which made him, Dori had once told him, a despot. A nice despot, a rational despot, but a despot nevertheless, because his rule over his emotions and his mind was abso-lute. "Most of us poor benighted folk," she had said, "are al-ways taking Gallup polls of our own constituent opinions before we can finally point to one as the probable winner." He had agreed that he generally spared himself the wear and tear of inner conflict and had said it in a way that told her she would do well to start doing the same.

But all that was a long time ago and a general observation. He wouldn't need to admonish her now, she thought, as she picked up the telephone to call him. She was still at Cele's. How the day had vanished she did not know; they had gone out to lunch together and ordered celebratory champagne cocktails; they had gone to a music store for some records they each wanted for Christmas gifts and then to a book-store as well. Now suddenly it was four and the early twilight of winter had begun and she was afraid she had waited too late in the day.

"Professor Varley, please." She almost never called him at the university, for she never knew his schedule of classes, seminars or student meetings. He picked up the phone, sounding affable. "It's me, Gene. I wondered if I could come over tonight. There's something I'd love to talk over if you're free."

She heard him ask his secretary whether there was anything on his calendar and knew there would not be. Ellen long ago had learned to compress their social life into the weekends, since he was so opposed to any ordained activity during the evenings of his bursting workweek. The university aside, he was a voracious reader; he loved music; he could spend hours in his darkroom, developing the dozens of extremely good pictures he had managed somehow to take since his last bout with his cameras. Bout was the wrong word, for his addiction was chronic and endless, with nothing intermittent about it, though with Jim and Dan both grown and gone from home, his favorite and handiest subjects were no longer easily available and his addiction harder to support.

"Looks okay tonight," he said. "Around seven?"

"I'd thought about eight, eight thirty. I'm at Cele's for dinner but I can leave right after. They're going to the theater."

"Fine. Then come whenever."

"Thanks. I hoped it could be tonight."

"Anything wrong?"

"Quite the opposite. Something great."

"You got fired!"

"You idiot." She laughed and thought, How like Gene. He was even more unequivocal than Cele about urging her to try free-lancing, and with a tougher practicality in his argument. "You've got a certain leverage, Dori, though I wish you'd cut out from that savings bank and into this boiling bull market. But even so unless you want to try for the *Times* or the *News*, neither of which would have the sense to want your kind of stuff, what sort of future is there for newspapering in New York?"

"No future, but don't crowd me."

He never crowded her. She did have a certain leverage—and some part of her training by her businessman father made her hold back from chipping it away on frivolity or risking it in the market like everybody else. She had never regretted rejecting alimony; to her lawyer's astonished protests, she had only said, "I happen not to be the alimony type."

Over the years she had discovered that she liked having something solid, liked seeing the interest mount up, a few hundred dollars a year, liked it when intangibles like inflation forced banks to raise interest rates on loans she had never yet made and on deposits she had never yet depleted. Oh hypocrisy, she sometimes thought. It's a wartime inflation because of an undeclared war you despise. But you don't refuse the interest, you don't give it away, you would be embarrassed to be such a crank, such a high-principled nut. You like it. You like the feeling it gives you. Especially when something comes up that takes money. Like now.

If she had had to go to Cele asking for a loan, how different today would have been. If she were going now to Gene to ask for support, how she would dread this visit. If she were penniless, unable to give up her weekly pay, how fearful a problem would be facing her. Suddenly she imagined a procession of frightened girls, as if they were figures on a frieze, their heads bowed, their faces tight with terror, all caught in the horror of unsought and unwanted pregnancy. Was it only money that made the difference?

"What's the big news?" her brother asked as she arrived. "Here, I'll take that." He took her coat, and then threw it at one of the chairs in the square entrance hall of the apartment.

"You're a help," Dori said, retrieving it and hanging it up in the coat closet. From the living room Ellen called, "Coffee—come on in," and almost at once Dori was repeating the opening words she had used that morning with Celia. "The most incredible thing has happened." But as she went on swiftly to tell them, Ellen said, "Oh, *no,*" her eyes wretched. Gene said, "Good Lord, that is news," and did something she had never seen him do. He began to pace the room. Up and down, back and forth, in silence, he crossed and re-crossed it, going off to the windows, coming back to them on the sofa, but turning quickly as if he were forbidden to sit down.

Dori thought, For once it's me who's without conflict. Under the bravado she felt a distance from them, not un-expected from Ellen but lonely and unlooked-for from her brother. He was now standing at the windows, drawing the draperies back and looking carefully out at the night as if the slow drift of snow had become a matter of professional concern.

"The one thing I do know," he said at last, coming back to them, "the one sure thing is that keeping it a secret won't work. Whether you go to Wyoming or some town in Ver-mont or even go visit Ron and Maude in England—no mat-ter where you try to hide out, this is bound to get out."

"Why? Who'd want to do me in the eye enough to tell it?"

"Nobody would want to. Say you don't have one enemy in the world. Say you don't know one gossip in the world. Say you don't even know one careless person in the world. Just the same it's going to get talked about somehow, by somebody, either viciously or innocently as hell, with no faintest ulterior motive. In any case, goodbye secret."

"Then okay," Dori said vigorously. "If it's 'goodbye se-cret,' it's goodbye. I can't see why it has to, though. Only you two and the Dukes are going to know. Maybe not Mar-shall—Cele wasn't sure she'd tell him."

"Why not?" Ellen said, not looking at her.

"He's pretty conventional, under all that modern talk."

Ellen seemed about to defend Marshall but changed her mind. "What about Jim and Dan? You don't want us to keep it from them or their wives, the way Cele intends to keep it from Marshall?"

Before Dori could answer, Gene put in mildly, "Dori hasn't had time to even consider Jim and Ruth or Dan and Amy. What we do about them can be put off for just now, can't it?"

"I was only thinking," Ellen said quickly. Then she addressed herself to Dori once more. "Not that they couldn't be trusted to keep a secret. I'm sure nobody would *want* to do you in the eye. Heavens. But I think Gene is right—somebody is bound to forget and say something—"

"Would you forget?"

"Don't sound that way," Ellen answered.

"What way?"

"I don't know."

But Dori knew. She had been so sure of warmth and approval, and she had been suddenly reminded that neither warmth nor approval was as automatically bestowed as one wanted them to be. She glanced up at her brother, but he had resumed his pacing. There was again a silence and Ellen said, "We all need a drink. I'll go get ice cubes." Dori looked after her. There had always been some basic distance between herself and Ellen, what she jokingly called "the in-law mile," but usually it was bridged over by the civilized cement of good manners because of Gene and the boys. To find Gene distant as well was another matter entirely, and inside her something ached and something else was angry.

As if he had suddenly realized that Ellen had left them alone, Gene turned and spoke hurriedly. "The grocer might talk, in whatever small town you go to, the postman, the next-door neighbor, the druggist, whatever story you tell them about your missing husband. That's what Ellen meant, that somehow it would get out and start being a nice juicy scandal. Why can't you come here?"

"Here?"

"Right here with us, for the duration. You can have Jim's old room, or Dan's, and if we have guests, you can lock your door and stay put."

"Oh Gene." Unexpectedly her eyes stung. She should

have known, through all the pacing and all the silence. "Thanks for asking me, but of course that's impossible."

"What's so impossible about it? Here, you'd never have to go near a postman or grocer or druggist—"

"But what about Norah—are you going to fire her and let me be the cleaning woman? What about your nice talkative doorman? I would have to get out to street level once in a while, wouldn't I? And what about your Miss Pulley, when she comes here to work?"

"None of that is what you mean. You mean Ellen. I can make her see it; she was caught short just now, but she'll adjust. I don't think you ought to hold it against Ellen that her reaction time is slower than ours on something like this."

"I don't, I really don't." She looked at him earnestly, but she knew he did not believe her, and could not believe her because of course she did hold it against Ellen. "If I were a hippie or yippie, Ellen would say, 'Oh, well, what do you expect of those dirty long-haired slobs?' and then she'd be tolerant about it. But being *me*—good family, New England background, forty years old—why, it's unthinkable."

She broke off. She never permitted herself the indulgence of complaining to any man about his wife—why should she think it permissible with her own brother? He must know, as she did, that Ellen's "reaction time" was rooted in a kind of class snobbery—"people like us simply don't have illegitimate children"—and knowing it about his wife, he must regret it. Aloud she said, "Excuse it, please. I didn't mean to give a lecture about Ellen. I do think it would be tough as all get-out for both of you with me here, locked away like crazy Aunt Hattie up in the attic when guests come." He laughed and she went on, hurrying to consolidate her small victory over her blunder. "Once I find the right place to go on the lam, Gene, you'll agree it's best all round."

"Maybe so." He looked dubious and then suddenly more positive than he had looked all evening. "Why isn't it better yet to tell the whole world to go to hell? Then you'd stay right in your own apartment, lead a normal life, see people you like, get help from anybody who gives a damn about you and stop all this clowning about hideouts and secrets."

"Oh Gene, it sounds so wonderful. Today, in a phone booth, I imagined just that. I imagined calling the paper and telling them, calling everybody I know, telling them, even calling Tony just to say, Look, I did it, I always knew that someday I'd be able to."

Ellen came back with the ice bucket and there were drinks to be made. Dori's expression signaled Gene not to reopen the subject and he talked of student restlessness at Columbia and at half the other campuses in the land, liking it. Students were fed to the teeth with "the biggest bureaucracy there is except the army." From students they went to the restlessness among civil rights leaders, the growing fury of the blacks—"I still can't say 'blacks' without forcing myself," Dori said—and by the time she left, she had nearly forgotten the constraint between herself and Ellen, thinking instead of what Gene had offered as the best plan of all.

Why don't I? she thought as she walked home. He had put into words just what she had felt as she saw the shine of the telephone booth on the street that morning. Cele had wondered about it too, obliquely raising the point and then backing away from the risk of influencing her. But why not tell the world to go jump in the lake and have nothing to do with the whole complicated twisty business of living a secret?

She glanced around as if expecting a sign, a directive. It was still snowing, easily, and the city lay in the white hush any snowfall lends its streets. Why didn't she? Why shouldn't she? She was no poor frightened girl in trouble. She was not ashamed. Nobody on earth could make her feel this as disgrace. Then why did she not obey her instinct and shout it from the rooftops? She glanced up at the snow-touched terraces atop the apartment buildings. From right up there—why don't I?

She had thought there was no need for Jesskin's three thinkings. She had made the one decision, the only decision: to go ahead. Wrong—she had not made it; it had sprung full-blown, a new being in her life, strong, firm, beautiful.

There had been no gestation period needed, no elapsing of time, no birth pangs. In the same instant that her mirror had gleamed its faint signal to her, in that instant the *yes* was born.

Now came conflict. A secret or not a secret? Keep silent or shout it out? She had taken it for granted that this was private, but this wasn't something you announced on a loudspeaker, but all day today there had come the pull of other desires, to tell Tony, to phone the paper, to agree with Cele, with Gene, with those snowy terraces up there in the sky. Would there be other conflicts? She wanted no others, she would hate them if they came, hate herself if she shilly-shallied until they took on size and shape and substance. There were matters to be solved, certainly, the logistics of the whole thing, all sorts of matter-of-factnesses to be disposed of, but these were merely the practical considerations, not to be dignified by the concept Conflict.

She must not let real conflict get a foothold, she knew herself well enough to know that. She had gone through periods in the past where she couldn't be decisive about the simplest things, whether to wash her hair, whether to go for a walk, how to phrase a letter, and she remembered them with a horror and a dread. Of course they had come only in times of sadness and depression, not in a buoyant time like this, but perhaps the mysterious process of growth was the same—she mustn't risk it—perhaps if the seed of conflict were embedded at all, it would attach itself to the flesh of life and expand and grow until there was no way to abort it.

Her own metaphor made her suddenly smile. When to tell Matthew, how to tell him, that was also a problem to be solved well and thoughtfully, with care but without conflict.

She glanced at her watch as she drew near a streetlight. It was nearly eleven. Off and on, all day long, Matthew had kept returning to her mind, kept claiming part of her through the excitements and celebrating and discussing, Matthew the unnamed, Matthew the unspoken. Even with

56

her entire attention apparently on Cele, on Gene or Ellen, he had been there, an interior presence to whom she would any moment return. Now that she was alone, tired from the massive day, eager for bed and rest and silence, it was as if she were going fully toward him once again.

❈   ❈   ❈

There was a letter slipped under her door when she got to her apartment and for a moment she thought, The Christmas rush already? Does it start this early in the month, and so late in the afternoon? This must have come after Nellie had left for the day.

It was a business envelope, its upper left corner engraved *Weston, Solomon, Jones and Poole,* over which, in longhand, he had written "Poole—personal." Her name was handwritten too, and there was no stamp on the envelope; he had sent it by boy or come by and left it himself. She lifted the flap easily; it was barely glued, as if it were not very private, and there was no salutation.

> I tried several times to phone you today, but this may be better. Have you any idea how remarkable you are? How beautiful and how responsive? At forty-two a man is not likely to be misled about love. I know that it is not a constant, that it can diminish or grow, and that at the start nobody can be certain which of the two it will do. But having bought in this careful coin an alibi for the future, I think I may tell you that I am not a diminisher by nature. I will be telephoning tomorrow.
>
> MATTHEW

It was written in a strong flowing hand easy to read except for the *m*'s and *n*'s which looked like linked and topless *o*'s in the middle of words but not at either the beginning or end, so that she did not have to pause over "man" but did over "diminish" which rippled along as if it were *diminish.*

Somehow this was endearing, and she looked at the two words, diminish and diminisher, with a fondness that set them apart from all the rest. Then she began to read his note at the beginning once more, but suddenly realized her neck was moist and knew she was still in her snow-wisped coat, standing there inside her front door reading her first letter from Matthew. She slipped out of the coat, threw it down on a chair, remembered saying "You're a help" to Gene and hung it up properly in the closet, finding some small amusement in this repeated ritual. Then she went into the living room, sat down on the sofa—the sofa she could never look at without remembering him there with her—and read the letter once more.

—Lots of women in the history of the world have told somebody who wasn't the father that he was—

—Just pick somebody off the street?

—You could start an affair and then tell him and get married.

—I'm such a rotten liar. . . .

Again conflict, again, another kind, a horror in it and a sudden magnetic power, pulling her forward, beckoning, tempting. She started slightly as if at a noise and went to her room quickly, tossing the letter on her turned-down bed and tapping the tiny ON switch of her radio. Mozart came into the room, fresh and bright, and again she started, for it was so similar to the quintet they had heard Monday evening. Monday, Thursday—three days, seventy-two hours, and an entire new world spinning in the infinite space of the unexpected? All at once she felt unreal, felt unable to manage, not fitted for so profound a change in all her patterns and all her abilities. What made her so sure she could go ahead? How could anybody manage alone and in silence? Nature had never intended it for solitude, God had never.

Oh cut that out, she thought roughly, the one damn thing you're never going to do is go sentimental. You can feel good or bad, happy or horrible, afraid or not afraid, but you can never, not even once, feel sorry for yourself.

She felt better at once. She went to her desk, took out from the upper drawer a small oblong package which her newspaper and stationery store had delivered earlier in the week. She opened it and drew out a refill for her desk calendar and also a narrow little book in a red cover that matched a row of ten or twelve other narrow little books in red covers in a small bookcase behind her. *Daily Reminder* was stamped on all of them, and on this, in bright gold letters, the numerals *1968*. The combination looked strange and she paused over it for a moment. She leafed through the pages quickly until she came to July, and then more slowly until she came to the twenty-third. It was a Tuesday. She remembered Dr. Jesskin's warning that July 23rd was "a theoretical date," that it might be a few days earlier or later, but she stared at that one page and then, in the upper right corner she wrote, very lightly, very small, *280*. She smiled at the figure as if in salute and began to undress. Without looking directly toward her bed she could see Matthew's letter, a small white marker lying there as if to denote a particular presence.

How completely good it was, to have a letter like this, and how long it had been since she had received one. Dick Towson rarely wrote because he was a telephoner. When she did hear from him it was by a telegram, cable or picture postcard, and she had never even remarked on it until now, so usual had non-letter-writing become in this age of speed and terseness. ARRIVING NINE THIRTY STOP FLIGHT EIGHT FOUR ZERO STOP LOVE YOU STOP

She laughed and glanced again at the letter waiting for her on her bed. Out in the kitchen the house buzzer sounded its raucous clatter and she went to it, surprised. The kitchen clock showed eleven thirty; unexpected callers didn't appear at eleven thirty, and she had long ago told the doorman not to announce people he recognized as her friends. "Some flowers," he said now, pompous as always. "They're in the package room. I missed you when you came in, so will I send them up now?"

"Thanks, please do."

They were odd spidery-looking great discs, as round across as large chrysanthemums, white and tall and fragile, their hearts edging into a young yellow green. She had seen them in florists' windows but did not know their name, and now she touched them with her fingertips as if some tactile recognition would suddenly inform her. She arranged them in her tallest vase, an etched crystal vase that had been a wedding present—the continuity of physical things—and carried them into the living room, to set them upon the coffee table in front of the sofa.

Flowers and a note from your lover. How old-fashioned, how outmoded; as the young would have it, what a drag. She could hear the derision in the word and automatically moved toward her dictionary. One of her hobbies was language, the derivation and shifting usage of words and phrases, and she knew all the *in* slang because it was part of her writer's need to know it. She rarely used any of it when writing or talking, but tracking it down was always amusing. She remembered how astonished she had been, on reading a Trollope novel recently, to see that one of the fashionable words a century ago, borrowed from the people in the pubs, was "gammon." Gammon as an expletive, gammon as a rebuke, gammon as a mild oath. Then too she had gone straight to her bedroom where, on a tallish mahogany stand, her great unabridged dictionary reposed, always open, and found eight or ten meanings for that surprising word. Now as she turned the left-hand pages back to the *d*'s, the telephone rang. Before she reached it, she knew it would be Matthew, and before she answered, she knew she would say, Oh, of course, even for an hour.

CHAPTER FOUR

"I've thought out all the things you told me to think out, Dr. Jesskin. You were right, there were so many more than I had dreamed there would be. But I did. I've talked to my brother and to my closest friend."

"And the result?"

They looked at each other in silence. His face was still what she had thought of as neutral. It was a waiting face, an interested face, not the face of an advocate or of a dissuader. Suddenly she looked again at this calm, unruffled man and found what she had always found. He was involved forever with life in its most primitive facets, conception and then birth, and nothing, nothing at all, would make him put up obstacles to either.

"And I am going ahead. Will you help me?"

Awkwardly he put his hand out on the desk and took hers as if in a handshake. "I am proud of you."

"And will you?"

"You have known that I would." His voice was still without stress but an animation shone in his eyes. "We will work it out step by step, between us."

"Oh thank you." Her voice shook but he did not notice.

"Is it going to be awkward for you in any way, taking me? Miss Mack and Miss Stein knowing I am not married—"

"We will not start by worrying about me," he said. "What are the worries about you?"

"Well, I do wonder about one thing. I've heard it's a little risky to have a first baby as late as forty—is that true?"

"Certainly not. You are a fine healthy girl and forty is not regarded as anything but young today. Medically, that is. Cosmetically—that is perhaps another matter."

She laughed outright. He was talkative. He sounded happy. "And another thing. I haven't had any morning sickness yet—when does that start?"

"It is a variable. Sometimes it is immediate, sometimes it is never. In my own belief—I have no scientific data, just my belief—it is worst where the pregnancy is resented or unwanted and it is often not experienced at all when the woman is overjoyed to be pregnant."

He made a note in the folder; she knew it was the medical equivalent of "no morning sickness," and in her mind added a parenthesis: "(overjoyed)." She suddenly had a need to confide in him about matters more real than these two, and the certainty that he would permit it, find time for it, perhaps welcome it. "I do have one problem that I get a different answer to every day," she said. "The biggest one so far." He nodded, silent and expectant, as if he knew perfectly well that once the preliminaries were out of the way the real questions would come. "Things like where to go, when to go, what name to go under—those aren't answered yet either, but I know they will be. The great big one pushes them all to one side." Again she paused.

"You cannot quite make yourself tell me?" He put the pen down and shoved the folder away.

"It's just that something in me doesn't want this to be a secret, wants to tell it to everybody, wants to let everybody see me later on, big and pregnant, and let them think whatever they want to think."

"Then why do you not?"

At once she felt combative as if he had said, "That would be better; that is the best thing to do."

"Because where everybody knows," she said with new stress, naming a famous actor, a famous painter, a famous movie star, all of whom had, willingly or via scandal and law suits, proclaimed to the world their indifference to conventional marriage—"because their children grew up to be neurotic wrecks. At school they must have been called 'dirty little bastard' from the first minute, and been taunted and whispered about and goggled at."

"School-age children are savages," Dr. Jesskin agreed, but unemphatically as if again he were turning neutral. His eyes strayed to the two photographs, easel-framed, standing on his desk before him, and he seemed to be studying their faces for reasons of his own. One was of a pretty woman, whom Dori took to be his wife, and the other was of a boy and a girl, about ten or twelve years old, looking enough like him to proclaim themselves his children. Were they savages too?

Dori felt rebuked by his speculative look as he gazed at the photographs. The stress and ardor of her words seemed girlish, the point she had raised suddenly tangential in this office, before this man.

"Oh, Dr. Jesskin, forgive me. These are things I shouldn't bother you with at all; I forgot for a minute. I'll decide for myself, and I suppose you will not disapprove either way."

"That is so. I will not." He pulled the folder back within writing distance and briefly she wondered what he had expected to hear from her that would not bear the recording in her history, already so full of other unrecordables. "In a moment," he said, "I will have a look at you for some measurements, for the technical chart. For the next three months, I will want to see you every fourth week. Miss Stein will give you an appointment card and Miss Mack will take a blood sample, for hemoglobin, for an Rh test and so forth. This is all routine. Have you any directives to ask of me? Most patients do."

"Directives?"

"You want to know whether you may continue to have intercourse. The answer is yes. It is normal. Indeed as the pregnancy progresses, the increased production of hormones is stimulating to sexual activity. That is, unless there is anger over the pregnancy, when resistance, even hostility, becomes a factor."

This was so surprising a dissertation and so precisely to the point, though she would have had to make a conscious effort to raise the point herself, that she felt a remarkable surge of new confidence in Dr. Jesskin. Always before he had avoided any overlay of psychoanalytical talk; today he had spoken twice of resistance and hostility, or of the good normal opposites. He was giving her his blessings to go ahead and be made love to, but he was thinking of the "awfully decent man, no scoundrel betraying me," while she was thinking of Matthew. She suddenly felt wanton, promiscuous and secretly pleased, but she looked down as if she were too shy to meet his glance.

"For the moment," he went on with no perceptible change in tone, "I have only two prescriptions for you, but they are both important and both to start at once, please. First, to begin a regimen of long walks, daily walks, brisk, not ambling, but a positive kind of walking. Three miles a day would be best. Second, begin now to do this." He stood up, turned half away from her so that he stood in profile, unceremoniously held back his starched white coat, and then visibly pulled in his slightly flabby stomach, pulled it in with a sudden jerk, then released it, then pulled it in again, released it. Tall and thin, he was totally free of self-consciousness as he performed for her, and it was all she could do not to laugh. Automatically she imitated him, sitting as she was, watching him, fascinated at the unexpected sight. He saw that she was keeping time with him and nodded in approval.

"'Suck in the gut' is the not so elegant way to describe this exercise," he said, dropping his hold on his coat and sitting down again. "The effectiveness is remarkable. You want taut muscles, strong, tough, and if you work faithfully at it,

64

you will have them. As you see, you can do this exercise standing or sitting, wherever you are, in a car, at the movies, at your desk, when you are watching television, even in bed. I want you to do it ten, twelve times a day, beginning today, in batches of ten or twelve times each."

She did laugh. She put her hands on her stomach and sat there practicing. She saw her hands jerk inward and she felt an immediate tightening of her muscles.

"The best maternity girdle of all," Dr. Jesskin said with satisfaction. "You will build it right into you, just this way, and keep strengthening it and toughening it right to the end."

"Couldn't it do any damage to the baby? Pulling in that hard?"

He waved the baby out of consideration. "You can't compress fluid," he said as if he had suddenly turned physics teacher. "You can't squeeze or pinch or decrease it." He touched the buzzer and Miss Mack appeared, competent as always, her manner as always, her eyes revealing nothing.

*   *   *

School-age children are savages. As she walked home the phrase sounded again and again in her mind, spoken in the mild voice designed neither to urge nor to exhort, and each time a phrase of her own replied, I won't let them be.

She had it within her own power to prevent those school-age savages from hurting, perhaps damaging, a five- or six-year-old boy or girl, and there was suddenly no question that she would exercise that power in the one sure way open to her.

Those future tormentors would never know. Their parents would never tell them because their parents would never know. Nobody would tell the parents. No shred of gossip would inform them, no hint would be whispered to them, no weapons would be handed them to be handed over to their school-age offspring. This much was at last settled.

Dori felt relieved. She walked quickly past shopwindows

bright and commercial with Christmas green and red and tinsel, seeing no particularities, only a brightness to match her mood. As she reached her front door she could hear her telephone ringing brassily inside and she dived for her keys, sure she would be tantalized by silence once she reached her desk. But the ringing persisted, patient, stubborn, and when she breathlessly said "Hello?" it was Ellen, sounding embarrassed, sounding serious, asking if they might meet, perhaps today.

"Of course. Whenever."

"Are you working? Or could I drop in now?"

"Come on, I haven't even started." But she braced herself and looked at her watch as if time had become a factor. Had Ellen ever before come over alone to talk to her? She could not remember even one occasion in all the twenty-four years she had been married to Gene. They had usually been congenial enough in a loose casual way that was only a cut above indifference, but private talks between them, private visits, private anythings, never happened. Since the night she had told them her news two weeks ago, she had heard several times from Gene, asking how she was, asking genially, "Anything else new, for God's sake?" but from Ellen there had been only silence.

The sensation of being braced for trouble grew as she waited for Ellen's arrival, and during their greetings and their exchange of mechanical cheer about Christmas shopping and Christmas plans, it became acute enough to be uncomfortable. "What is it, Ellen?" she finally asked. "We seem to be ducking it."

"I've tried to avoid it altogether," Ellen said. "For two whole weeks I've gone crazy trying to just put it out of my mind. But I had that awful feeling that time was running out—"

"Running out on what?"

"On telling you the truth about this. Gene won't, not ever. Your friend Cele won't either." She looked defiant but also wretched.

"What truth?"

66

Ellen remained silent, managing to give off an aura of reluctance as if her being there was no doing of her own, as if this conversation were no choice of her own but rather a distasteful trap into which she had somehow been inveigled.

"Is this some truth about including Jim and Dan?" Dori prompted. "And their wives?"

"That too," Ellen said with such a pounce that Dori knew she had not even been thinking of her sons. "You can't ask Gene and me to tell lies to our own children."

"I didn't ask you."

"It's far more involved than just keeping this to ourselves for now. For now that might be possible, but then there comes one lie, and then another, a whole series of fakes—we've *never* led them up the garden path—they would never trust a word we said from that minute on."

In her indignation at being asked to behave so abominably, Ellen raced on about bringing up two boys like Jim and Dan, how basic, how indispensable, complete trust was between parent and child, until Dori finally interrupted to say, "You were going to tell me what it was that Cele would never tell me, or Gene either."

"Yes I was. Somebody simply has to, and of all the things they're saying, they absolutely are not coming out with what they really feel down deep, what they instinctively feel—that you're making the most awful mistake, that this is the most terrible thing you can do."

"Terrible?"

"Yes, terrible."

"Terrible for whom?"

"For everybody. For yourself and for Gene and me, for—for the future."

"The word you can't say is 'baby,'" Dori said. "A terrible mistake for the baby."

"All right then. For the baby. For the whole family. For yourself most of all. A terrible mistake."

"I don't think Cele feels that and isn't telling me. Or Gene

67

either." Ellen looked away. "Does he? Does Gene? Or are you guessing?"

"Apart from Gene—look, now that you know you *can* have a baby, don't you see how different things are? You wouldn't ever again have the awful feeling you used to have, don't you see that?"

"Now wait a minute." There was a warning note in her tone but Ellen missed it and again raced on, immersed in her own earnestness.

"You would know that you're cured at last and just knowing would make a whole new situation. So even if you—there's still time, it's still safe—even if you didn't go on with this now, you'd know you could, and you might even marry faster, knowing it. And be so much happier in the long run."

"You are telling me to have an abortion."

"I'm only pointing out the true—"

"Did Gene know you were going to say this?"

"I don't discuss everything with him."

"Does he know you feel this way?"

"I've told him, of course I have. We're family, Dori, what affects you affects all of us together."

"Oh no it doesn't, not from now on it doesn't." Dori stood up, her voice suddenly loud. "This is nothing you need have one more minute of, not one more word of, not one more bit of news about. I will see you when it's all over, a year from now, two years, but now let's for God's sake call it quits." She started from the room.

"You might consider the way other people feel," Ellen said behind her.

"And vice versa."

"You're being utterly selfish."

"And vice versa."

She waited at the door from the living room, not looking at her sister-in-law, not thinking, wanting only to be alone once more. As Ellen passed her, saying, "I should have known," she answered, "That's right. You should have known," and opened the hall door. A moment later she was leaning against it, feeling for the first time the rise and swell of nausea.

School-age children are savages. They're not the only ones, she thought furiously. Just now in these few haggling minutes, here in her own house, she had heard the taunt of "Shame, shame!" Damn it, Ellen, shame on *you.*

* * *

She had stood her ground, she had said the right things. Off and on for the next hour she warmed to a small private glow of accomplishment, and then suddenly she accepted the truth: she was shaken through and through.

How many thousands and thousands lived through shame, humiliation and contempt because they were pregnant without being married? Why wasn't there a worldwide campaign to remake attitudes and emotions about it? They tested for the Rh factor, they watched for it, they knew it could be fatal to new life, but did anybody in authority check for the shame factor, the poisoning guilt that could be equally lethal, if not in the physical sense, then lethal to pride and self-worth?

The shame factor—if it were absent, how few young lives would be wrecked, how few hideous abortions there would be, the awful self-inflicted ones, the filthy unsterile ones, the slicing agony at the hands of the doctor who would not risk an anesthetic?

Dori shuddered. She hated Ellen for plunging her into these thoughts. Then she knew Ellen as Ellen wasn't the point, only Ellen as symbol. If Ellen, why not somebody else? Not Matthew, of course not Matthew. But was Marshall Duke saying this sort of rubbish to Cele? Was Ellen giving Gene a nightly burst for being so easy and acquiescent?

Matthew was no Ellen, not even a Marshall Duke, but he was in love with her, or, to be properly wary of large phrases, he was falling more surely in love with her, and any news of this magnitude might jar him through and through too. It was such a fragile process, that transition from "I'm in love with you" to the simple solid "I love you." Was it foolhardy to put it to any unusual strain so soon?

Day after day for the past two weeks she had been playing with opening phrases for the moment when she would tell him, but it had been a pleasant sort of daydreaming, with no sense of haste to prod her. Not just yet, it was too near Christmas, which he would be spending with his family; not right after Christmas either—he had promised to take his family off on a skiing weekend over New Year's. He had told her all this with a care, as if in a wish to say *"en garde"* to her, do not let these family patterns distress you; they were established long before we met. She had understood, had told him that she knew why he was telling her so carefully, so far in advance, and that she liked his doing it. And she had thought, liking this too, that after the holidays were done with at last, the timing would be just right for her news, and that she also would use care and love in the telling, and then had gone on half luxuriating in imagining the moment when at last he knew.

Her hand felt again the pressure of Dr. Jesskin's fingers, as if he were reaching out to congratulate her. *I'm proud of you.* She could hear the words again, but this time they were in Matthew's voice.

She drew back. Over them, through them, around them, a shrillness sounded: *You are making a terrible mistake. Terrible for whom? Terrible for everybody.*

Oh yes, she had stood her ground, she had said the right things, but Ellen had won something just the same. If Ellen had not come over, would there now be this sudden anxiety about what Matthew would say? She was seeing him this evening and for a moment she wished she were not going to.

Almost automatically she turned to her desk. Work, the anodyne. The piece on Martha Litton was too long and she had been having trouble cutting it. Usually she could be dispassionate about cutting her own work, looking at each sentence with a skeptical eye that asked it, What's your reason for existing? But this time that stern editor within her had gone fishing and a friendly defender had remained, rooting for each phrase, urging her to see its charm, if not its necessity. Now she turned on it in a violence of energy, slashing out entire paragraphs, rearranging sequences, slinging in new transitions as if she were back on the defunct *Trib*, on some late-breaking story, with a copyboy waiting at her elbow to rush each take down to the pressroom. When she saw that she was at last on the edge of completing the job, she telephoned the paper and told Tad Jonas she was in the neighborhood and could she drop in at four with the completed piece?

"Sure, come on. Remember—I liked it the way it was."

By the time she got there she felt sure of herself again. She again had a sense of accomplishment, but this time it was real and it lasted. This came from work, her own work, and she knew how to do it, and when it went wrong she knew how to set about correcting it. This was not taking a good stance, striking the right note, this was her own self in operation, and despite her occasional envy of people with bigger talents, the mysterious something that might make her more than the writer of good pieces for a paper or a magazine, she found a full satisfaction in what her own self did manage to do well.

"Hi, Tad," she greeted her editor, "I think you'll like this better." She opened a flat manila envelope, drew out about fifteen typed pages and laid them on his desk. "Two thousand words shorter and less wobbly." He read the first paragraph and the last before he looked up.

"I didn't think it was all that wobbly."

"Maybe it's me who's wobbly. Or just plain stale. I think I need a vacation."

"When are you taking off?" He sounded mock resigned to it. "Tough, not having enough dough in the bank to swing a winter vacation."

She laughed. She liked Tad; they had worked together for years on the *Trib* and he had never let their friendship interfere with cutting her work when cutting was indicated. He was an editor with a built-in discontent, for he wanted either to be on a huge city daily again or else to have a fat advance from a publisher to write the novel he was always talking about, but he did precisely nothing about either desire except suffer over its denial. Despite his own failures, he was pleasant enough to work for, generous about telling you he liked something, never needling or mean-spirited about finding fault. If he disapproved of a piece of work he said so, roundly, vulgarly, but straightforwardly to you, with his reasons for thinking so, usually cogent. It didn't happen very often with Dori but she was good at forestalling it by behaving just as she had with the Martha Litton piece.

"Maybe longer than a winter vacation," she said. "Tad, don't get caught short if I do something wild one of these days. I just might."

"Like what?"

"Like quitting."

"You've got to be kidding. I thought you finally decided you liked working here on a nice slow weekly schedule."

"I do, in that sense. But of late I seem to think of tread-mills awfully often, and of getting into ruts. That means something, doesn't it?"

"I guess it does. Maybe that you're in love or that you're going to write a book."

"Heaven forfend. Forfend the book anyway." She saw him look at her with the sudden attention that the first whiff of news or gossip commands in the human animal, especially the human animal trained to sniff out news. She slapped together the sheets of the Litton piece again and said, "Well, we'll see. I hope you'll agree this thing is better for all the rewrite."

As she left, she thought, Laying the groundwork, that's what I was doing. Write a book indeed. Poor Tad, that's all he thinks of, so he ascribes it to me. He can't face the fact that if he really wanted to, had to, he'd have done it years ago, the way other people have done, after hours, mornings, weekends. But me! Never.

This sounded a little defiant to her, a little dishonest, for she recognized, and had for a long time, that it was something she regretted, that her natural scope was the smaller scope of articles, that she would never be able to encompass a sustained piece of work, hundreds of pages of work, on some given subject. What if she had to write a whole book about a Martha Litton, or even about a Benjamin Spock? There must be some mechanism within the talents of other people that kept them wound up for a longer duration of interest and energy, but that mechanism was missing in her.

Fine. It was good to know what your limitations were. Knowing kept you comfortably back from the abyss of frustration that so many people lived with. She had had her one private abyss for too many years to play around the edges of a second one. She felt superior and it was delicious. Let Tad know frustration, let everybody and anybody; for the next few months at least she was safe.

Laying the groundwork. It might be wise to follow through rather quickly, before she needed to leave the paper. She might line up one or two actual magazine pieces right now, with some actual editors and some actual deadlines; the deadlines could always be extended if enough notice was given. She could choose topics which she would have to research abroad, so when somebody said, "Where's Dori?" the answer would be "Oh, she's doing a piece in Rome," or Honolulu or Africa. People accepted such answers without paying too much attention; she had done it herself, except for people who were close to her. Casual people could be gone a year and when she saw them again, she had no idea of whether it had been a month or a few weeks or a matter of days.

Matthew was not one of the casuals. Matthew would know to the week how long she had been gone, just as she would know if he were to step out of her life now with some story about a law case that would take him away from New York. That could work with Tad Jonas and the staff, with most of her acquaintances and friends—how much fewer were the people one called friends with the passing of the years and the pruning of the tree. Was that merely a concomitant of maturity, or was it a dark kind of in-turning

73

that robbed one of companionships and parties and amusements?

She didn't turn from anybody who mattered. Her heart thudded as she looked at her watch; in three hours, soon after dinner, she would see him. He came to her deep in the evenings usually, about ten, staying until midnight. Saturdays and Sundays, not. She knew that pattern so well; like the big holidays, the weekends were for his children. It had been that way with Dick Towson too; before Dick, she had not yet been wise enough to accept the pattern. It used to affront her that she had to spend weekends and holidays alone, and all the timeworn clichés about affairs were really true. Then for no reason that she could name, some buried good sense had struggled up through the gravelly muck and had come to her rescue with Dick, making her see without rancor or confusion that this was part of the contract one made with life if one had an affair with a man who was married. And the only men any woman was likely to be drawn to, once the carefree teens and twenties were gone, were men who were already married. Conveniently widowed men were for television serials; in actual life the only bachelors of thirty or forty were the neurotics and misfits, the mothers' boys, the homosexuals, the cranks.

It was intelligent, then, not to be confused or "insulted" by the necessities about weekends and holidays, and Dick had remarked on the fact that she wasn't, complimenting her for "not being a Friday squawker like most dames." Matthew had never spoken of it, but he couldn't have felt any unspoken pressure upon him to see her over weekends, for it was nonexistent. Nor could he have felt any pressure to tell her about his family either, for she knew better than to ask about them. He still said little about Joan; it was his children that he enjoyed telling her about, and his work. When he spoke of his life apart from his kids or his cases, he still seemed watchful and less than free. One night he had told her a little about his boyhood, but he had grown somehow nervous and hurried and had ended, "I think I was so anxious to prove that I wasn't drawn to the law by two silver cords that I got pretty rough about it at times."

"That sounds natural enough," she had said.

"Maybe so. But I can be a selfish bastard—better not expect too much of me in the nobility line."

"I never expect nobility nohow." They had laughed, but she had listened with all her antennae out, searching for the unspoken message behind his words. Now some faraway signal seemed to say, Don't rush, take it a day at a time, think of the right way, there are plenty of other things you haven't decided yet either. She actually enjoyed keeping some of them in suspension; it was pleasant to leave pending the matter of where to hide out, a kind of game as if she were thumbing her way idly through travel folders, trying to choose between a vacation in Jamaica and one in Europe.

By the time Matthew came, the anguish that had begun with Ellen in the morning had disappeared and Dori felt euphoric. It was the day before the Christmas weekend and tonight they would exchange their first presents. She could give him nothing that needed to be hidden or explained at home. After hours of telephoning and scurrying around and searching out of reliable opinion, she had collected for him the best recording known of each piece of music they had heard at their first concert. Actually, though she would only tell him this later, she had bought a duplicate of each of the four records for herself, so that she too might have that same concert whenever memory and emotion combined to ask for its rebirth.

He was touched, as she had hoped he would be, and he offered her his gift hesitantly, as if it were banal compared to the thought that had gone into hers. It was a pair of earrings of smooth white coral, domed and shining, thinly outlined in gold; she loved his wanting to adorn her, loved the earrings themselves and though she did not say so, loved him for knowing that she would have been disturbed if he had brought her something that cost more than she could have spent easily for herself.

She put them on and turned toward him. "How did you know I'm mad for white coral?"

"I know things about you."

"How *did* you know? You couldn't have asked Cele." Before he could answer, she said in a rush, "You *do* know about me. That I'm Victorian about things like too expensive presents, for instance."

"Books and flowers only?"

"And something lovely like these, but—"

"Not a mink coat?"

"Not a mink coat. Oh Matthew—you know so much about me, but there are some things still that you don't and—"

"Important things?"

She suddenly went somber, and for a moment there was silence in the room. The records lay spread on the carpet, four glistening squares of color and design, and on the coffee table the small elongated jeweler's box in which the earrings had come. He saw her hand go to her throat as if to quiet a too lively pulse there and he said, "Don't answer that, darling." It was the way he said it that moved her, the offer of patience and trust. "Don't even try until you're good and ready," he went on. "If ever I start cross-examining you, on anything, no matter what—"

"You weren't cross-examining. I brought it up in the first place, and it was a perfectly natural question with anybody you're this close to."

"But don't answer it anyway." Slowly he added, "Let's try not to make all the young mistakes, Dori. We can't crawl inside each other's minds and feelings, and past and present, the way kids think they can. We can't be in the same cocoon."

"We'd fit though."

They made love then and later, lying beside him, curled inside the curve of his body, she thought again, We would fit. A vision flashed bright, of herself tucked in an arc within the arc of his being while, unknown to him, another being, not yet an inch long, was curving within her own.

Suddenly she felt a sweeping singing sureness that everything about this would go well, would go smoothly, would be happy and good. She turned toward him again. "Oh, Matthew, even without you on Christmas or New Year's, it's being the happiest Christmas and New Year's of my life."

*　*　*

It was past midnight when Matthew got home; Joan was still dressed, waiting for him, though normally she was either asleep or in bed, watching some television celebrity show or an old movie.

"You weren't at your office," she said. "I tried three times."

"No. Is anything wrong?"

"The school suspended Johnny."

"Damn it. For how long?"

"The rest of the semester."

"Does he know?"

"I told him. He raised the roof."

"Did he know it was coming?"

"No more than we did. A fine time for them to do it, just to make sure we had a happy Christmas. I had a lovely evening with Johnny, you can believe it."

"I'm sorry I wasn't here too."

"You're never here."

She sounded bitter and he could not blame her. Not ten minutes after he had left to return to the office, she said, Mr. Garry, Johnny's homeroom teacher, had telephoned and told her the news. A formal letter was in the mail, apparently lost in the Christmas rush, since there had been no response from the Pooles before school had closed for the vacation, and finally, though Garry had left town on his own holiday, he had decided he ought to make sure they were notified without further delay.

"Was it about the hockey?"

"That and all the other things. 'Repeated insubordination,' Garry said."

His heart contracted. He had seen it coming, had talked it out with Johnny, not too insistently, not too often. The boy had been in a roil of rebellion against going out for hockey practice, just as in the fall he had refused football practice and in the spring, baseball. "All that crap about team spirit, Dad, just makes me puke."

"Suppose everybody at school just dropped things they didn't like—what kind of school would you have?"

"You didn't dish out that kind of stuff up in Boston to Jim Benting—the draft makes *him* puke."

Anger had flared between them, but in him admiration too. Formidable at thirteen, that kind of logic. Johnny was growing into a loner anyway, aside from his rebellion against authority in any of its forms. His abiding interests were making ship models and reading, the one unexpectedly expert and detailed, the other unexpectedly catholic and widespread. In the past two years he had raced through not only all the *Hornblowers* but also *Lord Jim* and half a dozen others by Conrad, also *David Copperfield* and half a dozen others by Dickens. But making friends came hard; most boys made him bridle, most girls bored him, and except for his favorite subjects, his chief comment about school was, "Forget it." Most of his teachers he dismissed as finks. The school rebels were his heroes, and the university rebels beyond them his gods. He was never going to be anything but a rebel himself, and like all rebels anywhere in any period of history, in any milieu, he was going to be hurt. And the people who loved him and valued him were going to be hurt with him.

My turn, Matthew thought, not pausing over the phrase. All parents knew pain as well as joy through their children; he had often wondered whether there was any greater joy in the world than that which came through a beloved child; now he thought that if that was true, then the corollary and opposite must also be true.

"Let's have some coffee," he said to Joan, "and talk. I'm sorry you had to take this on by yourself. I didn't dream anything like this was about to descend."

She didn't answer and he knew he had protested too

much. He either did that in troubled times or fell silent, speaking as if to somebody he hardly knew, as if speech came hard to him, as if he were a man of monosyllables.

"When things go wrong, you just clam up." That had become her accusation of recent years and it was true enough, particularly when a quarrel threatened. He could not stand the discussions, the explanations, the repetitions, but-you-said, but-you-never-said. The maddening paraphernalia of a quarrel stifled him, choked down his capacity to yield, to understand, and left him in stone-hard silence.

Except when it came to a fight for a client. In court he could feel the flow of power and will to proceed as the attack deepened; it was like a perceptible surge of adrenalin that he could see, a bright emission, life-rich and potent. Perhaps because he was himself not under attack, that withdrawal never occurred in court; on the contrary, words bubbled up, arguments, rebuttal, all urgent, clamoring to be spoken, leaving him with a sense of release and elation.

He felt again the racing exhilaration that had flooded him as he had argued for Jim Benting; he had felt an endless strength, to fight all the way, right up to the Supreme Court. Whatever one thought of Benting's turning in his draft card to symbolize his protest against war, surely no just man could condone the draft board for wiping out his student deferment, reclassifying him for immediate military service, using the draft as a whip to flog a dissenter.

No, he hadn't clammed up on the Benting case, he never did on something that deeply mattered to him. Perhaps that was the key clue, that phrase "deeply mattered." He glanced at Joan, silently drinking her coffee. As she habitually did when she entered the kitchen, she had flicked on the switch of her record player and he tried not to see the pile of song records on the turntable, or the upper stack, pegged up in the air waiting. The volume was low as it always was and it should have been easy to ignore the ceaseless thread of sound, but an unwelcome snobbery climbed within him. From morning to night she listened to this kind

79

of thing, twelve hours a day as a background for cooking and cleaning and knitting and sewing and all the things she said she really enjoyed. It mystified him, this difference between them about music, to name just one difference that had not been there at the beginning; for years her music had seemed mindless to him, automatic, just there, like humidity or sunshine, cloying or pleasant but mindless. He thought of the four records in his briefcase.

Again he was mystified at the many other distances that had grown so inexorably between them—music was only one of twenty such distances. How had it all happened, when they had started out as closely knit as any young couple in the first rapture of love?

And since it had, then how could any reasonable man ever expect any love to endure beyond its first beginnings? Could it endure between him and Dori? Given enough time, given life together in one household? In the deepest sense he was glad that this one valid test could not be made, would never be made. He was in love now with the insistence of a young man's love, the continuing desire of a young man's passion, and the fantasies and imaginings of a boy. But he knew, as a boy could not know, that there was no future for this kind of love, and that knowledge was his protection.

The affairs in between had never raised these questions; they had been for the most part brief and manageable; he was, he supposed, a selfish man when it came to emotional entanglement. He had been quick always to sense the shifting of the gears, as it were, in the mechanism of any affair; when the going was effortless and smooth, all was well, but when it became necessary to shift into middle gear and then into low because ease and smoothness were disappearing, then he grew watchful and unwilling. He had wanted no basic entanglements. He wanted no guilt. He wanted never again to reproach himself for being callous or cruel.

"I'll call Garry in the morning," he said at last.

"He's in Ohio for the holiday. He called from there."

"I can call Ohio. I'll talk to Johnny first."

80

"I've shopped so, for Christmas."

He saw through the non sequitur, and again he could not blame her.

*   *   *

If it wasn't Christmas night, he would phone Dori, late as it was. It had been an exhausting and endless effort to keep the semblances of a happy Christmas day; the two days before had been bad for everybody, edgy at best, violent and hostile at worst. Johnny was miserable and infuriating. Today had been a farce of Tolstoy's happy family, all the proper sounds of joy and surprise and gratitude at each new present, and underneath always the heaviness. And there had been no sudden collapse at suppertime into baby-sleepiness; Hildy was still awake in her room and Johnny had just slammed off to his.

Joan was exhausted too. Matthew sat sprawled in a big chair, silent. To say now that he was going to the office would be insulting, so palpably untrue would it be. Yet he had to get off for a while; he had been with them all through every moment of three nights and days and he needed to get off as he needed to breathe.

"I'm going for a walk," he said. "Want to come?"

Joan looked up in quick surprise and said, "I think I'll straighten up the rest of this mess."

He was glad and knew it. Outside he walked in the direction of his office—so much for habit—but for the first time in all that troubled stretch of days he could think fully of Dori. It was going to be a crowded week, one trip to Washington, another to Boston; if it were not so late now he would call her, but she probably had had a strenuous time of it too. Any number of times during yesterday and today he had longed to talk with her, to hear her voice, to tell her about Johnny and the blow it was, not for anything practical like advice or counsel, just for solace and the sense of sharing a problem. But how much could she understand this sort of thing, since she had never had children? How much could anybody understand who had never known the sweeping pride or the fierce dismay your child could give you, so dissimilar from any other pride or dismay in the world? How much did she regret not having children? The one subject she rather shied away from was this one of children; she had told him of her marriage and her divorce with enough completeness to make him see both clearly, but about the marriage being childless she had sounded constrained and somehow artificial.

"We did want children," she had said. "The one mistake was the timing. Practically the first minute after we got married, so we stopped it. But then when we did want to start a family—"

He could still see her palms outflung, to gesture "nothing." He remembered his discomfort at having embarrassed her and again thought, as he had then, But why embarrassed? He would have understood regret, or relief that there had been no child to suffer from the divorce, but there had been something else that he could not understand.

He glanced once more at his watch. Twenty after eleven. Much too late. It was a clear cold night, dry and frosty; around the streetlights, the air seemed to sparkle and the crisp night renewed him. At Fifty-eighth he paused and looked about him. A block to the west, across Fifth Avenue, the old bulk of the Plaza rose to its modest height, dwarfed by the new skyscraper being flung up across from it, and he turned toward the hotel, planless except for the idea of stopping in for a drink to feel better. Inside he ignored the bar and made for the row of telephone booths. A drink with her instead, a half hour of talk, no bed, no sex, just being with her for a little while; suddenly he wanted nothing else.

Five minutes later she was opening the door to him, a short wrap of some kind over her brief nightgown, her legs bare in the abbreviated wisp she wore, as short as a little girl's party dress. How beautiful she was this way, without makeup, with her hair loose, and how important in his life, and in so swift a time.

"The school suspended Johnny," he said abruptly. "Once before they warned him, but it's bad to have it really happen."

"Oh Matthew, why did they? When?"

He told her about the last two years of growing worry over his son, finding comfort in the intensity of her listening, the absorption of her listening. As if she'd been through it herself, as if she knew the sinking of the heart that came with this sort of trouble.

"Dori, don't you get bored hearing about somebody's kids?" he asked unexpectedly. "Most people get bored; you can't talk to them about that part of your life at all."

"Of course I'm not bored. If I had had children, I can't imagine—" She broke off abruptly as if the thread of her thought had been snipped by shears and now fluttered, dangling, in separated halves.

"What is it, Dori?" He reached for her hand and held it between his own. "There's something that makes you change, whenever we talk about kids. What happens? What sort of thing is it?"

"I didn't know I changed. What do you mean, 'change'?"

"I can't say exactly. But two or three times already I've come smash up to a stone wall closing you off. If you want that wall there, all right, but if it's something you want to talk about—"

She felt her eyes sting, and she thought, But don't blurt it out, not now, not ever. Wait one more day, wait until tomorrow—just to be sure you're not acting on impulse, not now, not ever.

"Oh, Matthew," she said, "you don't know about one of the greatest parts of my life, that started when I was married, when we began to want children, and didn't have any, and didn't, and didn't, until I finally went to a doctor to see why I wasn't getting pregnant, a Dr. Jesskin, who was specializing in that branch of medicine. Nearly thirteen years ago, it was, the first time I went."

Now it was Matthew who listened with the intensity of total absorption. Talking, she lived again through the long-ago tests, the long-ago promises, the disappointment and hope and disappointment again, the fearful pendulum. She felt again what she had so often felt as she watched women and girls going and coming in Dr. Jesskin's office, some happy, some disgruntled, some with an anxious look about them that made her sure they were there not because they were pregnant but because they could not be.

"My poor girl," he said once.

At his words, at the tightened handclasp, her eyes filled with tears. But she felt good because she hadn't lost control, hadn't blurted out too much; now when she did tell him about being pregnant he would know the whole story of it, know the years behind it, see it as she saw it.

"Did you ever think of adopting a child?" he asked at last.

"We had even set a timetable. We were going to give Dr. Jesskin one more year, and then if it was still nothing, we were going to start seeing adoption agencies. But after the divorce even that was finished." She looked at him in sudden curiosity. "Could I have gone ahead? Could a woman alone adopt a baby? Or is it true that only couples are allowed to?"

"Not that I know of." He became the attorney, alert, wary of the quick reply. "I'd want to check out New York adoption laws at the office with people who specialize in them, but I seem to have read of cases where single women did adopt."

"Don't bother looking it up. I just wondered." She suddenly sprang to her feet. "I haven't even given you a drink. We got talking right at the front door. But oh Matthew, I'm so glad we did."

CHAPTER FIVE

I should have told him, she thought the moment he left. This would have been such a natural time to tell him, when he was hearing all the rest of it, caring about it, knowing how it must have been. He would have known about this too, he would have seen why, he would have been as sure as I am about it.

Why didn't I? What made me pull back? I've got this fixed idea about waiting until the holidays are done with, but what's so sacred about that particular timetable? I'm using it as some sort of excuse. I'm big and brave when it comes to Cele or Gene, but I run like a rabbit—

Oh nonsense. You didn't know what it would do to him if you went on then and there, you wanted to give him time. You still don't know whether it will infuriate him or hurt him or put him off you completely. You daydream that he will understand and approve, but suppose he did just the opposite?

How little she knew of him after all, despite knowing so much. Twenty days of being in love made you positive—if you were twenty—that you knew an entire human being, but at forty you had learned better, at forty you knew how complex and involuted and shifting any love could be, at forty you knew the awful risks in the unexpected.

Unexpected? That was understatement for you. Poor Matthew.

The brush of depression feathered across her mind. It wasn't only with Matthew that she was being timid; she was putting off a dozen lesser problems that were still there to be solved, leaving them strewn all around her like assorted notes and reminders on a crowded desk, waiting to be picked up and disposed of. Suddenly that tranquil "one day at a time" seemed to be approaching its end, a bright bubble floating toward a brick wall.

In a week a new year would start and she would be in the eleventh week; her own body would be forcing her to positive action. She stripped off her nightgown and crossed to the dressing table, staring with clinical detachment as if at a stranger. She still looked, in this dimmed light, much as she had looked the first night Matthew had seen her, Matthew who had already wondered that she liked them to make love in the dark, who would one day hear that she loved to be made love to in the blazing sunlight. But even in the half-light there was more definition to the orbing, instantly seeable perhaps only to her own eyes but surely there. In a few days more he would see it too.

She slept restlessly as if she were in transit, in a plane or ship or train, always on the surface of sleep instead of burrowed down in the good depth of it. In the morning she woke suddenly, with a decisiveness of relief, as if she had at last solved some mystery while she slept. She jumped out of bed, thinking, If ever I was on an inexorable schedule, I'm on one now, and I'd better go in for some inexorables of my own. She crossed to her desk, dated a sheet of typing paper 12/26, and wrote:

DECISIONS TO BE MADE BEFORE Jan. 2, 1968

The tingle of danger ran along her nerves. This was no document to leave blithely around for Nellie to find. Nellie!

What to do about Nellie was one of the decisions, minor, but one of them.

"Minor," she wrote. "Nellie to go; two weeks' notice today."

Major: Hideout for Feb. 1 through July.

Major: Costs? Jesskin's fee? Hospital? Can't use Blue Cross under false name.

Major: Tell Dick T in letter? Wait till return? Not tell at all?

Minor: When Cele to shop for maternity clothes?

Major: Matthew.

My poor girl. He had felt how it must have been for her, he would know that following all those years there could be now no alternative for her, he would see that she had to go ahead, unmarried, married, alone, not alone, rich, poor, no matter any of those outer things. The primitive thing is what he would have seen, would have felt it as anybody feels the choice of life over nothingness, of birth over nothingness, of the filled vessel over the empty one.

She looked at the telephone. But he had a crammed week ahead, with only snatches of time between clients and flights and whatever bouts he would be having with Johnny; there was, after all, some good sense in the timetable she was following; it had to be right for Matthew too.

How different love was from sex itself, and how this with Matthew had transformed her life and needs in just three weeks. All the years with Tony seemed shorter in retrospect; Tony and she had been so young during their marriage—she saw it now and could even forgive him for tossing it all aside, for he had been operating then on the same young values. The young were always so sure they alone knew about love, but when they got to be thirty and then forty, they would see how much their lives had drawn from the passing years, how white and innocent and thin their first youth had been, and how muscled and complex and durable love could become.

She returned to her list. Major: Matthew. Her mind

balked at anything beyond Matthew, but she thought, Oh no you don't, no more stalling.

Minor: Pseudonym, alias.

Major: Mail forwarding; answers mailed from where?

Major: Bank and checks. New account under new name.

She stood up, read her list through with satisfaction and then went to the front door for her morning newspaper. In the kitchen for breakfast, she shivered; the window had been left open by Nellie and a nightful of blasting cold had come in through the careless half inch of space. She went back to her room for a long flannel robe and thought of flats in the ghetto with inadequate heat or no heat, their tenants endlessly calling up janitors to complain and threaten and beg.

Suddenly she knew where her hideout would be.

Not the Grand Tetons, not the Cape, not Washington—all these were fantasy places, absurd, impractical, valid in the first days of dream unreality but not worth serious thought now in the sure status of the third month. She was not the type to go unnoticed in any small town at any time; suddenly she remembered the vacation that had made her fall in love with Jackson Hole and the Grand Tetons so long ago. One sentence from her and somebody would ask, "Where are you from in the East? Boston? New York?"

Her clothes, the license plates on her old car, her letters, all from New York—everything would give her away now, and in the big months ahead. Alone, not staying at any dude ranch with a lot of other Easterners but really alone, living in some small rented cottage in a small town, she would within weeks trail question marks wherever she went. No matter what story she told—husband off in Vietnam, husband killed in an air crash—she would soon turn into a mystery lady, a personality, a Somebody Interesting.

Where did criminals go when they had to hide out?

Suddenly she laughed aloud. Why, she had had the answer all along, had seen it in a hundred movies, in a hundred crime shows on television, had read it in a hundred detective stories.

They hid out in the biggest city of all.

Not her own New York, not Madison and Park and Fifth, not in the Village, not in her own attractive neighborhood where all her friends were. Certainly not. But what about a furnished room in the Bronx for the six big months? How many of her friends would she run into in a grocery store up on Mosholu Parkway?

New York—it would be New York. There was something momentous in the decision. To stay right in New York, to abandon the travel folders of her imagination, to know she was half an hour away from Matthew, that she could phone Cele and ask her over, see Gene—

So of course, New York. If not the Bronx, then Brooklyn, out in Bay Ridge or near Coney Island. Perhaps good old Manhattan, just across the park, over on the West Side. Apart from Lincoln Center, she could probably wander all those side streets and avenues for hours every day without seeing one soul she knew.

The fact startled her. Life in New York was stratified, sectionalized, "segregated" not only as to black and white but also as to income, general style, general background. That awful word *status*. She knew her own segment of the city, that one narrow strip of attractive clean streets just east of Fifth and Central Park, where she had always lived, and where most of the people she knew had always lived too. There was a snobbery in it, suddenly horrid, a snobbery she had never caught before. She was angry at it now, glad to awaken to it at last. She would break through it, had to, wanted to. It would be part of the newness and goodness of everything else so suddenly happening.

She turned to the back pages of the *Times,* but at once realized she would do better with the Sunday *Times* where the real estate ads would be in the hundreds instead of in the weekday dozens. If not this Sunday which was the always shrunken post-Christmas paper, then in the next. Too early to look seriously, but just about right for some self-education.

She returned once more to her list of minors and majors

and telephoned Cele. "Hi, I've decided to do it for myself. Do you want to come with me?"

"Do what yourself?"

"Get my own clothes."

"Suppose you run into somebody, from the paper or wherever?"

"Couldn't I be in a maternity shop buying a gift for a dear pregnant friend?"

"Sure you could. Okay, I'll go along and buy one for a dear pregnant friend."

They met in an hour and by noon Dori had chosen everything she would be likely to need for the half year ahead. This was a new world to her, a world of the young, judging by the other customers, a world she had never even shared beyond a passing glance at some coy headline in an advertisement about "lady-in-waiting" or "blessed eventuality." She was not surprised that the clothes were so pretty, but their prices astounded her. A navy dress in a ribbed silk was a hundred dollars; a red checked housecoat, sixty; there seemed to be nothing for anybody poor. Suddenly she thought again of the girl who "got caught" and had to go on with her job, thought of her looking at these clothes, these price tags, thought of her going away empty-handed. There were thousands of such girls at this very minute of time, maybe hundreds of thousands, with their fear, guilt, shame, anger at the man who had "knocked them up." She could suddenly see them as a group, as a part of society out there in the city, in all the cities.

There's a minority for you, she thought; I guess it's my minority from now on. She wondered how big it really was, what the world really knew about it. She might find out for herself, right away while she could still go to libraries and newspaper morgues, save up the research until she was ready to write a piece about it.

"That's enough," Celia said firmly. "You try these on before you get swamped." The saleswoman showed them into a cubicle of fitting room, said, "When you decide, call me," and disappeared.

Another surprise caught Dori as she tried on the navy dress, a distant pleasure she could foretell as she imagined herself bulky inside it one day, and an impatience for that bulk to come, meaningful, unmistakable, a commitment from which there was no escape except the good escape of completion.

A sudden desire to show herself to Matthew in this dress seized her and she unexpectedly announced, "This one I'll take home with me, Cele. I just might wear it right away."

"A preemie," Cele said, laughing. But to herself she thought, Is she still seeing him? I thought they were winding it all up.

*   *   *

At home that evening, with some vague talk of cutting expenses, Dori gave Nellie two weeks' pay in lieu of notice and then checked off on her list the *minor* about Nellie and the *minor* about clothes. Minor or not, victories. In the morning she slept late, relaxed and warm and free of wake-up compulsions; then, remembering, she dressed quickly and went to the library.

It was the main branch at Forty-second and Fifth, the very sight of which always gave her a rising sense of expectation. In the vast catalog room, she went to the B and C sections and searched the cards for *Birth* and *Childbirth*. A subhead on one card caught her eye: "Illegitimate birth; 302,400 in yr." Three hundred thousand in one year, she thought, in this country alone; my God, are any of those three hundred thousand girls *happy* about it? She started for the reading rooms to get the book, but as she passed the A cards, she hesitated. *Ab, Ac, Ad.* She pulled out the *Ad* drawer and riffled through it half guiltily, telling herself that Adoption Laws could wait for another time. But she kept on, pausing at last over a card for a magazine article on "Single Parent Adoptions."

As if she had no choice, she filled out a blank for it and went straight to the Periodical Room. She was excited, tingling and warm along her temples as if a pleasant headache were possible, and she began to read. Too quickly at first, her eyes racing ahead of her mind like searchlights on a road trying to pick up some valuable object far ahead. After a moment she made herself start again at the beginning.

There was nothing in the statutes of New York State that prohibited a single person from adopting a child, though it rarely happened. The public adoption agencies still clung to their old standards of what constituted acceptability in adoptive parents; the optimum still was the married couple with a reasonably good income, happy in marriage, stable in personality, still young though not so young that they had been childless for fewer than three years. But an experiment begun in Los Angeles a few years back had proved that single-parent adoptions could and did work, and that they were often the only way to place the children most optimum parents didn't wish to adopt: the handicapped child, the Negro child, the Mexican child, the child of mixed bloods or mixed religions.

After Los Angeles the new concept had been ventured upon in half a dozen other cities; by now eight states had shifted from their rigid two-parent rule, and New York was one of them.

Change, changing, she thought, new mores, new wisdoms. She read the article once more, this time taking notes. The agencies all were officialdom itself—she would never go near officialdom. Would that make a difference?

Matthew would know. Or a partner in his office would know. The moment she told him, he would begin to help her. Suddenly she wished this was not a crowded week for him, wished there were no clients, no crisis with Johnny, no three-day family weekend off there in the snow.

Cut that out too, she thought a moment later. Futile wishing is one more thing you're never going to do.

*   *   *

"So, somewhere in this city," Dr. Jesskin said slowly, "you will get thee to a nunnery, so to speak. That is very good. Certainly for the sake of this baby who will be your child, it is very good. You have thought it out, in my opinion, to a decision that is wise. I am glad."

The grave tone, the unexpected quote, inappropriate to the point of being ludicrous—there was something so straightforward and so simple in the way he used them that she thought, I love him. He is so good and kind I really love him. He reached for his calendar and she waited.

"I have thought out some matters too," he said. "In April, the start of the sixth month, you will no longer come here to the office, even as my first morning appointment. I will instead start making house calls. Hideout calls, you might say."

"Oh, Dr. Jesskin."

"And for your confinement in July," he went on, glancing at her open folder, "where do you intend to go?"

"I hadn't even thought that far ahead."

"I already have to. Now that you do think of it, have you any idea where you will go to give birth?"

"Some small private hospital, I suppose."

"My dear Mrs. Gray, no. You are not going to have this baby in some little medical setup somewhere, and certainly not in your rented room."

"Then where? You have it all decided!"

"Yes, I think so. But it depends." He checked himself. His face was animated again and she thought. He's not only good, he's quite good-looking.

"It depends on money," he said firmly. "We must first consider money. My fee of course will be at your convenience, but I do not know if you can—if you are pressed—"

"I have thirteen thousand dollars in a savings bank," she said simply. "Not from alimony—I hate alimony. My father left us each—" She broke off in confusion. She wanted his help and his approval, but why was she telling him this much, why putting in her proud little bit about no-alimony? She glanced at him in embarrassment. He was again his usual self, attentive, waiting, absorbed. "I mean, within reason I can afford whatever you think best."

"Well then," he said, "we can dismiss the rented room and the little medical setup." The first hint of irony sounded. "In that case you are going to have this baby right in Harkness Pavilion, right on the eighth floor, the maternity floor. That is where."

"Harkness?" She could not think he was joking, but Harkness? City editors always kept an eye on Harkness. The wealthy went to Harkness, the celebrated, the illustrious, people who made news, whose deaths and births and illnesses and recoveries were minutely reported in the press.

He was watching her, with delight in her disbelief. "One does not expect an illegitimate birth at Harkness, so that is where you will go, one of the pampered ladies there."

Suddenly she laughed. "How marvelous! I wouldn't have dreamed of it."

"The one thing different from the other ladies is that you will not be on orders to walk the corridors for exercise. You will stay behind your closed door all the time, before and after, and a NO VISITORS sign on the door. You see I am considering matters." He held up his hand to ward off her thanks. "One more thing. On that door, along with the sign of NO VISITORS, will be two names. One will be Jesskin, but yours will be—what?"

"My false name? I've thought of a dozen—"

"I will need to know soon, to reserve a room for July twenty-third or thereabouts."

Suddenly she leaned toward him, her eyes anxious. "There will have to be a false birth certificate, won't there? Under whatever name I choose?"

"Yes."

"But you will be signing it?"

"Of course."

"Couldn't you be disbarred or whatever it is, for signing a legal document you know is false?"

He picked up the paperweight, apparently examining its many facets. When he spoke, his voice was dry, remote, as if he had all at once become very nearly a stranger.

"We will be very clever," he said, "and this will remain our personal business. But if I am found out, and charged with

94

signing a false birth certificate, I would have to find a way to manage that."

"But have I the right to let you run such a risk?"

"My dear girl, it is not you alone who are involved." He rose and she thought, It's the first time he's sounded sentimental about the baby. "The other person now involved," he continued as he nodded to her in farewell, "is me."

* * *

It was a wild idea but she could not resist it. She had to see it, look up at it, imagine herself there on a hot blue summer day. The bus to take was the No. 4, and she walked from Dr. Jesskin's office to the bus stop on Madison and waited.

Harkness, eighth floor, the maternity floor—just saying the words made July twenty-third closer. Everything since she had made her list had done that, piling reality on reality. How much more there was to tell Matthew tonight than there had been one week ago.

At nine or ten tonight she would be telling him. This time there would be no backing away. She was suddenly impatient. If only it could be this moment instead. Or at lunchtime or at five. A No. 4 bus was bearing down on her but suddenly she drew back from the curb. They had never had luncheon together and they had never even met for cocktails.

She found a phone and dialed his office. She had called him only once before but she recognized his secretary's voice and said, "Is Mr. Poole in? This is Theodora Gray."

"Yes he is, Mrs. Gray. Just a moment."

It was several moments before he came on and her heart began its familiar thudding. She must not think now of how he would take it; she never should have wondered how he would take it.

"Hello," Matthew said in the receiver, and she said, "I hate disturbing you at your office. Happy New Year," and he said, "I like to be disturbed," in an artificial bright tone that was for his secretary. "Happy New Year to you."

"I wonder if—I wanted to talk to you about something and

I thought maybe you could drop by for a drink after the office."

There was a pause, and then, almost formally, he said, "If you think best, I could make a free hour right now."

"You could? In the middle of everything?"

"Of course I could."

"Oh, Matthew, thanks."

"I have a couple of phone calls first, and then I'll be there. Let's say about twelve. Perhaps you'd give me a sandwich."

She hurried home and changed into the navy dress, finding a rightness in wearing it now for the first time. He was dropping everything, perhaps canceling a luncheon appointment; he had instantly understood that this was no idle impulse and he was responding without pause. It was part of him, part of what drew her to him, this responsiveness in him awakening total response from her.

The navy dress seemed frivolously short, shorter than she had thought it when she had tried it on in the store, shorter than her usual clothes, but she rather liked the frivolity of it. And she liked herself in it—if she stood tall in it, holding in hard, there was still nothing but the flat straight planes of the navy silk.

Making sandwiches and coffee, she tried not to rehearse what she would say. Rehearsed lines were always false, glib, revealing a poor thin worried tension in the speaker. But she rehearsed it anyway, framing the first thing she would say, then the next, hearing her voice speaking to him, his answering her, until by the time he arrived and asked, "What is it, darling?" she felt confusedly that she had, by some telepathic miracle, already revealed everything she had to tell him.

"It's something I've been wanting to tell you, but kept putting off and off."

His face was sober and he looked at her with a concentrated attentiveness. She said, "Oh Matthew, thank you for coming right over," and preceded him into the living room. His concern was so total. Men always expected total attention from the girl they were with, but so few returned it when it was the girl speaking. Her throat was dry but she ignored the bar table and sat beside him on the sofa, suddenly floundering for any words at all.

"What, Dori?"

"Oh Matthew, I'm suddenly so nervous, it's so important to me."

"Is it about us?"

"Not really, and yet it is, the way anything is now." She saw her own fingers interlacing and clutching at each other. "You were so marvelous when I told you about all that time of my trying to get pregnant, you understood it, you really saw how it must have been."

"Darling, are you pregnant now?"

He said it so swiftly, the impression of eagerness in his way of saying it was so fleeting, that she could never be sure it was there. For one flashing moment she thought, Women all over the world, but she flinched from it and the instant was lost.

"That first night we made love, I didn't know yet—I was afraid to believe it. I had been to Dr. Jesskin that very morning for tests but the results weren't in yet and it could have been nothing, a skipped period, it's happened before—"

"That first night?"

"I'd seen Jesskin in the morning but he couldn't know without tests—"

He stood up abruptly. He seemed very tall standing above her, tall and rigid and alien. He was not looking at her, he was not looking at anything, he seemed not to be breathing. Then he said, in a rough voice she had never heard, "Are you pregnant by another man? Is that what you're telling me?"

"If I'd already known for sure that first night, I would have told you then and there—no, I couldn't have told you yet, but I wouldn't have let us start."

"Are you saying you *are* pregnant?"

"Oh yes, and I—"

"Pregnant by somebody else. You are saying that too?"

"You see, I was coming to the end of an affair, and usually

97

with me, a year or so will go by before I even meet anybody who interests me again, but this time you—"

He caught her wrist. "You are going to have a baby from that other affair and you've known it and you let us go ahead, deeper and deeper, with me not knowing one goddam thing about it. Christ!"

He flung her wrist free and she was hot with anger at the rage in his words. She squeezed her lids shut as if to hold back tears but she heard him cross the room to the bar table, heard him open the whiskey carafe and pour a splash of Scotch and drink it, without bothering with ice or soda.

"I meant to be more careful," she said, "about the way I told you, I didn't dream it would suddenly be said. For a long time I meant to write something to you first, or maybe just say I was going away for a while because of something that had happened before I ever met you." He said nothing. His hand rested on the neck of the whiskey carafe, fingers tight around its filigreed silver collar. "But ever since I told you the first part of it I wondered what had made me pull back and then it all seemed banal to wait and try to think how to say it, as if I were afraid or ashamed."

"Damn it, you're thinking exclusively of what you felt and how you feel."

"I'm not. I've thought a million times about how you would take it, I've worried so about the way you might feel, I kept thinking, 'Just for one more week, and then I'll find the right way to tell him—'"

"So you blast me with it like a load of buckshot."

Dori winced at his roughness, but thought, You did blast him. How had it happened? How could things go so wrong? "I didn't mean to blast you. I'm sorry—oh you have to know I'm sorry it came out that way."

He made no reply. He went to the window and stood staring out at the raw winter day, the streets grayed with sooted snow. She suddenly thought of her brother Gene staring out the window that night she had told him and Ellen, and the dearness of Gene ever since, even after Ellen's visit. But Gene was her brother.

98

She felt sad and compassionate toward him, a new sense of Matthew despite his rage. She started toward him, but halted. Everything she said now came out wrong.

He suddenly left the window. "Why don't you look pregnant?" He looked pointedly at her stomach. "How long has it been?"

"I do look it when I'm not standing this way, straight up this way, holding myself in. It's part of the exercises I do, it's sort of a habit already." She hesitated and then said, "See?" As she let her muscles relax, the flat planes of the navy dress altered; a delicate sphere took shape.

He looked away sharply. "How long has it been?"

"This is the eleventh week."

"Then every time we've been together—oh my goddam Christ."

She remembered his talk about cross-examining and nearly cried out that he had no right to put her through this quizzing. But he did have the right. She had given him the right by loving him and letting him love her.

"Are you going to marry the—the whoover ho was?"

"I haven't even told him. He's away now."

"Going to blast him with it too?"

"I don't know whether I will ever tell him at all."

He started to speak but thought better of it. He went to the bar again and splashed more Scotch into the glass he had left there, still not bothering with ice or soda. Then he said, "I'd better not stick around. I'll call you when I get this into some sort of shape."

Dori watched him go to the front door where she had so often met him with an upsurging of pleasure, and the drag of depression pulled downward throughout her body. He took up his coat and hat, not putting them on, and left.

She turned back to the living room. On the coffee table the pretty plate of sandwiches, the fruit and coffee suddenly repelled her. She remembered the way he had looked at her after asking why she didn't look pregnant. Again she squeezed her eyelids shut but this time the tears came anyway. She went to her room, took off the navy dress, hung it

99

deep in her closet as if it were something to be hidden even from herself, and went back aimlessly to the living room. The thought of food was repugnant. She drank a cup of coffee, took everything out to the kitchen and started to wash the dishes. It was important at times like this to have something essential to do.

* * *

An hour later she was on the street once more, on the corner of Madison, waiting for the No. 4 bus. This time she took it eagerly, as if it contained some miracle comfort she could find nowhere else. She watched the store windows go by, watched the people, watched the traffic lights, her mind emptied by some primitive mechanism, draining it of pain and guilt. She felt guilty because she had failed in the way she had told him. Matthew deserved more of her, anybody deserved more of the person he loved, for there was an unwritten treaty between two people in love, to spare the other needless pain and shock. Pain and shock there might have been for him no matter how gentle she had been in the telling of this news, but she had multiplied them both by "blasting him with it."

Defensive, Dori, always defensive. For such a long time now those words had not sounded in her mind, not once, but here they were again, like old antagonists one had hoped to be rid of forever but who persisted in coming back at unlikely times, unbidden but undismissable. But this time she could not ignore them.

This was a *major,* more major than anything she had written into her happy list. She knew that losing Matthew for good was what she had been afraid of all along, the threat through all her delays and timetables. And she also knew that to lose him for good would entail no minor adjustment; it would be no peaceful and willing ending of an affair as it had been with Dick Towson, but total upheaval as at the end of her marriage. She shuddered.

Outside the bus window the streets grew unfamiliar and strange. Dori tried to pin her attention to them, like some sightseer from a foreign land, but she could not concentrate. Delay was so false, so much the opposite of what she really was. She should have told him that first night, before they had ever touched each other, there on the red sofa; she should have blurted it out right then, "It's probably all a mistake, but there is one chance in a billion that I am pregnant, and I won't even know until Thursday." That would have been shock too, but a protective one keeping them back from a worse danger.

Instead she had thought, Just this once, and then through the hours that followed, just these wonderful days. No matter how natural that had been, no matter what her motives, the delay and then the planning were so out of character for her, she should have known better than to rely on them even for a short while. She had been called tactless too often not to know that she lacked the small graces of subterfuge. And she had been called oversensitive too often not to know that she was not one of the thick-skinned of the world who never got hurt. Faults, both of them, but together they added up to something that was the basic truth about her.

For the first time, Dori felt comforted, and by the time she left the bus and stood looking up at the great blocks of white buildings between her and the river, she began to recapture at least part of the eagerness she had felt that morning when she had left Dr. Jesskin's office.

There was Harkness Pavilion, a separate unit from the main hospital, closer to the river. She counted upwards; there was the eighth floor. The maternity floor. The arctic wind whipping at her from the Palisades across the Hudson suddenly lost its meaning; she could imagine a July day of piercing blue sky and yellow morning light and somewhere in there herself in the very act, the everyday, commonplace, unbelievable act of giving birth.

She began to walk toward the river. She stood at the crest of Riverside Drive and looked up once more. One, two, three, four, five, six, seven, eight—one of those windows on the eighth floor may belong to my room. She could see herself standing by the window, looking out at the water, and something in her seemed to stretch forward toward that distant day, as if one could crane toward a point in time.

She retraced her steps and again stood on the Broadway corner where she had left the bus. But she was too restless to enclose herself in the specific space of a taxi or bus, and she began to walk, not the crisp positive walking she did every day as part of her orders, but an aimless, sightseeing walk, not ambling only because the wind was too sharp for meandering along. The stores interested her, the movie houses, the neighborhood in general. For all she knew she might find her furnished room somewhere near here; this might become the hideaway.

A store caught her eye because of its name, Tots and Toddlers, and though she smiled at the mawkishness, she stopped to look at the window display. Then with no prior decision to do so, she went in and said to the only clerk there, "I'd like to buy a present for a newborn baby."

"Boy or girl?"

"I don't know." She laughed in confusion and said, "It just happened and I haven't even heard that much. Does it matter?"

"Not if you don't care about blue or pink. What sort of present were you thinking of?"

"Anything, nothing fancy."

The woman looked at her with less interest, as if she had received a code message that this customer was not ready to be lavish. She turned to a series of shelves behind her, stacked one above the other, but each open on its front face like a bookcase. "A wrapper," she said. "Like a bathrobe, you know?"

Dori accepted the scrap of white flannel she had handed her and instantly said, "Why, the whole sleeve isn't as long as my middle finger."

With a voice tinged with the faintest scorn, the woman said, "Have you ever seen a real newborn baby?"

Dori laughed outright. "Only from a distance," she said. "This will be the first time close up. I'll take it."

CHAPTER SIX

Matthew woke up as if a fire alarm had shot off at his ear. It had happened every night for the ten nights since she had told him. Each time he heard a voice jeering, her voice, often his own, sometimes an unknown's, but always taunting and raucous.

"That's right, buddy, always blame the other person." This time it was his own voice, needling, insulting. Here he was blaming Dori for this ripping tearing clawing of his entrails, as if she had planned this butchery of jealousy, had planned it weeks before she knew he existed, had begun to plan it with Jesskin years before.

But he could not stop his anger. Hour after hour he could not; try as he would to return to thought and clarity, he could not. There was no way. He would have to forget it, forget her. He would have to get over her, never see her again, rid himself of her once and for all.

For almost a week he knew that this was what he had to do. It was a nightmare matched by the alternative nightmare of continuing with her. See her again? Love her again? Glory in her body?

He shook with fury at his own fury; he should not have let himself fall into this pit, should have stayed remote, a man having an affair with a damn sexy responsive appealing female, but nothing more, as with all the other affairs. He had instead let this become different, let his whole being become fettered and tethered by need, by love, by some positive sense that here again was the thing he had never thought to know again.

Pain, goddam it, pain and grief and suffering always, when you had done nothing to deserve it, when you knew yourself free of causing it. Every damn life anywhere had its damnable quota of it, not to be exorcised, only to be endured.

Like one of the split-second images flashed across a movie screen, he remembered his mother holding a tiny Hildy, looking down at her, sitting alone there looking down at her first grandchild.

Jesus, why now? Why see that lonely posture now, springing into reality again? Over the years at mad irrelevant intervals, that image would suddenly stand before him again, clear, silent, there. He would flinch and it would go, but for an instant it was there. His mother who had never hurt him had hurt him indeed in the end.

And now Dori, whose gleaming slender body possessed his mind and filled his memory. She was no longer his, basically she had never been his, not even that first time on the red sofa.

Be fair, be fair. That first time she didn't know herself. You came down from Boston with one determination, admit it, you couldn't wait, you wanted her then, that night, she did hesitate, you felt it and spoke of it to her and nobly offered to wait if she wasn't as uninvolved as she had thought. But *this* was what was holding her back, and you gave her as much chance as a snowball, so now you're blaming her for going ahead. You knew all along you wouldn't let her fight you off on that damn red sofa. You knew it then and you know it now, you always have made love to the women you wanted to make love to, you always make them want you to, and now—goddam it, damn it, damn it, damn this for happening.

He would call her when he got this into some sort of shape. That's what he had said, thinking that if only he could get off by himself, away from the sight of her, the God-given processes of reason and enlightenment would come into play and help him accept this as another one of life's problems, to be handled, absorbed, reconciled to, like a verdict gone against you, like Johnny's suspension from school. But he didn't really believe it.

I'm not a diminisher by nature. He had written that to her in his first letter, faintly enamored of the sound of it, but meaning it, feeling sure of himself with her, sure of them together. Now he was truly diminished, withdrawn, dry with coldness and fevered at the same time, half of himself gone dead and still.

The word *diminished* infuriated him. Abruptly he got up from bed, slid his feet into his slippers, nearly gasping at the first sting of their frozen leather, and went into the kitchen. Night after night he had done this also; twice Joan had waked too, to admonish him not to be too concerned about Johnny or even about Hildy's sudden demands for a bigger allowance when her next birthday came. "It's more than that," he had said, but when she had looked attentive, interested, he had quickly added, "You know how things stick in your mind and won't come unstuck."

Now he waited for a moment to be sure she did not wake and follow him. From the icebox he got half a glass of milk, took it into the living room, and then he unlocked his briefcase. In an inner compartment was the letter that had come yesterday morning at the office. He had read it a dozen times already:

DEAR MATTHEW,
I would give anything not to have started with you without telling you first that Dr. Jesskin had just begun tests and that I would not know for sure until Thursday. I cannot, even now, be sorry about *it*, but I am wretched about you.

Always,
D.

A dozen times, too, he had tried to answer it, but he would write, "Dear Dori," and then his pen would go still. He would look at the phone but wonder what possibly to say. The specific idea of going to see her, of talking to her, of trying to put into words—he could do nothing.

He needed more time. He could not think of these new complexities. Never had his own life been so filled with complexities: Johnny, the Benting case, the sudden vision of Hildy as a sixteen-year-old and all at once not a child any more. Maybe later on, the time would come when he was calm enough again to see this about Dori in an acceptable light. But not now.

He tore her note across and then again across. He looked about for a place to throw the scraps, then aligned them, put them back into his briefcase, and locked it once more.

* * *

On the fifteenth, Dori told Tad Jonas she was quitting to try herself at free-lancing. She would of course stay as long as he needed her, but because there was one piece with an early deadline, she would appreciate it if she could pull out pretty soon. Jonas said, "Anytime, cookie, I knew it was coming," and she left the office for the last time.

She had heard nothing from Matthew.

The one note she had written him was short, almost too short by the time she got through tearing sentences from it. She had sent it to his office, marked *Personal*, wondering how sacred that word on an envelope was in his secretary's opinion. The very next morning she had waited for the mail; he had not answered it. Nor the morning after, nor the morning after.

It's a fascinating time to be alive anyway, she told herself, not only because of being pregnant and watching it happen, but because of a million things outside me. There was hideous news or wonderful news every day: hideous, like the indictment that week of Dr. Spock and the four others, with trial to come in April or May; wonderful, like the story from South Africa about transplanting the heart of a man newly dead into the body of that dying dentist. Her own blood had pumped in some wild hope at this bizarre story; a new world was opening for the future, with new chances, new possibles. Maybe by the time any 1968 baby grew up, there would be a hundred such miracles, a cure for cancer found, the end of pain, the end of war.

The end of pain? Not since the despairing days just after Tony's departure had she felt this gnawing sensation of emptiness, and this seemed sharper now, more unremitting. Or was that because you could only remember past pain, never reinvoke it? Every moment of thought now said *Matthew*, the soft hush at the core of his name like a brush across her heart. Never before had she heard the sound made on the ear by Matthew's name; now she heard it constantly, and constantly it brought with it its cousin sounds, *breath, death, ethic, ethical.* Ethic, ethical—what was right here, what wrong?

She had foreseen that he might leave her when he knew but she had never believed in it. She had been vain, loving his praise of her body, wondering only whether that would lessen, and by how much. She had told Cele what Dr. Jesskin had said about sex and pregnancy and Cele had said, "Oh, yes, right up to maybe the last few weeks." There was a special quality, Cele had told her, a new intensity. But Cele was remembering herself and Marshall as a young couple; it had been "their" pregnancy and had made them both happy.

That flash of eagerness in Matthew's first question, "Darling, are you pregnant now?"—she had not imagined it, and now it was too poignant to bear. If she had been able to let him think it was "their" pregnancy, that instinctive eagerness might have expanded and grown, thrusting, strong enough to endure through all the clutch and twist of problems that would face him because of it. He would never leave Hildy and Johnny; his devotion to them was an absolute. But he would have become involved too with *this* child, would never have walked out this way, would not now be silent and absent and lost.

But oh God, I couldn't. I couldn't lie to him and pretend

and go on letting him think, and then go through with the terrible lie about a premature baby in July.

There were women who could and she marveled at them and also despised them. She half envied them their shrewdness and ability to manage life and she also detested them for it. She herself had had no choice. Her options had lain only in method, and there she had proved a failure.

She could not sleep. At each shrill ring of the telephone she told herself it would not be Matthew, but when it was not she had to force her "hello" to sound normal. Irrationally, she summoned telephone repairmen to muffle the ring, but the new sound was no less rasping. The doorbell, the morning mail, a florist's delivery boy in the elevator—each became a hazard to be met and overcome. Within hours of mailing her letter to him she began rewriting it in her mind, adding phrases she had not thought of in time, letting herself argue with him, plead, even at last accuse him. *Don't let us make all the young mistakes?* But at the first real difficulty, Matthew, you cut away in a rage like a boy of twenty, ignore a decent letter or throw it into the nearest trash basket.

Rebuttal at once, defense of him; perhaps he needed silence and absence to regroup his forces, to rearrange his life with Joan—

Come on, cut that out, she thought, the one damn thing you're never going to do is to think about any future with Matthew. You can love him or hate him, see him or not see him, fight or make up, but the one thing you are never going to do is to think about being married to him.

She felt better. Vaguely she was reminded of something else that had once comforted her, but she could not catch hold of what it had been. It had come at some other time when she was becoming overemotional, and she had seen then that she need not give in to it.

Weekends were easier; she had never seen him on Saturdays or Sundays. On the third Sunday of his absence she turned determinedly to the voluminous real estate ads in the paper. Houses—Manhattan, Houses—Brooklyn,

Houses—Queens, page after page of houses for sale, for rent, everything houses. Also apartments: Furnished, Unfurnished, Six Rooms, Four Rooms, Two Rooms, Apartments Wanted, Apartments to Share. At last she came to Furnished Rooms, East Side, West Side. There were only a few of each, and most of these in hotels, hotels with unknown names in side streets, but all belonging to the same family of third-rateness. Hotels were out anyway; she had to do without even a shabby lobby, without a front desk and elevator man.

That meant a room in a brownstone. In half an hour she had underlined half a dozen. One was in the Bronx, on West 253rd Street, and she wondered if it were near Bronx Park; another was rather close, on West Ninety-fifth, definitely near Central Park; another was in a remodeled brownstone in the old Chelsea district. That was too close to the Village. If she could find something near one of the great parks, she could do her brisk three miles in the early morning or evening; she was free of the usual fears and alarms about the dangers of the streets and the parks. She had always been a lone walker in the city, and not once had she encountered anything more suspect than a weaving drunk.

She reread the ad about the place on West Ninety-fifth. It was not a furnished room but a "2 rm studio, gd. fl, all new furn," and suddenly she thought, On the ground floor I'd never have to meet people on the stairs. The $180 rent astonished her but she stared at the telephone number which served as signature to the ad and almost without volition dialed it.

A foreign voice answered, perhaps Italian, perhaps Spanish, but there was no difficulty in understanding. Yes, just renovated, repainted, new icebox, new bed, new everything, very big studio room and kitchen. No roaches. Nobody had lived there since the new furniture. All first time for the new tenant.

"When could I see it?"

"Anytime. Ring the super's bell."

"I'll be there in about a half hour."

"What name, please?"

She hesitated. She had been choosing and discarding names for so long and now suddenly she had to decide. "Grange," she said. "Mrs. Grange—I'll be there right away." "If it's rented, don't blame me. First come, first served." "I'll hurry."

She dressed quickly, a spurt of new interest lifting her spirits. The time ahead is still good, she thought, nothing can change that. How strange that she could feel, at the core of surrounding pain and loss, this persistent quiet rightness. It was almost as if she were, somewhere, still happy.

As the taxi turned off Central Park West into Ninety-fifth, she looked out in anticipation. The street looked bare and almost clean; with the temperature below twenty, the bareness was not surprising. In summer there would be ear-piercing children screaming to each other as they played, music blaring from open windows, jammed traffic, the usual hullaballoo of city streets in hot weather. But by then, with only days to go, why should she mind anything?

Dori stopped in front of the house. Its brick front was already shabby, mean, its windows dirty against an assortment of lace curtains, chintz curtains, drawn shades. Two great garbage cans stood at the curb where the taxi stopped, lidded and faintly odoriferous, a pair of horrid welcomers. She ignored them and went into the small vestibule where an astonishing expanse of brass letterboxes stretched across one wall. She counted sixteen and thought, At these rents, people room together. She pressed the bell over the typed card, *Steffani, SUPER*, and at once the foreign voice of the telephone queried through the round grating in the brass: "Who is it?" And she made herself wait a second, rehearsing, before she said, "Mrs. Grange."

A moment later the landlady appeared and without a word of greeting led the way to a door at the rear of the hallway. "Everything new," she said as she opened it, and as Dori went by her a chill of disappointment seized her. It was a large room, with low ceilings and two windows on a cement-paved backyard; it might once have been the kitchen of the house, as at Cele's, and the floor was covered with yellow-and-brown linoleum as if it were still a kitchen. But it was furnished like a studio bedroom-living room in the drab good taste of a bargain furniture store. A stiff squared-off sofa that the landlady proclaimed "a convertible, a double," was flanked by a pair of ladderback chairs in a shiny veneer, obviously new, and there was a corner table, also shiny new. Where a fireplace might have been was one armchair near a home-made platform of wood, oblong, twelve inches from the floor, empty, devoid of meaning until the landlady said, "For the television."

"And is there an outlet for an air conditioner?"

"Don't need no special outlet." Mrs. Steffani gave her a closer look, a scrutiny as if to make some judgment. A television set was expected, but not an air conditioner? By what yardstick? This was no slum neighborhood; actually it was a rather pretty street with several other remodeled houses, and she certainly would not be the only tenant on the block with an air conditioner. Then why that second look as if she had asked for a private garage?

Mrs. Steffani led her to the kitchen, a sliver of a room, also facing the cemented yard, and then to another sliver, the bathroom, the walls of both a staring dead white. Here too was the same unused look, with no fingerprint, no frayed edge, no smudge.

"Did you just paint it?"

Mrs. Steffani nodded. "All the furniture new, every stick. Look here, this new stove and icebox. Brand-new."

"Lovely," Dori said, going back to the big room. But how ugly, she thought; I'd simply die in such an ugly place.

Behind her Mrs. Steffani said, "You want it? Or you don't want it? The lease is one year. First and last month in advance."

"I won't need it for a whole year. My husband—"

"A year's lease. Here, nothing by the month. You want your husband to see? Okay. It could be rented the next twenty minutes. First come—"

"Yes, I know." She cast one last glance around as if trying to decide. "I'll let you know. I have one other place to see."

At once Mrs. Steffani dropped any show of interest, going back into the hallway, Dori dismissed and forgotten even as she passed by her to the front door. Out in the street she paused, relieved to be away from the unspoken pressure she had felt inside. A hundred and eighty a month for *that?* Because it was remodeled and not subject to rent control! This dreadful housing shortage let such rents happen. But a year's lease would run over two thousand. Unthinkable to start off that way. She certainly could find something that cost less.

In the bus uptown to her next address she reminded herself that there was still no great rush; she could look again next Sunday and the next. But the moment she arrived at the furnished room on West 253rd, she was nervous. A smell of mildew and frying fat rushed out at her, filthy walls appalled her and she fled, suddenly exhausted, her one thought to go home. But she did not go home. By bus, subway, taxi, she continued on the rounds of her addresses, from one impossible to another.

Her nervousness deepened. Suppose that a place like Mrs. Steffani's really was unique, and that after a few more Sundays when there was no more time for being choosy, suppose that then she could find nothing but the ones with frying fat and filth?

Suddenly the "just renovated, everything new, no roaches" seemed a treasure she had wholly underestimated. Suddenly the linoleum on the floor, the varnish, the bargain-basement taste seemed admirable, utterly desirable. Quiet, clean, a few of her own things strewn about—why had she ever left this paragon of a place for somebody else to snatch up? Perhaps after July she could sublease it—better not raise that question now. She hailed a taxi.

"Is it rented?" she asked over the brass announcer in the hall, and then said, "Wonderful," at Mrs. Steffani's reply.

Mrs. Steffani demanded a deposit until the lease was ready tomorrow or Tuesday. "Check or cash, twenty-five down."

Dori opened her purse. But I can't write a check signed

Grange, she thought, and nearly said so out loud. "Here's the cash," she said. "May I have a receipt?"

For the first time Dori felt optimistic. Tomorrow she would find a bank in the neighborhood and open an account in the name of Dorothy Grange. A bank account under an assumed name. She might move in right away, this week, the moment the lease was signed and a telephone connected. There would be a sense here of a new start, of getting down to it, of cutting all the trains of thought to the past. Here if the phone rang, she wouldn't leap for it as if it might be Matthew. He would not even know her number.

*   *   *

Four evenings later, she glanced around her bedroom, disheveled as it was with its still-open suitcases and a dozen odds and ends. The telephone rang and a voice said, "Towson, home from the wars."

"Dick! When did you get in?"

"Yesterday, and does this city look good."

"You've been gone, let's see, three whole months. Your pieces have been great."

"Thanks. I just heard you'd copped out on your paper. Is that true?"

"Tell me I'm crazy. I'm going to free-lance."

"Why didn't you drop me a line about it? I'd have told you then."

"I should have written." She added quickly, "But I've thought of you lots."

"I'll bet."

"I really have."

"When do I get to see you? How about a drink tomorrow around five?"

"I can't, Dick, I'm sorry."

"Then when? How about after dinner? Have you a date tomorrow night?"

"I can't think. Wait a minute." Automatically she turned toward her calendar as if she really were looking for a free afternoon or evening in a crowded life. But her eyes were closed. Automatically too, as she did so many times every single day, she tightened her muscles over her stomach, feeling the good tautness, releasing, tightening, knowing that now even when they were tight there were no bland flat planes any longer. "Dick, could I give you a raincheck?" she said at last. "I'm sort of swamped with things right now."

For a moment there was no answer. Then he said, "Well, okay, if that's the way it is." His voice brightened as he added, "Have fun, whatever."

"I'll do that."

"Think of me."

"Oh I will." Suddenly she laughed a little. "I truly will."

So are decisions made, she thought as she hung up. It's as if your active mind had nothing to do, as if you just put the problem into the miracle-computer of your unconscious, fed it in, left it there through all the mysterious whirrings and clackings and tumblings, and then as if there came, at the proper time, the desired *output*, your decision, firm, clear, authoritative.

Input and output, technology's new words for a process as old as man, as old as conscience. How could it possibly be right to tell Dick Towson that I am going to have a baby that he unwittingly sired? To what end? To make him feel guilty? Responsible for its support? Honor-bound to get a divorce and make an honest woman out of me? I am an honest woman.

And suppose he did, what about that other honest woman, his wife?

She left the telephone and returned to her packing. She was moving in the morning, and Cele had been over all day to help. Clothes were easy; two suitcases were ample. There had been a problem about the pots and pans and dishes and books she wanted, because cartons or a barrel would scarcely go with her official story to the building, that she was off on a world cruise by plane and ship for ten weeks, but Cele had solved it by lending her a huge plaid carryall that concealed awkward shapes. Cele was known to the doorman; she would be coming over every few days to pick up her mail.

"A hard and fast itinerary is out," Dori had explained. "It's a crazy kind of trip with a crazy schedule."

"I wouldn't mind taking a trip like that myself, Mrs. Gray."

"I'm dying to get started, Bill." It would be the longest ten weeks on record. The stretchingest, she thought, and smiled.

Now she checked once more to see that she had overlooked nothing. She glanced longingly at her record player; it was a fine true system and she wanted it with her. But one didn't take hi-fi equipment on world cruises and Cele was going to lend her one of Marshall's the moment she was installed. Into the carryall she had slid half a dozen records; now, almost as a final rite, she added her set of the four she had hunted down so happily to give to Matthew at Christmas.

The packing had tired her but she was too keyed up to consider sleep and she made one last tour around each of her four rooms, in one last search for some forgotten object she would sorely miss. This was what made packing difficult, the selecting and choosing, this I must take, that I needn't, yes, but I might need it. Now, looking down at the mahogany stand near her desk where there reposed in all its grand solidity her vast unabridged Webster's, she hesitated once more. Cele had ridiculed her for considering it an essential on West Ninety-fifth Street, and she had yielded. "But don't I deserve one or two fetishisms?" and Cele had raucously declaimed in an exaggerated Jewish accent, "Fetishisms yet! On a world cruise she needs a hundred-pound dictionary, plus whatever else she's carrying."

They had laughed and now Dori smiled, remembering. Cele was that rarest of creatures, a friend who was there when help was needed. She would be there in the morning for the actual move; she would do the unpacking at the new place, she would do the first marketing for her, stow supplies in cupboards and cabinets. "Sugar and soap flakes and canned goods weigh tons, Dori—you can do nice things like fruit and steak."

This final rambling search for any forgotten object was oddly pleasing. Closing her apartment, locking the door behind her, and leaving everything behind was soothing, as if she were leaving her pain about Matthew there too.

She glanced at the silent telephone. After tomorrow if he should try to call her, it would ring and ring and ring. That maddening secret sound of a telephone ringing on and on and on, giving no reason for its futility, offering only a "no comment" to the caller—a sudden sympathy for Matthew awoke in her, quenched by an ironic query somewhere: "And what makes you think he'll be calling?"

She had vetoed the frugal step of stopping service for half a year just to preserve that "no comment" and prevent the singsong revelation that service has been temporarily discontinued. Frugality could be costly on the scale of real values; she had already begun another list of majors and minors headed "Possible Tattlers."

Had she overlooked any? Her suitcases were monogrammed TVG, as were the towels and napkins and few pieces of silverware she was taking, two knives, two forks, two soupspoons, four teaspoons; it would take more than a Mrs. Steffani to prove that those initials had ever stood for anything other than Dorothy V. Grange, though she might, in a brilliant moment, pause over the *T*. The dozen or so books she had to have with her were not so perfect, for in them all had once been written either T. Gray or Dori Gray or D. V. Gray, this from a school-bred ritual of writing her name inside the front cover of any book or notebook or exercise book she had ever acquired, but she had methodically inked them all out and written Grange in, instead, using various pencils, pens and marking crayons to avoid obvious similarity.

Her new checkbook on a big neighborhood bank on Columbus Avenue would be the only one kept in the shiny new desk, her real checkbook for her "real bank" being stored in one of her suitcases, always locked. Deposits in her Grange bank, as she thought of it, would never be her own checks, signed Gray, drawn on her real bank. She would write out her real checks to either Cele or Gene and get their checks in return to be deposited or mailed to her Grange bank. She would even have to pay her hospital bills by Grange checks.

When she had first realized that she could not use her Blue Cross hospital insurance, she had been worried, but it was a brief worry vanquished by the reality that nowhere on any public record in any bank, store, organization, nowhere on any punch card of any computer, could the connection between Gray and Grange ever be set forth for even impersonal eyes to see. Except in that one ultimate document of adoption which, she knew somehow, was to be held *in camera* forever by the courts and the laws of the land.

But for the rest, it was to be Gray and Grange. It was all legal; her newspaper years told her that. You could take any pseudonym you wanted, any pen name, any stage name, do anything in that name and still be legal—unless you planned to commit a crime or did commit a crime. All she planned to commit, she thought cheerfully, was one small baby.

She had overlooked nothing. If Mrs. Steffani and her passkey ever did enter the apartment while she was out, she would find not one detail that could point to any tenant except Dorothy V. Grange. And if she should overhear Gene or Cele call her Dori or Dorr—who said that every Dorothy had to be nicknamed Dot?

Only once so far had she made a slip that might have raised a question. For a moment only, at the signing of the lease, there was the fleeting pause over a question not properly answered, and it had gone by quickly enough to be nothing.

"Your husband to sign here," Mrs. Steffani had said, accepting the first and last month's rent and pointing to a dotted line on the document.

"He's in the Air Force," she had replied, a split second late. "I'll sign."

Mrs. Steffani looked uncertain. Then she shrugged, accepted her copy of the lease and departed. Dori had intended to say that he was in the Air Force and off on duty in Vietnam, and how awful that he had to be away at such a time, but her half answer, sufficing, taught her something: the less you explain the more real it sounds. She had determined to be frugal with her words.

At last she undressed and went to bed. As the light went out, she thought of Matthew. Why had he done this? She had imagined every kind of reaction from him, but this continuing silence, this continuing absence, with never an answer to her letter—this she had not foreseen.

I can't be sorry about *it*, she repeated silently, remembering the words she had written, but I am wretched about you. Wretched. What a word, what a cheating, mealymouthed, uncomplaining word. I resent the way you've taken this is what she had really meant, I'm shocked by it, and frightened too. I am forty and this may be my last passionate love, I will not be a girl any more, I will be a woman with a child, and you loved me, and now you stay away and say nothing, not a word, just this silence and absence and more silence and more absence.

I'm not wretched; I'm sore and insulted and let down. Not sore meaning riled, but *sore*, full of ache and hurt and woundedness. And you—what about your insight and care for other people and all the fine things I thought you stood for?—that you do stand for if it comes to a law case?

But this was sarcasm, hitting out, hitting back. Suddenly the thought of tomorrow was no longer a soothing thought; it became a desperate longing for the new beginning in the linoleum-floored room across the park.

*   *   *

From the beginning she liked it. It was a different world but she liked it for being different. She did not feel removed from regret or pain about Matthew but she did feel somehow insulated as by a protective cooling layer. It was more than that, she thought after a few days in her new place;

here she felt encapsulated somehow, the cocoon again and safe. I am creating my own womb for me to curl up inside, that's what I'm doing. There was a harmony in the notion; she let herself think about it.

She had Cele for dinner the first night and Gene the second. She had always liked cooking and now she gave herself to all the lengthier processes of it, ignoring the shortcuts she used to stoop to in the press of time, the pre-prepared seasoning, the pre-chopped chives, the canned and frozen and freeze-dried everythings. She never felt too tired to market and cook, she even liked washing up afterward and doing the daily housework. She had promised Cele that she would exchange her weekly cleaning woman for a daily part-time maid "later when I'm a big hulk," but for now she could manage very well alone and for some obscure reason needed to. It was part of the different world she had come to.

Not physically different so much; there were just as many streets like this half-tended, half-neglected one over on the East Side, if you walked away from Fifth and Madison and Park over to Lexington and Third and Second, just as many there where the snow still stood blocked and solid and graying in the gutters. In fact this new street of hers, this West Ninety-fifth, was rather handsome, certainly the near-the-park half of it which included her house. The old apartment houses on the corner gave way on each side to a quartet not of brownstones but of white stone houses, pale and clean as if they had been newly sandblasted. There were signs of remodeling, but fortunately the old bay windows on their upper floors and their mansard roofs were unchanged, and on one or two there were wrought-iron picket fences around the step-down areas at the kitchen entrances, with window boxes or privet hedges dusted with snow. At the street level all doors and windows were barred with iron grillwork, but brass knobs and number plates and bells gleamed from faithful polishing.

Off to the west at the Columbus Avenue end of the long block, a modern apartment house was nearing completion.

It promised to be attractive, with its tan brick and white stone walls, its picture windows and terraces, and she was relieved to hear that it wouldn't be ready for tenants until the end of the year. This, and some other new or nearly new buildings sticking up out of the rubbish of old tenements up and down Columbus Avenue—why had she not noticed them when she came to answer the ad?—all these new buildings, tagged "middle-income housing," all looked inviting. She'd better keep an eye out for friends and acquaintances after all.

Walking, marketing, going to Broadway to a movie, she kept a particular watch on passing faces. In an old fur coat lent her by Cele, needlessly ample thus far, and from under the flopping brim of a dated felt sports hat, she looked out at all approaching people, ready to cross the street at the first sight of anybody familiar. The faces too were different from the faces of home across the park; there were many dark faces here but so were there on Madison and Park. But over there they were the faces of delivery boys and maids whereas over here they were of people living in the neighborhood, mothers with small children, school kids tearing along with their books or on skates or sleds, old people. There still were more whites here than blacks and Puerto Ricans, but for the first time in all her life she was living in a really integrated neighborhood. Better than talking about it, she thought vaguely, not stopping to inquire what she meant. It all added to the sense of difference, of actually being a traveler, as if the lies about the crazy world cruise were in part true and she were far from home and greedy for new sights and new experiences.

When she said "home," she never thought of the linoleum-floored studio room she now lived in. Home still meant the apartment she had locked up and left, still meant her books, her music, her desk, her dear familiar paintings and furniture and colors. But soon she came to see, embarrassingly enough, that home also meant certain other things which brainwashed you with a subtle sense of privilege and upper-classness.

At home you mailed a letter right up on your own floor, going down a carpeted hallway in your dressing gown to the brass chute ten steps from your own front door; here you dressed and went outdoors to the corner mailbox, and if it was late at night you didn't go at all until next morning because of the horrendous tales you were always hearing about crime in the streets. At home you ordered food from the grocer and butcher by phone and had it delivered, the tomatoes, the perfect pears, the apples, the lettuce wrapped separately in glossy white paper before being put in the carton, to isolate and protect it; here you went out yourself in good weather or foul, to the stores on Columbus, saw all your vegetables and fruit dumped into one great brown bag, and were careful not to choose too heavy a load to carry. At home there was always the doorman to tell you the weather or whistle up a cab; here there was the bolted door and the announcer beside it and the peephole through the door and the latch chain always slid into the groove before you opened more than an inch to anyone whose voice or face you did not know.

And yet day by day she liked it more, liked it for being different. In daylight hours at least she disregarded the horrendous tales and walked freely in the nearly deserted park, striding out as she had been ordered to do, feeling immune to danger as if nobody ever could possibly hurt her.

* * *

And then one Sunday morning in early February, she suddenly found herself shaken by something else she had heard horrendous tales about. In the twenty days that she had been walking in the park, she had always turned south, instinctively turning toward the skyline which stood clear and sharp and beautiful at its southern rim. She would walk hard, as Dr. Jesskin had ordered, following the winding, dipping, curving walks to the old casino near Sixty-seventh, and then with more than half her mileage accounted for, leave the curving route within the park and return outside on the special pavement of Central Park West, six-sided stone plaques cemented together, like gears meshed one to the next. In bitter weather, with the temperature in the twenties or below, these daily three miles were test enough of her will and stamina, but there was a sense of accomplishment afterward as well as a glowing well-being. So far she had had not a minute of illness; early in the fourth month it was still too early for any discomfort of bulk.

On this particular Sunday morning she idly turned north instead of south when she entered the park, her back to the skyline, nothing ahead but winter-stripped trees on mildly rolling hills and the sky itself. It was an easy sky, a blue sky, wind-cleansed of soot and haze and lowering gray. It filled her with longing for spring and then summer, for trees leafing gently and then richly, for shade arching again over green park benches, for movement and sound everywhere instead of this sparse winter stillness and emptiness.

Because it was the weekend, with the roadway closed to automobiles, she walked in the road itself, long cleared of the last snow which still lay patchily on the ground and pedestrian paths. An occasional cyclist, dressed like a skier against the cold, came whistling by, and on the shallow slopes still under snow, a few children were tumbling around on sleds or skis.

She had gone in at Ninety-sixth as she always did and soon found that there were more people about than she had at first thought. Off at her right lay a vast playing field that she had never in all her years as a New Yorker seen before; there was a game in progress, voices rose shrill and bright, largely in Spanish, and she wondered if today were some Puerto Rican holiday or field day. The roadway led up a sharp hill and then down; she glanced occasionally at the aluminum light poles, each marked with numerals and letters to guide police or repairmen or park maintenance men to a specific site. The playing field ended at about 100th Street. She had worked out the system of the poles for herself in the first days of her walking; W 9601 meant that it was the first pole inside the park at West Ninety-sixth Street; if it had read E 7202 it would have meant the second pole inside at the East Seventy-second Street entrance, and M 6703 would have meant the Mall around Sixty-seventh, the third pole in a cluster of half a dozen.

This small decoding for herself had given her a spasm of childlike pleasure; every day she found some new small pleasure in the park, always with a thready surprise stitching along her senses, for she had always lived near it and had assumed that there was nothing about it that was new or unexpected. Now she was seeing things one did not see from taxis racing against the lights to get you to a theater or concert, and up here to the north and west it was like finding a new park entirely. Here were playgrounds she had never seen, playing fields she had never seen; there ahead now, down far below in a great hollow, was the first shine of the new skating rink she had heard about in the past year or two but had never seen.

Dori heard voices, sharp young voices, gleeful, laughing over nothing, the climbing shouts of children at play. It was a large rink, and crowded, somewhere music was playing, and she thought of the older rink down at the other end of the park near Fifth Avenue and Sixtieth, where she herself had so often skated. *Hans Brinker, or the Silver Skates;* there was always something shining and lovely about gleaming ice and twinkling blades, red scarves and mittens, eyes aglow, ruddy faces whipped by the wind. She was being sentimental and knew it and did not chide herself.

The roadway curved sharply and as she came around a bend she was suddenly close enough to the rink to see it not as panorama but as a specific scene. There was something strange about it, and she did not know at once what it was. She looked beyond the roadway toward the rusty old tenements fringing the far border of the park and even without consulting the nearest aluminum pole she suddenly realized that she was approaching the northern boundary of Central Park at 110th Street. Harlem. The skyline here was Harlem. And then suddenly she knew what was strange about this skating rink on this shining blue morning.

All the faces were dark. All the children were Negro or

Puerto Rican. Perhaps one child was white, perhaps two, out of the hundreds down below the rising ground where she stood, but it was a whole world of brown and tan and black young faces.

De facto segregation. Once somebody had asked her what, exactly, de facto segregation meant and she had thought it a stupid unwilling question, as if anybody could possibly not understand what de facto segregation was. Now suddenly she thought, If you were here this minute you'd never have to ask that question again.

She shuddered. Those Spanish voices back at the playing field weren't celebrating some fete day, they were there because that was about where it started, in the Nineties on the West Side, and she had passed it by without thinking. All over the rest of the park these past twenty days, wherever she had passed some group of kids out with a teacher for athletics, she had seen how many faces were dark, except when the group wore the blazers or uniforms of some private school, when the faces were nearly always white with only a few black—as tokens? She had always known all about the city's population, had always assumed there could be no surprises.

But this was a surprise. This was solid and ugly and she wanted to turn quickly away and would not let herself. She walked closer, listening now as well as watching, hearing the young shouting voices, hearing the excited cries and laughter, seeing the little playing animals on the ice who did not even know that on this lovely sunny Sunday morning there was something hideous in their shining skating rink.

❃   ❃   ❃

"Can't we have one hour without that damn music?" Matthew demanded.

"Why of course," Joan said. "I didn't realize you minded."

"This whole damn weekend we haven't had five minutes without it."

"You might have said so before you got this worked up about it."

Both children stared at him as their mother left the table and went out to the record player. There was the crisp click of a switch and a declining wail as the turntable came to a stop. The mournful sound told the story, for normally Joan pampered the machine and would have lifted the tone arm properly, and pressed the stop button only when the needle was safely disengaged. Now she did not even wait for the record to stop; she went out of the kitchen and down the hall to her own room.

Matthew grunted. It had been a foul weekend all round, foul roaring wind and rain, the children indoors, the house roaring with their voices, their intermittent spats, their incessant motion. When he was a boy and landlocked by weather, he had had none of the noisemakers that were the appurtenances of today, no transistor radio, no television, no stereo; he had doubtless been a nuisance in whatever ways children can be nuisances to their parents, but he had no recollection of incessant noise accompanying every activity. I used to read, he thought, everybody used to read.

Hildy rose from the table, her face wearing the injured look that told him she found life hard to bear in this household. She started from the room and he said, "What about the dishes?" She turned back, still injured, not answering but beginning to clear the table. "I'll dry," Johnny said, and disappeared. With the new semester he was reinstated at school, impenitent, still saying that basketball and hockey made him puke. The school had "compromised" by capitulating. He would do shop and painting, favorites both, instead of sports.

Matthew watched his daughter as she moved between the table and the kitchen. She was wearing a skirt so short that it barely cleared her tiny buttocks, and again it startled him that he lived in an age that permitted its young girls such flagrant narcissism. For he was sure that the ever-briefer skirts of Hildy and her friends revealed not only their desire to attract boys but their own enormous self-approval; they knew very well how delectable their slim young thighs could be to the male eye, the young male eyes of their sixteen-year-old admirers as well as the startled eyes of their fathers and uncles and other supposedly immune observers. But they also found them rather delectable themselves, when they gazed into shopwindows or long mirrors.

Next week, on the first of March, Hildy would be sixteen; recently she had put a definable distance between herself and her parents, natural enough, not meant to be hostile, not meant to be troubling. Yet to him it announced a milestone. She was grown up. In an earlier age, sixteen would have been merely another stage in the gradual process of becoming an adult, but in the rushing years of the late nineteen-sixties, the message to most parents was "I'm an adult now." In Hildy it had come abruptly; last year she was still his loving little girl, now she was at best an amiable relative, at worst a cool remarker of his faults and frailties and a cooler critic of his decisions.

Alienation. The word was all over the place, already a nonce word, a slogan, a piece of verbal claptrap uttered so easily and so often it had forfeited its original force. Blacks and whites, alienated; doves and hawks, alienated; young and old, alienated. It was a kind of shorthand no longer fully decipherable by people who sought meaning underneath the hooks and curves and dots and squiggles.

It was a world in turmoil and here he was, alienated right out of it. His turmoil was his alone; he seethed in it; it seethed in him; he could not control it and rejoin that other world, those other turmoils, could not get back to living as he was living before—before—

Damn it, he had ordered his mind not to do this, and his mind kept doing it anyhow. Before Dori, before wreckage, before catastrophe. He was pierced with longing for that flashing of happiness in the first instant of her telling him, before he caught what she really meant, and he was pierced too with desire, not sexual desire but a desire as poignant, to be back before this had happened, back there somewhere with her before, before, while there was still time for them.

This backward-longing was something he had never known before, a something not in the schedules and manifests of life as he knew it.

Last night he had spent two hours drinking with Jack Henning and Jack had finally said, "What's eating you, for God's sake?" To his own complete astonishment, he had told him to go to hell. But then, in a few brusque sentences he had told Jack about Dori, not naming her, told it harshly, the essentials only, of their affair, of her swift importance to him, of her sudden announcement that she was already pregnant when they met, and that he had found himself staggered in a way he had never known before.

Jack had been staggered too. "You offered to help her." It was a simple statement, bearing no question mark.

"She wasn't looking for help." He had then summed up her history of doctors and tests and waiting, and had ended, "so help was the last thing she wanted. She was happy about it." He had seen Jack's eyes fill with some new expression that he meant to query him about, but in another minute Jack was ordering more drinks for them both and the moment passed.

Later, alone and in a half-drunk reverie, he had thought, Alienation, that's it. Dori and I are alienated—what a farce of a word. Distance from, distance between, separation and silence, that is alienation. We are alienated one from the other.

The phrase still haunted him, even now, weeks later. It was feeble and false, but it was also true. Why? Why did it remain true? Over and over he had assured himself that this was no typical male jealousy but something else, yet he could not find what that something else was. Over and over, like a scientist, like a detective, like a trial lawyer preparing for court, he had searched through the whole body of evidence for the one clue that had evaded him, and each time he wound up defeated. If she had lied to him about her life these past years—but she had told him all he needed to know about herself and men, more than he had told her in return. He hadn't felt a qualm about those infrequent and apparently none-too-meaningful affairs of hers, had known she was just getting over one. He had wasted no time thinking of them, any more than if she had told him about her first kiss, though he had not let himself visualize her responsiveness to anyone else, knowing as he did that if it were required of him that he answer yes or no as to whether sex had moved her, he would have had to say, Yes, always. It never was possible to think of her as unmoved about sex, cool, remote, contained about sex. One of the holds she had on you was the depth of her response, the readiness, the complexity, like your own, the totality of drive toward the top of it and then the totality of the moment itself.

Remembering was still a savagery, and then fury that she should have—

Should have what? He still could not state it, this crime he charged her with. If he once could frame it in the containing rim of words and phrases, he might at last manage it, accept it, view it as reality and then come to terms with it. But he could get no closer than his own certainty that what looked like an onslaught of male jealousy was more complicated.

He still did not know what it was. And until he did, he was immobilized.

CHAPTER SEVEN

Suddenly it was warm and in Central Park the first green tinged the winter-brown earth. Spring had not officially arrived, but each day offered another indicator that the equinox was coming, the season filling. Dori began to go out earlier in the morning, no longer needing to wait for the sun to cancel rawness and cold; she stopped at bushes to stare at their thickening buds and wonder when the first burst of color would come. Her daily walk became a sought pleasure now, and though she pulled herself at intervals out of her lazy watching and renewed the ordained briskness of her step, she saw proof each day that she had always libeled the city by saying that the change of seasons was imperceptible in it.

All at once the yellow feathering of forsythia sprayed the bushes she had been pausing before, and a day or two later on the last Sunday of March, a small tree was pinkly white with blossom. Was it dogwood? She had always been too much a city dweller to be sure, and she wanted to stop a mounted policeman and ask, but as she approached him she could imagine the words "Officer, is that dogwood?" and was embarrassed and passed him by. Other trees were budding, and with a start she noticed that every one gauzy with green was a young tree, still slim in its trunk, still slender in the spread of its branches. The old trees remained dead with winter, the great oaks and elms and maples, all caught tight with their years, slower to move and change, stolidly patient amidst the burst and thrust of life around them.

At home she telephoned her brother at the university. "Gene, don't laugh at me, but could you ask Miss Pulley to get the name of the best book on trees and plants and flowers from the Botany Department? A beginner's book, what things are named and when they bloom, that kind of thing. I've gone all-over interested and could order a copy."

"My God, Dori, I thought it was pickles or something you were supposed to crave."

"That comes later. Please do, Gene, and let me find out when a dogwood really blossoms. Maybe it's magnolia."

"If Pulley can swipe a copy up here I'll drop it off on the way home. Have courage, hang on."

She took his teasing cheerfully and felt an elation of interest. Who knew where hobbies had their genesis? Maybe this would become one of the lifelong kind that would never leave her. She was reading everything else these days, she might as well read about trees and shrubs.

She picked up the *Times* which she had only glanced at during breakfast, and prepared another cup of coffee to read it by. This had become a small ritual for the morning return from her walk; she recognized that it was quickly forming into a pattern, perhaps an unvarying pattern, and could only feel indulgent toward it. Surely you had the right to help things along with little rituals?

And then she stopped reading. She held the paper as if it were a bar of metal to cling to in a moment of weakness. She did not move. She forgot to breathe. It was true—she had not imagined it.

The smallest thump. Not a kick, it was nothing as firm and sure as a kick despite everything anybody had ever said or written. From within her, against the wall of her being, there was a small thump. The first one.

She waited unmoving. The newspaper slipped to her lap, the coffee was forgotten, she was electric with the waiting and then there it was once more. She suddenly realized that she was grinning like a maniac.

This was where the happy young wife was supposed to take the happy young husband's hand and put it over her swelling body so that he too might feel the kick. But she wasn't young and she wasn't a wife and she hadn't a husband. It must be marvelous, to share it. But it was also marvelous all in itself.

She sat on, immobile, inviting it, pleading with it to happen again. It did not, and she thought, Stubborn, hey? and a swell of feeling loosed itself in her.

It wasn't a kick. It was more like, like—she tried to reproduce the sensation. With the knuckle of her index finger she tapped the muscle of her left arm; that was something like, but not exact. With the flat part of her thumb, she gently poked at her hard rounding and still small stomach, as if she were prodding a melon. That too was something like, but still not right. With the edge of her hand she lightly struck her kneecap, a doctor testing reflexes, and dismissed the result: too bony. It had been a tap, firm but not bony, a thwack, a tapped signal, a magic telemetry across the incalculable space between nonbeing and being.

She had an impulse to call Dr. Jesskin and tell him, but she held back. He had told her it would be happening soon, "the end of the fourth month, the beginning of the fifth, these are individual matters also." She had been expecting it and yet it was totally unexpected in its arrival. It would happen again, but whether in minutes or in hours, there was no one to say. She would report to Jesskin after it had gone on for another day or two.

Once more she tried to remember just how it had felt. Without knowing it, she again sent her fingers tapping at her flesh and bone, seeking, testing, trying for approximation. And then, her lips accidentally apart, she tapped her right cheek with the middle finger of her right hand, and thought, That's it. She tried it again, this time opening her mouth wide and stiffening her cheeks so that the cavity within made a small hollow shell. She tapped again with a stiffened finger and at once thought with delight, If it came from the inside that would really be it. Life.

❖   ❖   ❖

The movie would end in three or four minutes and as always she rose and made her way to the exit before the house lights came on, seeing the final scene standing, poised for instant departure. Under the brightness of the marquee, she paused, swiftly looking about her, seeing the faces of passing strangers with the familiar sense of satisfaction. All as it should be. It always was.

The sky was clouded and once she moved away from the lights of Broadway, the night was murky, warmer than early April evenings usually were. As she turned into her own street, the din of radio and TV voices seemed more insistent than usual, but she had already trained herself not to listen to them. Cars lined the curbs, their consecutive bumpers faintly shining, inches apart, but the usual beehive look of early evening was missing, the street empty of children as if some Pied Piper had passed through only a moment before and seduced them all away. Far ahead, at her own corner, a car deliberately double-parked, and she wondered at the gall of the driver until she remembered the doctor's shingle in the window.

"The assassin's bullet—"

One of the radio voices suddenly cut free from the surrounding din and pierced her wall of non-listening. The air was always vicious with shows of crime or terror or bang-bang-you're-dead, but there was a horror in the voice speaking these words, a shaken excitement that proclaimed that this was truth, not playacting, and an answering horror and excitement rose in her through the jerking next words until she heard "Martin Luther King was shot."

Oh God no. She heard her own cry, wrenched from her,

torn out of her throat, and suddenly the circumambient din of voices that had been overlapping in the evening air turned into an unbearable repetition: Martin Luther King, Martin Luther King, Martin Luther King was shot and killed, Martin Luther King, Martin Luther King—

She began to run in a dark invisible need to get behind walls, to close out the voices. Running reminded her that she must not run, and she changed to a rushing, gasping walking. She was filled with fear, with pain, with hatred for the killer, for all killers, for all haters except the haters of haters; they were different, they were the good, the decent, the reasonable and loving, the ones who were flooded with fury at hate and death and killing.

She unlocked her door and bolted it instantly behind her and saw the night gleam on the shiny linoleum but before she clicked the switch of the lamp, she crossed to the low wood platform and clicked on the television instead. In the seconds that had to elapse before sound and image could appear she sank into the armchair as if she had been wounded, and when the first words came they were spurts of words clustered around the same shaken excitement she had heard on the street. "The assassin's bullet" . . . "ambulance rushed to the hospital" . . . "possible conspiracy." She was hurled back to that November day not five years before when other shaken voices were telling of bullets and blood splashing and assassination and conspiracy, and the two became one and she could scarcely see the small lighted screen through the scald of her sudden tears.

After a time she remembered that the room was still dark except for that one oblong at her knees and she rose to turn on the lights. The telephone rang. It was Gene.

"Do you know?"

"Oh Gene, I can't bear it."

"I'll come over. I tried to call you before."

"I was at a movie. Oh please come, Gene, it's so horrible."

She heard her voice waver, the "horrible" broken in half by the suck of her breath, and she thought, It's the first time, and did not ask what first time she meant. Relief poured through her belatedly; this was no thing to bear alone and Gene had known it and was coming to sit it out with her, a loving wisdom making him do it. The telephone rang again. It was Cele.

"Are you all right, Dorr?"

"Yes, are you?"

"It's brought back the whole thing about Kennedy."

"For me too."

"Where were you, how'd you hear it?"

"Coming home from the movies, I heard it on somebody's radio and didn't take it in until his name."

"We were just leaving the house and Minnie began to scream, 'They shot him, they shot Martin Luther,' and we both rushed into the kitchen to her radio and the kids heard it on theirs and I've been trying to calm them all and wondered about you."

"Gene is coming over."

"Then I'll come tomorrow night. God, do you remember at school, everybody telling just where they were when they heard about Roosevelt?"

"But that wasn't assassination. He was old and sick and he died, but Kennedy and now—oh Cele, what's *happening?*"

There was a pause. Then Cele said, "Don't go out for a day or two, will you? They say rioting is starting in Washington and Memphis already."

Long after she hung up, she sat staring at the television set as if in hypnosis. Gene was slow getting there, and obscurely she was glad. She needed time; she had to absorb, hear, let the tears come unheeded through the rerun of old scenes where Martin Luther King alive was speaking in the curiously rhythmic chant of his careful enunciation—movement, chil-dren, moun-tain—words grown familiar and dear by repetition. She had been right there in Washington on that hot August day in 1963 when he had first said those words and she had gulped over his dream. *One day on the red hills of Georgia . . . one day even the state of Mississippi . . . a dream that one day my four little children—*

134

now she listened again to a replay of the same words and her throat locked. She had gone on the great march without knowing exactly why she went, knowing only that she had to be there too, had to walk with strangers too, bearing witness, peacefully. She remembered their walking, almost amiable along the wide and beautiful stretches of the capital's avenues, remembered the sudden sting of tears when up ahead somebody started, "Mine eyes have seen the glory," remembered the new song, "We Shall Overcome," whose words and melody she had never heard before and could not then know she would hear so many times again.

And now this, unbearable. Again she thought, It's the first time, but now she knew suddenly what the phrase meant. It's the first time since Matthew that anything horrible has happened in the world, and he's not here to go through it with me, not here to talk about it, not here to help me bear it, or want me to help him.

Her heart pounded, but this was not the happy beat of excitement and expectation; this was new, this was a heavy acknowledgment of disappointment, of disapproval. Could it be of something more than that? Of, perhaps, dislike?

She quivered at the thought, shrinking back as if she were the recipient of the word instead of its bestower. "Dislike" was too strong, but there was something. It was fine to say that you should never put your own yardstick along the stretch of another being's acts, ticking off in a kind of lineal moralizing how much you approved and how much you found less than worthy. But that was theory. And right now at this harrowing moment there *was* something for the first time that made her draw back.

Gene arrived then. She was dry-eyed as she opened the door to him, but the first sight of his darkly somber eyes filled hers. "Oh, Gene, what's happening to us?"

"It's a good question, damn it." He slung his coat off unceremoniously and asked for coffee. He sank into the armchair in front of the television set and began to listen again to the details he had already heard and heard and heard again, the white car speeding away, the Lorraine Motel balcony, the dirty brick flophouse across the street, the tall white man who was particular about the dollar-a-day room he had rented that afternoon, turning down one that faced a blank wall and choosing another that looked across the bare mimosa trees to the porch of the motel, owned by Negroes, for Negroes only.

"If he'd been able to stay anywhere he chose," she said, "they might not have known where to go to pick him off."

"It was bound to happen. He knew it. I suppose we have all known it all along."

"Here's coffee. Would you like a drink too?"

"Not yet." He continued to watch the screen and she pulled a cushion from the sofa and sat on the floor to one side. There was silence between them and she thought, This is all anybody needs, to share it, not to take it square alone. But that was going back to her accusations, and she cut sharply away from that direction of her thinking, like a driver taking a corner on squeaking tires.

For perhaps an hour they listened and talked, listened again and talked again. They talked of violence and non-violence, of the whiplash of white hatreds and the new militants in the ghettos, of the growing rebellions of the young everywhere, on every campus, in every nation, and of the burden those young felt, to put to right the world into which they had been born.

"Gene," she said, sure he would follow the unspoken transition, "do you know a good lawyer I could go to, for the actual adoption?"

"Not offhand, but I'll ask Dave Weiss. I think it's a special field."

"How much would you have to tell him?" Professor Weiss was on the law faculty and a close friend of Gene's, but she had never met him.

"That somebody I know wants the name of a lawyer for adopting a child. What else did you think?"

"He'd assume it would be through the usual adoption bureaus."

"I'd tell him it wouldn't be."

"He'd assume it was a married couple."

"I'd tell him it wasn't."

"Wouldn't he need to know anything more than the simple fact that 'somebody you know' wants a lawyer for adopting some little old baby?"

"Probably whether I'd got myself into a jam, but he wouldn't ask me." Unexpectedly he laughed. It was a blessed relief to be talking of this instead of the other. "I'd assumed this was all arranged by now, the way you've arranged everything else."

She looked suddenly away. "I sort of had assumed it too, that a man I know, a lawyer, would help me with the legal part of it. But I—I've lost touch with him."

He glanced at her inquiringly but said nothing. For a moment he turned back to the television screen, thought better of it, and without asking her, went to her small kitchen for more coffee. She followed him with both their cups.

"He's not the villain who's responsible," she said, too lightly.

"I didn't think there was a villain."

"There isn't. I don't know why I'm trying to make jokes."

"I do."

"Oh, Gene, thank God you came over tonight. Was it all right for you to be here with me all evening?"

"Ellen isn't pregnant," he said shortly. He heard the snap in his own voice and added, without emphasis, "Anyway, she has more sense than we have about something like this. If you call it sense."

He stayed for the eleven o'clock news and then on for another hour until he saw that she was getting sleepy. She had not pretended the sleepiness but the moment he left, drowsiness vanished and she turned compulsively back to the set. There was a necessity she could not explain, to hear all of it again, and once more, and then once more, as she had done during the hours and days after Kennedy was assassinated, right through until the first flicker of flame upon his grave.

At one thirty she went to bed exhausted. But the dreaming began, as it had begun that other time, the sudden start came again, the clutch of shock, the piercing longing that it had not happened, that it was only nightmare. The horror had been greater over President Kennedy's assassination because he *was* the President, but the jagged edge of this shock was just as bloody, and the next morning on the street when she passed a Negro woman she wanted to stop and say, "I feel just the way you do." But she thought, It would sound patronizing and I would die.

* * *

It was during the final mile of her walk that morning that she was suddenly driven by the need to settle the matter of the lawyer. She had not even thought of it as one of the problems during those early days when hideouts and false names and new banks and mail had preoccupied her. So sure had she been then that her lawyer would be Matthew, or if a specialist were needed in this field, then somebody Matthew would select and recommend and, in a sense, watch over.

All at once the thought of Gene's asking Professor Weiss was distasteful. If she herself knew Weiss, if he were her own friend, it might be good and right and natural to turn to him, but for her brother to be delegated by her as an agent to a stranger—suddenly the idea upset her. This was too personal, this matter of the attorney who would have to know all about it, who would guide her through the maze of papers and documents and laws and statutes—she should have realized that going to an unknown lawyer recommended by an unknown colleague of Gene's was an agitating notion at best. She had not thought the thing through at all; she had let it slide; never had she put it on any list of majors and minors, and suddenly it loomed very major indeed.

She hurried home and telephoned the university. Gene was in class; she said to Miss Pulley, "Would you just ask him to delay on that legal matter for a day or two—he'll know what I mean. Thanks a lot." She hung up, convinced that he had already had it all out with Professor Weiss, and her spirits fell. This sudden preoccupation with the matter of a lawyer was excessive, but that insight did not end the preoccupation. Was she still remembering Matthew's quick offer to check out New York adoption laws with people at his office? Was she still assuming that somehow, some way, it would still be Matthew who would see her through this final, and tremendous, chapter?

She drew back sharply. The one rule, the basis, the foundation: no sentimentalism, no daydreams, no girlish refusal to face whatever reality there was. And God knew one reality was that there was no Matthew.

On her next visit to Dr. Jesskin she could ask him about the final step of the adoption itself. Why had she not thought of asking Jesskin long before this—she had asked him about everything else. Probably, he saw ahead to it as clearly as he had seen ahead to that room on the eighth floor of Harkness and the two names on the door.

The knowledge soothed her, pacified her, and yet a few moments later she thought, My next visit is on the fifteenth, a Monday, and this is the fifth, a Friday. That's two weekends to get through and the week in between.

She dialed quickly. "Miss Mack," she said, "this isn't any emergency, but something's come up, and do you think I could talk to Dr. Jesskin before he goes off for the weekend?"

"Can we call you back? He's with a patient."

"Of course. If he's not too rushed."

"About one or one thirty then. You sure you can wait till then? Nothing going wrong?"

"Really not. Thank you."

She looked at the clock and then at the morning paper, black with headlines about the assassination. She still had not come to grips with it in print; she had read headlines and set it all aside for later, just as she had permitted herself radio news for a few minutes this morning and then set that aside for later too. The assassin had not been caught. Knowing that single fact, she had forced herself to wait through breakfast and through her walk. Now she edged toward the *Times*, unwilling to open herself to pain again.

The telephone rang and it was Dr. Jesskin. "Miss Mack said you sounded ill though you said you were not," he stated quietly. "I thought it best not to wait till one o'clock to call back."

"Oh Doctor, I'm not ill, but I had such a hideous night, I was so horrified, I couldn't sleep—"

"I think many of us couldn't sleep last night," he said. "Have you any physical symptoms? Miss Mack said you did not sound like yourself at all."

"No physical symptoms, only terribly upset, and that seemed to tie into something else upsetting and I—well, I wondered, Doctor, if I could possibly see you for ten minutes today, or if you weren't too rushed now to talk a little by phone."

"I'm not too rushed."

"It's just that I had thought at the start that a lawyer I know would take charge of the formal adoption process, in court or however they do it. But that's all been changed and I haven't faced up to it and when I got upset last night I also got awfully upset that anything so important should still be up in the air as late as this and I got wondering if by any chance you might know a good lawyer who—"

"Miss Mack was correct," he said calmly. "You do not sound yourself. But you do know how one anxiety tends to trigger off another?"

"I'm sorry."

"Do not be sorry. Will it quiet that anxiety if I say that some weeks ago, for my own education, I did already discuss with a first-rate attorney how one would go about legally adopting one's own child? He does not know the name of my patient, but he is my good friend and he did educate me completely. It is entirely feasible and if you should wish me to arrange a meeting between you and him, that is simple."

"Oh Dr. Jesskin, there never was a doctor like you."

"There is a disadvantage," he said and she thought he

chuckled. "As with Harkness, I seem to run to expensive solutions. This lawyer is a senior partner at Cox, Wheaton, Fairchild, Tulliver."

"I know of them." It was one of the great law firms in the country.

"Just as one does not expect an illegitimate birth at Harkness," he went on, "so one does not expect an illegitimate baby to become a client of Cox, Wheaton, Fairchild, Tulliver. Is that not correct?"

This time he did chuckle and she could only say, "It is correct and it's just marvelous. Would you go ahead and tell him about his new client and about me? Honestly, Doctor, I just don't know how to thank you."

❖   ❖   ❖

The day became bearable. For a long time after she hung up, she sat in a benign relief, like warmth. Then she turned to the telephone book to look up Cox, Wheaton, Fairchild, Tulliver and wrote on the last page of her desk calendar their address and telephone number. Which one was the senior partner who was Dr. Jesskin's friend? Would she one day be known to Mr. Cox or to Mr. Wheaton, Mr. Fairchild or Mr. Tulliver? Would that day come before July twenty-third, or afterward? Soon after or not for six months after when the time came to go to court?

In her research for her two articles, still only roughed out and nowhere near completion, she had found out that in New York State, unlike certain others, a waiting period of half a year was mandatory, a six-month trial period between the time any baby went into any adoptive home and the time the legal process of adoption could be taken to court. The city of New York would send a social worker of some kind once or twice during that trial period, to judge the prospective parents, the prospective home, the general prognosis for the baby's future.

Suppose one of them came to see us, Dori thought now, and turned me down? She began to laugh. It was impossible, of course, but it was high comedy even to think of such a scene. Or high horror.

Cox, Wheaton, Fairchild, Tulliver wouldn't let it happen. They would know, or one of them would know, their archives would know, where secret papers were held *in camera*, and they would not let the State of New York interfere. God bless Cox, Wheaton, Fairchild, Tulliver, separately and aggregately.

She smiled and her eyes fell on the deserted *Times*. A sweep of guilt invaded her, that she should so soon be turning from its intolerable burden to her own good fortune. But that's it, she thought, that's all part of it, the systole and diastole forever.

*   *   *

Cele came late in the afternoon, bringing three days' pile-up of mail from home. It was mostly requests for donations, but the April rent bill was there, a department store bill, the telephone bill, and a note from Tad Jonas saying the Martha Litton piece was still pulling mail and why the hell didn't she drop people at least a postcard and a clue about whether she'd like it forwarded or not? "I must write him," she said, showing Tad's note to Cele, "or it'll twig his attention, but for now, let's get on with these." She opened her locked suitcase for her real checkbook.

Rapidly she made out the checks, addressed envelopes bearing her real return address, handed them to Cele to put straight into her own purse again for mailing on the way home. She also returned all the original envelopes that had her name on them and any letters where her name was typed to show through the envelope window. These Cele also put back in her purse, to dispose of in some street bin.

Then only did Dori say, "I can't talk about it anymore, can you?"

Cele shook her head. They had talked of it already, before they began on the letters, talked until they each felt spent. Through supper they watched the evening news in silence; they listened as if bludgeoned to the inevitable re-

capitulation and then the nature of the programs changed;
now they were scenes of rioting in dozens of cities, of burning buildings in a dozen black ghettos, of crowds and looting
and tear gas, of the smashing of windows, of screaming
sirens and troops and police and the National Guard, called
out by this governor and that mayor, of havoc across the
face of the nation.

"Forty cities," Dori said once. "He said 'in forty cities.'
Did you hear that?"

"I heard a special bulletin that said 'sixty or more.'"

"All in ghettos?"

"Of course, ghettos."

"But it's their own neighborhoods they're wrecking."

"If it were white neighborhoods, they'd be shot by the
dozens."

"Sixty cities," Dori said, awed. "Could it be the start of
another civil war? *Time* would promptly dub it Civil War
Two."

"Let's quit talking about it. You look terrible. I'm going to
get the fruit and cheese." She snapped off the television set
and went to the kitchen. Dori went to the mirror in the
bathroom, combed her hair and freshened her lipstick.

She did indeed look terrible, frowning and tight-faced.
She also wanted to stop talking about it, and she made an
effort to sound more cheerful. "I do look fierce, face-wise,
as the ad boys might say. But figure-wise? It's five and a
half months, and sure, you can tell I'm pregnant, but not the
way I thought I'd be by now, not good and bulky and obvious. Are they holding out on me or what?"

"You're going to be the servant girl that carries on till the
last minute, with the mistress of the house not suspecting a
thing. You look great, if not yet 'great with.' So stop hurrying."

"First you say I look terrible, then that I look great.
Which do I believe?"

"Both."

"Okay, it's easiest that way." Then matter-of-factly she

143

added, "That lawyer I met at your house, Matthew Poole, have you seen him again?"

"Not since. Have you?"

"He asked me to a concert."

"Did you go?"

Dori nodded. "It wasn't long after I met him."

"We like him but he's not the social type and we don't see him often either."

"I liked him too." The brief interchange surprised her. Cele was gazing at her with the mildest air of encouragement but she ignored the invitation. She was not certain why she had never said anything to her about Matthew; she had known she would not talk about being in love, but she had not planned a specific reticence about seeing him. Now suddenly she was bringing him into the conversation without pretext of pertinence, just idly speaking his name, the trick of the loving—or lovelorn—and with, of all perceptive people, Celia Duke. She nearly laughed. Yet without meaning to, without even knowing how she had managed to, she certainly had given Cele the wrong impression. They didn't see him often either. Maybe if you once embarked on lies you became so adept at the techniques that you soon lied out of habit, in a fine promiscuity including people you had never deceived in your whole life.

There was a pause; they ate fruit and cheese.

"I wrote to my brother Ron in London yesterday," Dori said, again matter-of-fact, "and asked if I could use him for a mail drop for six weeks or so. I didn't say why, just asked if I could send him an occasional letter to put British stamps on and mail out from there."

"How will he take it?"

"He'll say yes. His secretary will do it—it won't be more than a few times at most. He'll decide I'm having an affair and need a cover for that, and he couldn't care less." She could see Cele trying to put this train of thought together with the one that had made her mention Matthew. But Cele remained matter-of-fact also.

"And Alan? Did you write him too?"

"I tried to write the same damn letter to him, actually typing off the same words. But it stuck tight; I could imagine his passing it over to Lucia and the look between them. I might just up and phone him at the office some day. This note of Tad's—it's his second one."

Cele glanced at her watch. "It's only ten of five out there."

"Call him now?"

"Obey my impulse, Dorr. Get it done. Get your mind off everything awful, and back onto yourself."

For a moment Dori hesitated. Then she went to the telephone. "Person to person to San Francisco," she said and gave the operator Alan's name and office address. "His sister calling." In less than a minute she was saying, "No, not a thing, Alan, everybody's fine here. I'll tell you in a minute why I called. How's everything with you?"

She listened and Cele, watching, thought how animated she looked again, how pretty; she had forgotten the TV set and the bulletins and the dead body lying in that final darkness—God, why should she not? She felt protective and loving as if Dori were her sister or her child.

"It's going to sound wicked as hell," Dori was saying into the telephone. "And I thought you might not want to tell Lucia, so I called you there instead of at the house." He said something that made her giggle. "Not a movie star, no, nor a millionaire. But for a few weeks I'd love it if I could mail a few letters to you, for you to mail out with a San Francisco postmark. Not many."

She looked even more animated; Cele thought, She's actually in a tizzy as if she really were going off with a lover. She waved a hand to catch Dori's eye. "Tell him it's secret even if he can't do it," she whispered. Dori nodded.

"Lucia of course, but not one single other? Oh your secretary, she'll have to—no, I know she won't. Well, thanks, Alan, thanks a lot."

When she hung up she said, musing, "It's the first time, I swear to you on the Koran, the Talmud and the Bible, the very first time he hasn't been a stuffed shirt."

"Then he will?"

"Yes, but he'd die of disappointment if he knew I wasn't having an affair at all." Suddenly she shoved away from the telephone. "Oh, Cele, I'm not having an affair, but I was, and it was real, and it meant everything and now it's over and—"

Her voice suddenly caught and she turned away so that her face was averted. Cele did nothing. It must be Matthew Poole. It couldn't be. Dori never had sudden loves; she was never casual about friends or politics or books or what she read in the morning paper, then how would she be casual about sex? With sudden concentration she tried to recall exactly what it was Dori had said about Matthew Poole and that concert, whether she had said that was the first time she had seen him or whether she had specifically said that was the only time she had seen him. Already it was too far back in the blur of the evening to remember precisely.

After another minute of silence, Dori said, "Let's see if there's anything new about it," and crossed the room to the TV set. The click of the knob was sharp in the quiet room.

*   *   *

Suddenly Matthew knew what it was. He was not thinking of Dori but suddenly there it was, the truth, the thing he had not been able to name. Perhaps because he had not been thinking of her, because he had not been at his relentless prodding of his thoughts about her, it suddenly skimmed along the surfaces of his mind, and he caught at it, netted it and held it carefully as if it were a fragile creature that could be wounded or destroyed.

It was an April night, raw, sensitive, and fresh, and he was walking home from his office, tired and dispirited. He had lost the Benting case; it would now go to appeal before the circuit court. He had never been trapped into hope on the first stage of the case and had been careful to prepare Jim and his parents for this first defeat, so that they too would know all along that the ultimate decision was still months

146

off, perhaps even a year. The Spock indictment had, curiously, encouraged them, though he had tried to explain why the idiot charge of conspiracy in that case cut through any bonds of similarity with Jim's own. Jim saw it, but his parents persisted in feeling that even if the Spock trial, coming up soon in Boston, ended in conviction for him and his codefendants, the verdict would be so outrageous it would certainly be reversed someday by a higher court, and thus by some esoteric logic it was more certain that a reversal would someday be forthcoming for their son as well.

How strange, parents. How strange the persistence of his own hope that the bad times now with Johnny would reverse in some golden process as time went on, that in three years or so when Johnny the boy became John the college student, there would be a magic shift in his son's personality.

His intelligence told him not to hope but he went on hoping. He knew as surely as astronomers know three years in advance just where a star will be in the cosmos, so he knew that on a day in 1971 his son would be part of some great campus protest, would be arrested or suspended or expelled from the college of his choice, and that he would applaud him for his courage and his principles and at the same time know the stricture in his own heart at his son's newest struggle. When your kid's in trouble your heart is lead. A lifetime went into making your children happy and when they were happy your whole world was right. You knew what it was all for, you had done it, or helped do it—

That was when he suddenly knew. Dori was happy and he had had no part in it.

Suddenly he remembered the change that had come over Jack's face that night he had told him about Dori. *And you offered to help her,* Jack had said. It wasn't like that, he had answered, she didn't want any help. He had gone on to give Jack the whole background, all the years of tests and doctors, and Jack's expression had altered; a kind of comprehension had entered it, as if something had suddenly opened. But Jack had only ordered more drinks and they had got rather drunker than was usual for either of them.

All at once he knew what Jack had thought, knew why he had kept still about it, thinking it better for him to come to it himself. If she were crying to you for help, Jack had thought, you'd have stood by her, but you couldn't take it that she was happy about it.

She was happy in the profoundest sense and he had had no part in it. She was pregnant at last, and in the profoundest sense also, he was excluded from it. She had done this without him and she would go on without him. She was already, on that day she told him, already going on without him.

There was the crux of it and he had not faced it until now. He had talked of a blast of buckshot, but that was only alibi for his protracted silence and absence. Buckshot? It was more like napalm, to sear and scar. But that was alibi too.

At last he had isolated the truth. He had at last "got it into some sort of shape." Twelve weeks had gone by in the attempt; it seemed twelve years, it seemed twelve minutes, so endless was it, yet so hot and new. He no longer sweated out nightmare hours, but he could not recall even one moment of peace, of pleasure. She was away somewhere; he had tried two or three times to call her, the last time the night of King's assassination. Not even that time did he know what he could say, once he got through talking of the murder. That he was still trying to get this into some sort of shape? That he was still on hell's own wheel? That this was merely an interim call, meaning nothing? Each time he had been relieved that she did not answer. Now he suddenly felt that he could wait not an hour longer to face her and say, God forgive me, I've been in hell because you're happy.

CHAPTER EIGHT

It was ten thirty that night when the phone rang and Celia thought, Dorr, something's wrong. The one worry that still fretted her was that Dori might suddenly wake up one night, sick, and be there all alone, without even a maid to summon help. But the voice on the phone was a man's voice, not very familiar.

"Celia, it's Matthew Poole. I didn't wake you, did I?"

"Heavens. In this house?" She laughed. "Even the kids are awake."

"I gathered you were night owls. Something Marshall said once about *Nachtmusik*."

"And not always *kleine*." She was ridiculously glad to hear from Matthew Poole. All at once she knew she had been right at Dori's a couple of weeks ago, though they had not referred to it since. "It's rather fun to get late phone calls, unless it's some drunk, so did you want Marshall?"

"As a matter of fact, it's you, not Marshall." He was keeping his voice light and wondered if she knew he was. "I've been trying to reach Dori Gray and having no luck, and I hoped you'd give me an address that would find her."

"She's away for a few weeks."

"That's what her doorman said; I went by there. Some sort of cruise, and you pick up her mail every few days."

"Yes, I do."

"But I'd like to wire or cable her and I wonder if you'd give me the next stop on her itinerary."

"I, well, you see—"

There was a pause. Like Dori she had rehearsed the answer to every foreseeable comment or question, but this was one she had not foreseen and she was caught. To say to Matthew Poole, You can't wire or cable her, all you can do is write her at her regular address and I'll forward it and she will get it in due time—this would be a rudeness so signal that it would flag his attention at once.

It was he who broke the silence. "Look here, Celia," he said, no longer casual. "I know about Dori. She told me the last time I saw her. So even if you're not telling anybody else where she is—"

"Know what about Dori?" It sounded cautious, and it was cautious. She did like Matthew Poole, but she did not know him very well, and how could she be sure that when he said he knew about Dori, he actually knew this? Dori certainly had not told her that he did.

"Know that Dori—I wish this weren't the telephone."

"We're not bugged. Are you?"

He laughed; the whole concept was uncomfortable. "It might be better if you could let me see you tomorrow or next day for a few minutes. Would you?"

"Tomorrow if you like."

"About five? For about ten minutes?"

"Even fifteen."

As she was putting up the receiver she glanced again at the clock. Only five minutes had passed; Dori would not be asleep. Of course she would consult her as to whether to tell him where she was; the only question was whether it would distress her to know he was trying to see her, and if so, whether she might not wait until morning so as not to risk Dori's having a worried night. Or ought she to keep it to herself until she had seen Matthew Poole, heard what he had to say and had something more informative to pass along to Dori than the mere fact of his telephone call?

She wished she could ask Marshall's opinion, but that would only end by irking her, as she had been irked when she had finally told him Dori was pregnant. "Is this for real?" he had said. "I thought she couldn't." She could hear again the instant curiosity in his voice, very satisfying indeed.

"It will be born in July."

"Is the guy willing to get married?"

"He is married, with four children."

"Who is it?"

"My guess is that it's a newspaperman she's been seeing for a year or so, but you know Dori about what she calls 'he-said-I-said' talk. I did gather they were winding up their affair when it happened."

"Did he walk out on her when he knew?"

"She didn't tell him."

He nodded as if to say, Sensible girl. Then he had asked how people were taking it.

"Nobody's 'taking it' because nobody knows about it except her brother Gene and me, and now you. She's not going to play Emancipated Female for her own ego and have her kid called 'dirty little bastard' all its life."

"Good for her." He had glanced down at his work then, and she had known that his brief curiosity was over. He knew everything he needed to know; malelike, he now was returning to important things like the contracts being drawn up for a subsidiary company specializing in cartridges of taped music. She had been irked then; a hundred times since she had been irked again for he never showed more than a perfunctory interest whenever she gave him any further news about how things were going. Nor would he now if she asked his advice about Poole's call.

She was irritated at her dear beloved husband. He was still, after eighteen years, the one man she could imagine being married to, was still, among the hundreds of men she had met through his large business connections, the only one she could imagine as an abiding and continuing person in her life. Mainly he was easy to get along with, though they had the usual number of spats and quarrels, and he was delighted with the kids, though he never had enough time for them. He seemed happy with her most of the time, though he was quickly bored if she talked about politics, and if he had ever had in those eighteen years an affair with another woman, he had had the wit and the skill to keep it to himself in every way, with no telltale absences or careless shreds of evidence. So he was a good husband and it was a good marriage but at times she wanted to scream at him or hit him for being so immersed in his big successful record business that his attention span for anything else was about four minutes long.

Now she gazed for a third time at the clock and then dialed Dori. "You're not asleep," she greeted her. "I can tell by your voice."

"Of course I'm not."

"Dori, for a minute I wondered whether to hold this back until tomorrow, but I decided not."

"Hold what back?"

"Well, Matthew Poole just phoned and asked for your address, and naturally I ducked and then he persisted and asked if he could stop in tomorrow."

"Stop in where tomorrow?"

"Oh here. I didn't give him your address or phone or anything, of course."

"Of course." She swallowed in a suddenly dry mouth. "What did he say, Cele?"

"Just that he's been anxious to get in touch with you and had phoned and phoned and then that he went by your house and asked your doorman and got the cruise bit and also that I picked up your mail to forward. So he wanted me to give him the next stop on your itinerary, as if he'd cable you or call you person-to-person at the North Pole or wherever."

"What did you say to that?"

"I got around it, sort of gulping 'Well, you see,' and not being too good about managing it. Then he switched tactics and said he 'knew' about you, that you'd told him the last time he'd seen you, so even if I wasn't giving your address to anybody else—"

"'Knew' about me? Did he say what he knew?"

"He was as cagey as I, as if he didn't know if I knew. Anyway, then I decided I'd have to clear it with you before he gets here. He's coming at five unless you tell me to head him off."

"Oh Cele." She fell silent, and Cele waited in silence too. The telephone line was live between them, they each knew it, nobody had to ask, "Are we cut off?" yet neither was ready to say the next word. Dori was waiting for order to come, for her heart to stop its lurching, for a decision to be made about what to say, how much to say. "He does know I'm pregnant," she said firmly at last. "He also knows that it had happened just before I met him. Remember the Martin Luther King night when I suddenly told you I had been having an affair and that it was all over—"

"Certainly I remember. But you barely started and then you clipped it short."

"I know I did. Well anyway, I haven't seen Matthew Poole, or heard from him, since New Year's, and I don't know what this call of his means, but of course give him my phone number and address if he wants them, and after he's been, will you call me and—" She burst into an embarrassed laughter. "Will you listen to me? Clickety-clack, clackety-click, like some gushing adolescent."

Cele laughed too. "That's not what adolescents sound like. Liz would say 'groovy' or 'hey, man,' or something lyric and poetic like that. Me, I'm glad you're shook up. I hope he's worth it; I told you we didn't know him very well but liked him."

"I *am* all shook up. Cele, what I'm trying to say is all of a sudden there was Matthew at your house and then three or four weeks later, there was no more Matthew, and I do want to tell you all about it but now I have to wait and see what any of this means."

"Sure you do."

"Call me."

"I might at that. Good night. I have a feeling of being *deus ex machina* or something, big sense of power."

Dori tried to go back to the book she had been reading, but couldn't keep her mind on it. She was wondering what Matthew's sudden determined effort to find her might mean.

That he loved her, that he had at last "got it into shape," that he was going to come to her in remorse and longing and renewed passion.

Her body swirled with her own sexuality at the thought, swirled and spun and swooped as it had not since the day they had parted. Except in dreaming, she had been devoid of sexuality, despite Dr. Jesskin's pronouncements on the heightened presence she could expect. Now suddenly she saw that it was still possible, instantly possible, waiting only to be summoned forth from whatever locked and frozen cell it had fled to on that fierce day when he had gone off with his coat over his arm.

But that was the day after New Year's and this was the middle of April. Three months to get it into "some sort of shape"? Three months to come to terms with it? There was something wrong in the equation. A week, two weeks—she would have understood that, have read nothing into it, would never have needed to excuse it or make allowances for it. But three months? A quarter of a year? A third of a pregnancy? Something was excessive about it, something in Matthew was all twisted round or knotted up, else he would not have needed three months.

But remember the way you blurted it out at him.

Now don't go blaming it on yourself; you can't always be in the wrong. Don't you go twisting it around and knotting it up until it's all your fault. You've always been too damn ready to be the hurt instead of the hurter and he did hurt you, and then kept on hurting you, on and on.

She felt restless and uneasy. She jumped up from the big chair and reached for her coat. She had to move, stir, stretch, not sit bound in that chair in this limited space.

Never since living here had she gone out for a walk at this hour but she was going out now. She threw a scarf over her hair, wondered briefly whether the heavy coat would be too warm, wore it anyway, and let herself out into the mild night.

There was still music drifting from open windows up and down the wide street but few people. She turned toward the park, knowing that she would not enter it, and began walking briskly down Central Park West. Ahead lay all the night splendor of the New York sky, the twinkling levels of whole lighted floors in some of the great buildings, the reckless fling of other lights as if they had been strewn from a wild hand at accidental windows. She loved it. No matter what happened to her in the future she would always live in New York. It was her city, her hometown, her world. For all its viciousness and crime and noise and filth and cruelty, it also was the core of all the life she really valued: music, theater, ideas, books, newspapers, people. London rebuked her at once, Paris, Rome, and she made obeisances and apologies to her memories of all three but still she walked on toward the great jagging skyline below the park, loving it.

She walked on the west side of the street, past one apartment building after another, their lobbies alight, nearly all presided over by doormen. She felt safe proceeding from one pool of lighted sidewalk to the next like a child jumping from rock to rock to cross a stream. If anybody did dart out at her from an intervening strip of shadow, one cry would bring help.

But nobody darted. Soon she felt foolish for having considered so dire a possibility; between the sheepishness and the exalted response to the night sky, she slowly regained an inner calm. The wariness was tempered, she suddenly saw; the rush of readiness for Matthew was still there but in some way it was tempered too.

She was changing. Not only her body, but she, the whole being that she was. These months over here alone had surprised her in some unfathomable depth of herself, far down, far below anything she had known of herself before. This loneliness of the three months over here had not been her old enemy, had not been arid, not a long spell of bleakness that would remain and remain and remain, not the old-style loneliness she had always fought off like a dark tenacious illness. This had been a factual aloneness, that was all. There had been many days and evenings when she saw not one soul but a grocery clerk, yet there had been no misery in the idea *alone*.

She was changing. She hadn't thought of that, but tonight, with Matthew once again entering her life, on whatever basis, tonight she wondered for the first time if it would be the same Dori Gray he would find.

*   *   *

She woke thinking, He may call me right after he sees Cele. But how to get through all the hours until five? She was due at Dr. Jesskin's at eight thirty and she was glad the day was starting with a specific task to do. Dr. Jesskin's house visits were to have started with this one but when she had seen him in March he had said, "You are splendidly thin and tight; your musculature is clearly of the highest order."

"The exercises you ordered. And the three hard miles every single day."

"It must have been there before the exercises. Are you an athlete?"

"I love tennis and swimming, and I've always done lots, but not as an athlete, on school teams or anything."

"They have served you. Sometimes it is simply a case of good health, and good construction to start with. At any rate you will still be able to come here next month and my house calls will start in May. So you see I have made one miscalculation already. I am glad."

Her good construction. Each time she had recalled the phrase again, she had smiled. That and the three thinkings were the things she would always remember about him probably, apart from the great thing. She knew nothing about him as a person, only as a doctor, and if there was

156

any flaw in him as a doctor, either through the long years of the "so-called sterility" period or now during these incredible months since the day of infamy, then it was a flaw too microscopic for her unaided vision. She remembered the smiling faces on his desk, his wife and children, and thought, No wonder.

She had switched from the old fur coat at last, to an old loosely cut tweed of her own that was equally shapeless and nonrevealing, but as her taxi drew up to Dr. Jesskin's office, she still looked quickly about, up and down the avenue, fumbling for her fare so that if there were a familiar face anywhere she could sit back unseen until any danger of a meeting was past. Here on Park Avenue, there was still danger; over there where she lived, she had long since learned that there was none.

She had quickly given up the old sports hat pulled down far on her face, realizing that in the scarf-over-the-hair environment there she was merely calling attention to herself. She had taken to scarves too, because of the severe cold, but since the first thaw of March, she had even given those up most of the time. She never had her hair done any longer; that was her only disguise. She let it grow, washed it every few days, let it hang loosely around her neck, and at times thought, I'll never go back to the damn beauty parlor racket again anyway. That final rinse they always give you "for highlights," really! Now she saw that her own hair was slightly deeper in tone, more really brown, and she liked it. Some sketchy gray had begun to come in at the temples, for so long toned away by the "rinse," and she saw it with some surprise, with some displeasure, and then, upon reflection, with acceptance and even with approval. It was becoming, just a faint grayish feather above the outer corner of each eye, and she had never even known before that the paired plumes were there.

There was nobody in sight on the street and she stepped quickly into the office. Miss Stein was not yet there but Miss Mack said, "There you are, always on the dot," and led her in to change. "The doctor is ready. He's always on the dot too—you'd better believe it."

The locution amused her. She was more and more fond of Miss Mack, increasingly impressed with her behavior. Not once in all the visits since that day of the lab report had Miss Mack betrayed the fact that she knew Dori was pregnant. She seemed to have perfected some trick of seeing her only from the neck up; even when her hands were busily draping that sheet around torso and legs, she directed her gaze only at the upper part of her body, above the pregnant belly, above the enlarged breasts, above any and all evidence, even avoiding any direct gaze into Dori's eyes, settling instead on a point just below her chin.

Now as she stripped, Dori had the mischievous impulse to turn naked to Miss Mack and say, "Hey, look, I'm pregnant," but to Miss Mack it would have been a gibe, a jeer at the way she did her job, so the impulse died. In the toga-like sheet, she stepped on the standing scale in the examining room, knowing in advance what her weight would be, and heard Miss Mack say, "Good, you're obeying orders; the fatties annoy us so."

For the first time Dori used the small step stool to get herself up on the table. A sign of progress! Again the stirrups, the hiss of the sterilizer, the clink of steel instruments, but how marvelously unrelated to the years of dogged persistence and fading hope. Even if she had been like some pregnant women, prey to a dozen ailments and miseries all through, this was what she would never have let herself forget, this blessed difference from that void time.

"Good morning, and how has it been going?"

"Good morning, Doctor." From the table, she twisted her head backward to where he was coming in by the door from his office. "Except for my panic call that day about a lawyer, I've been grand."

He ignored the reference. "No physical discomfort in any way?"

"Not really. I don't skip and hop and run, but nothing you could label physical discomfort."

"I expected not."

He began the examination, silent as always, swift, satisfied. Then he moved his stethoscope down from her rib cage to her protruding belly, gently pressing it here and there until suddenly he nodded and smiled. "Strong and clear," he said.

"Oh, Doctor!"

"Do you want to hear for yourself?"

"Of course I do. Can I?"

He reached for another stethoscope, saying, "This one is weighted, to amplify sound," and fitted the twin tubes to her ears. She raised her head, craning forward, and then sat up, lowering her head to shorten the distance. Dr. Jesskin was holding the rounded listening tip to the spot where he had heard the hidden heartbeat, and she waited to hear it too. But she heard nothing. She sat forward a little more. She could hear nothing.

"It is there," he said calmly. "Sometimes the untrained ear does not catch it, but it is there. Quite decided, quite clear."

She listened again and suddenly said, "I think, I really do think—I can't be sure."

"You undoubtedly did." Dr. Jesskin took the ear tubes back and turned toward the scale, stooping to read the precise quarter-pound. Then he said, "When you are dressed," and returned to his office. Dori glanced in triumph at Miss Mack who returned the glance with her air of knowing nothing, as if stethoscopes placed on stomachs sent no message to her brain. Even her remark about fatties annoying "us" had not been a definite admission that she knew Dori was pregnant; twelve years ago during the "sterility visits," if her weight had been what it should be in the charts of Miss Mack's mind, she would have been as likely to say, "Good, the fatties annoy us."

Dr. Jesskin stood as she went in to his desk. Sometimes he did this, with a courteous reach for the back of her chair, at other times he sat ignoring her entrance entirely, reading the opened folder and his last notations. Today his expression indicated that there were no notations on which he needed to refresh himself.

"You follow every textbook of normalcy," he said. "It would be extraordinary if any deviation showed up now. How do you sleep?"

"I take a couple of aspirin and then read until about twelve."

"You will later on want some help, and then I will prescribe." He looked at the ceiling as if to avoid a direct glance. "My friend Bob Cox is more than ready, I will say eager, to handle your case. This time I told him much, everything I know of you and the long history behind this birth. It is all in confidence, I need not say. Even from his partners."

She started to thank him but he waved off any such idea. "You will not need to consult him until much later, perhaps in September or October. And I miscalculated again; his fee will be no extravagance at all."

"But—"

"He feels some sort of vested interest: we are old friends. He was at Harvard Law while I was at Harvard Medical. Now his son and my son are finishing up at Law and in June they both become junior clerks in his office."

"Will they be working on my case too?"

"Neither one will ever hear your name or see your documents." He consulted his desk calendar, but only as a reflex action, hardly pausing over the riffling pages. "Now as to the next part of your schedule, the seventh and eighth months. You will of course no longer come to the office. I begin the house calls. Eight thirty in the morning, May thirteenth, on my way here—will that be convenient?"

"*Any* time is convenient."

"Do you know what the advent of the seventh month means?"

"That it would live."

The four words were so simple, so strong, that the sudden waver in her throat startled her. It was like the first time she had felt the small firm thump; again there was that chasm between what she had always known and the moment it became her private knowing, within her own blood and bones and ligaments.

"That is so," Dr. Jesskin said. "It would have achieved completion in the biological order, but of course you will go to full term and not need to prove that."

He sounded genial, pleased with her as if this advent of the seventh month were an achievement she was to be praised for, and she left feeling that she had been applauded by the one mentor whose good grades and good graces she most wanted in all the world. Only when she was once more tucked safely into a taxi did she suddenly think, I wonder if he'll take Miss Mack along on May thirteenth, to stand there, during the house call. She laughed aloud, and then for the first time since she had entered Dr. Jesskin's office she remembered that this afternoon at five Matthew would be talking about her to Cele.

* * *

The doorbell rang but she moved automatically toward the telephone and then stopped, knowing it had made no sound. Ever since Cele had called her two hours ago, she had waited for his call, even turning the evening news program down low so that the volume left wide margins for hearing her muted telephone bell at its first ring.

"He's just left," Cele had said. "He really is determined to see you. He said right off and flat out that you were in love. That was almost the way he greeted me, sort of, 'Thank you for letting me come. Look here, you see, Dori and I are in love, were in love, no, let me say I was in love with Dori' and then he went on to say he'd been going through a—'bad time' is what he called it, and he didn't once say 'pregnant' as if he still wasn't sure I knew and wasn't about to give you away. He sounded as if it had been pretty rough, and that it had baffled him, I mean his own feelings had, and that finally something had clued him into another way of looking at it, and that he wouldn't want me to give him your address without checking first with you, but would I call you long distance then and there wherever you were, at his expense, and ask you, and then give it to him. He nearly fell apart when I said you were right in New York and that I had already had your permission and then gave him your number and your address."

Ten times she had wanted to interrupt Cele's tumble of words but so sure was she that Matthew would telephone within minutes that she was afraid to tie up her own line and had held back all her questions. But then nothing. She had tried to eat and could not; she had bathed quickly, ready to go wringing wet to the telephone, but it had remained silent. She had dressed in the navy blue silk and put on the white coral earrings, just in case his call included a question about when he could see her, and as if there were some guarantee of continuity if she appeared now to him as she had appeared on that wrenched-off last visit.

Not the same. Now there was nothing faint and hesitant and uncertain. There still was her own slenderness in arms, legs, face, throat, but now there was a hard shining belly, not soft or pudgy or fat, but hard and gleaming like stretched silk.

The doorbell rang again and this time she moved swiftly to the door, hand on the knob, eye to the peephole. "Who is it?"

"Me, Matthew."

The deep voice, the Matthew sound, like no other sound. She drew the bolts and opened the door. There he stood, thinner, older, his face not happy in greeting. "Cele said you were alone, so I decided not to talk first on the telephone."

"Oh Matthew," she said, and all the wary words were lost. She stepped aside and he came in, saying nothing, looking at her, looking at her face as if to draw forth from it something sustaining, looking openly down to the bulk he had never seen, openly and easily and without pretense. Then he looked up again, saw the brush of gray he had never seen in her hair, saw her intent eyes.

"My God, you are beautiful," he said. He still did not

move toward her and she stood still, not wanting to make the first gesture, not wanting to offer him the first touch. "I thought you couldn't be the way I remembered, and you are."

He turned abruptly and looked at the room, also carefully and at length. "So here's where you've been all along." He made a sound that would have been a laugh at some other time. "And I was imagining you in England or France or Timbuktu. Celia Duke said you like being here."

"I've grown attached to it. Isn't it hideous?"

He suddenly laughed. There was a burst to the sound, a breaking of constriction, a freeing, and he stepped toward her and said, "Oh, my God, Dori." He put a hand on her shoulder and drew her toward him and felt her move within the drawing arm and suddenly she was tight against him and he felt the hard rounding bulk of her that he had never felt, and again he said, "My God, Dori," and the words were gritty in his throat.

"What about a drink?" she said, pulling back from him. "I need one too." He said, "Scotch, please," and the hesitant look returned. A thin strip of sympathy went around her throat like a cord, unexpected and tight, and she said, "You take the big chair. It's the only decent one in the place."

While she made their drinks he was silent and so was she. Then she sat down on the low wood platform and looked up at him and smiled. He was so strained and uncomfortable that the impulse rose in her to say, "Never mind, it's over now, don't feel awful about it, let's forget it." But something clamped down on the words—it was not over, not really, not until it was understood equally by each of them and accepted equally, if acceptable it proved to be. One could "understand" anything; long ago she had understood Tony and his sudden announcement that he was through, but that had been no protection from what lay ahead. Just the same she could not find it in her to insist here and now on an accounting.

"What about the Benting case?" she asked over her un-

163

touched Scotch. "And Johnny, is he all right again at school?"

He answered the second question first, and she saw his relief in the alacrity and detail with which he spoke. He talked of Hildy too, of her increasing aloofness and secretiveness; at her birthday party, he had not been astonished at the shaggy look of some of her friends, nor at the incessant twang of guitars, but he had once thought that he had smelled the acrid sweet smell of marijuana. He had wanted to go straight in and ask, "Is anybody smoking pot in here?" and had not done it, remembering Hildy's harsh scorn of "parents who thought they could run every minute of their children's lives." Had not done it, and felt not proud of his restraint but uncertain of his fitness for parenthood in the new universe of liberated youth. "If there was ever a classless society," he ended, "today's teen-agers are it— they're wonderful, they're impossible, all of them alike."

And then he told her briefly about Jim Benting and his parents, and the appeal, and again she heard relief in his voice, as at a reprieve. He really did not want to explain the three months, not yet at least; he did not want to go over the weeks of absence, he wanted only to forget them. He had come to some point with himself that had made him ashamed of his own behavior, and he was grateful that she was not standing there invincible and demanding, a Juno figure of outraged womanhood demanding explanations.

"Oh, Matthew," she suddenly said, "you don't really want to talk about it now. Cele said you called it 'a bad time,' and I thought you'd want to tell me but if you don't want to for a while, you don't need to."

He suddenly stood up, looking down at her. "It's nothing I'm proud of."

She put her hand out as if she were going to touch him but did not. "You once said we shouldn't make all the young mistakes, remember?"

"Yes, I do."

"Then let's not."

There was silence and then he was down beside her, his

164

arms around her, his mouth against hers. "Darling, I'll be careful," he said at last, and passion swirled again in her, a vortex, rotating upon itself, not to be resisted. She undressed, stood naked for a long time, letting him see her as she was, turning down no light, seeking no nightgown or covering. He looked at her and nodded as if in acceptance, and she nodded too, gazing down at her distended body, seeing gladly the gourd-like roundness, so purposeful with its silken taut stretch of skin.

*　*　*

Matthew stayed most of the night, making a telephone call after midnight which she could hear clearly from the bathroom where she had gone to give him a semblance of privacy when he said he'd better call home. "I'm sorry to call this late," he said almost formally into the telephone, "but I won't be in for a couple of hours yet." She wondered at the formality, and wondered for perhaps the first time what, exactly, was the actual status of his and Joan's relationship, when staying out half the night could be managed with one brief phone call after midnight. Obviously there was very little of any tight proprietary hold left. On both sides? Or only on his?

For the first time she wondered if this loose arrangement made Joan unhappy and wanted to ask him and could not. A swift memory flew across her mind of Dick Towson saying of his own absences from home, "I've got a damn good marriage in all the usual twenty-five-years-of-it ways, steady, and no surprises, and all the kids know I'll always be back, so it's okay and you and I don't ever have to worry about it." Perhaps Matthew could say the same thing about Joan and his kids and say, too, "You and I don't ever have to worry about it." As if he were saying, *That is intact.*

The family intactness. As if he were saying, Sure, I love you, but what's that got to do with anything—meaning his continuing patterns, his true life at home, apart from her. To her, *home* used to mean that closed apartment; *intact* used to mean her other life over there on the other side of the park, her real life, with her books and paintings and colors and continuity. Now home was here, right in this place where she lived day by day; the truest life she had ever known was this life, not the other one she had accepted for so many years as the only one.

Change. People did change, life did change, not everything remained intact and untouchable forever. She, in any case, had changed already. Was it only temporary, delusive, not to prove real later on, when July twenty-third had come and gone? It was the first time the question had presented itself, but at once it had stature and importance.

"Darling, are you all right?" Matthew called. With a start she realized that his telephone call had ended minutes ago, and that she had stayed shut away as if to hide her skimming thoughts. In the instant she returned to him she forgot them, so wonderful was it to see him there, sitting on the edge of the disheveled bed, eager for talk, eager for her presence, eager soon to make love again. He stayed until four in the morning and when he was leaving, he said, as if he had left a sentence dangling a moment before, "But it's no young mistake to put the 'bad time' on the record instead of evading it permanently."

"I meant only that you didn't want to talk about it tonight."

"Maybe tomorrow night I will. About nine thirty?"

But through the second evening he did not talk about it, nor on the third. He wanted to be "filled in" on everything she had done; she found it delightful to retrace each step for him, the dielmma of the hideout, the rejection of Wyoming and Washington and all the other far-flung ideas, the apartment hunt and Mrs. Steffani, the brotherly mail drops, the reservation already made at Harkness.

"If you want more exotic postmarks than California and London," he said, "we have some affiliate attorneys in Tokyo and Honolulu and Rio."

"That would really clinch it. I'm not keeping in touch with many people anyway; to let them forget about my being gone is better. But one or two judicious little letters from Tokyo or Rio would fill it in for fair."

Only afterward did she realize that she had said nothing about Cox, Wheaton, Fairchild, Tulliver and wondered that she had forgotten. She also wondered why Matthew had not asked her about her arrangements for the adoption. Was he still intending to check it out for her at the office, and proceed from there? And if he was, would she tell Dr. Jesskin to tell his Bob Cox that she wouldn't be needing his services after all?

She felt a most unexpected reluctance to do so. She had appealed to Dr. Jesskin in crisis, and he had given time and thought and care to this, which was no integral part of his function as her doctor. Now to brush it all aside—"the lawyer I mentioned has come back and will handle it for me, thanks anyway"—that was impossible.

Better not let it chivy her; better let time take charge, as time had taken charge of so many other things. She did not want to accost Matthew with it either: You're keeping awfully silent about lawyers on this adoption; are you trying to tell me something? Would you rather not get mixed up in it?

It was on Friday night, with the weekend separation facing them, that Matthew suddenly said, "I told you I could be a selfish bastard, and I guess that was the basis of this whole damn thing."

He had still not talked about the bad time; now she went quite still, waiting, a nervous longing in her to have it over with and let it slide backwards into the past again. But he was talking about the night Jack Henning had finally demanded to know what was eating him and how he had, to his own surprise, sat there and told Jack about her.

"Then Jack said, 'You offered to help her' and I said it wasn't like that, that you were a million miles from wanting help, and I told him why, and then a couple of weeks later, I suddenly remembered the way he had looked, comprehension dawning in him as if he had seen something basic and wondered what had kept me from seeing it. I knew he'd decided on the spot that it would be no good to spell it out for me, that I had to come on it all by myself. He was right."

He turned away from her, and she wished it were over. Resentment arose obscurely in her, that he was still in misery over this, letting her see he was, as if he were charging her with it still.

Tony had done that transfer too. The very day after he had smashed their marriage, he had sent a letter from his office, by messenger to speed it, saying he was sending for his clothes and moving to a hotel, that he could not "go through another such night." It was the letter of an ill-used man.

"And that basic thing," Matthew went on heavily, "was that if you had been in a state of misery about getting pregnant, I'd have come through like a brick."

"You would have. I never doubted it."

"I'd have stood by, I'd have been a hero. But you weren't miserable. You were happy, and I hadn't had a damn thing to do with it. There was the shutout right there."

"But Matthew—"

"I couldn't take it, that it hadn't anything to do with me, that it had happened for you before I even came along. That was the ultimate shutout, and nothing was going to change that, not ever."

"Didn't you know I'd have been ten times happier if you *had* been part of it? I wished so terribly that it had been you, I was on the verge of telling you it *was* you." He winced, but she could not be sure why. Was it simply regret that she had not lied to him?

"There's nothing about the whole damn story I can feel good about," he said at last. "I'm not going to cop any plea and rationalize my way out of it. Even when I finally saw it all, I also saw what it's like to love somebody the way you loved when you were a young man but without the freedom you had when you were young, to follow through and say, Let's marry." He compressed his lips; he looked angry. "I wish to God I could say it, darling."

"I wish to God you could, too." Joy leaped within her. It

was as if he had said it. He wants to, she thought, that's what matters. It's like being pregnant; the primitive thing is what matters, not the social thing of having people know. This is the same now with Matthew; what counts is the primitive thing that he wants to say it: Let's marry. He wants to say, Let's marry.

Aloud she said, "But from the first minute you made it clear that you would never leave your kids. I've known it, you've known it, it's been part of everything."

"Yes, everything." He looked the way he had looked the first night he had come back, older, thinner, not very happy. Long ago she had thought of him as a man who was not often happy, and then she had forgotten that. Now she remembered it again and her heart went out to him.

* * *

Cele finally said, "Matthew Poole put me into it, so you might as well get over your reticences and tell me about it."

Hesitantly at first, then more easily, Dori did. It was remarkable that she had needed to keep silent for so long, for she discovered now that there was a definite pleasure in talking about herself and Matthew, in talking separately about him, about his life, his family, his work.

There was no impulse to confide intimacy of detail, nor did Cele indicate any eagerness for it. Indeed at one point Cele interrupted to say, "Remember at school how I used to sit up half the night giving you a blow-by-blow of some new date and how you finally stopped me?"

"How did I?"

"By being brutal."

"Brutal how?"

"It was sophomore year and I'd just come back from a football weekend in New Haven, fairly snorting with triumph. You looked at me coldly and said, 'Okay, but not one word about Then he tried to kiss me.'"

They burst out laughing, and Dori said, "I don't remember that at all."

"I used to be god-awful," Cele said. "No taste, no asterisks,

I used to read love letters aloud to you until you said you wanted to throw up whenever I opened an envelope."

"I must have been god-awful too."

"There you go, defensive little Dori. I was a blabber-mouth slob, is the truth, and it took me years to learn what you knew all along. Anyway, go on about you and Matthew."

Dori did not spare herself when it came to "blasting him with it like a load of buckshot." She told it all, astonished anew that what she had so thoughtfully planned in advance should have got so out of hand and become so inept and abrupt. "I never blamed him for going off in a shock reaction."

"Oh Dori, you'll be the end of me."

Dori nodded as if in agreement. "The only thing I couldn't see was why it took him so much time to manage it. It took his friend Jack only that one evening to see what had hit him so hard and they were drunk."

"It's always easier to get to the heart of the matter when it's not your matter."

Dori was grateful, as if Cele were exonerating Matthew. It was all the more surprising, when she had come to the end of her recital, to have Cele say, "But there's something about your Matthew I don't quite get."

"What?"

"Why doesn't he get a divorce? Other men do."

"I know they do."

"Good men, not just rats."

"But Matthew—"

"Is he Catholic?"

"He's nothing. He was born Presbyterian. It's not religion, it's his children. Mostly his son."

"But his children are sixteen and fourteen."

"Even so. Johnny is a pretty troubled child and God knows what would happen if his father walked out on him now."

"Maybe one reason he's troubled is having a father who's unhappy, who hasn't been really happy for years."

170

"Matthew would never have said one word about that to either of them."

"He's not home much at night, is he? You think kids have no unconscious minds absorbing things like that?"

Dori was suddenly angry. Cele had no right to raise such questions; she didn't know enough about Matthew, could not know enough about him and his situation and his problems, yet here she was right spang in the middle of the forbidden territory of divorce and remarriage, territory Dori had put beyond the pale from the first moment, in her thoughts, in her fantasies, in her whole existence. Perhaps that was why she had been so reticent with Cele all along about Matthew, instinctively guarding those boundaries from casual assault, even with the most loving of motives.

They had to remain intact too.

Cele was apparently affected by her long silence. When she spoke again it was to say, almost carefully, with none of her usual good humor and vigor, "So much for that. You know more about it than I do."

"I do, Cele. I really do."

CHAPTER NINE

Matthew was there on the Thursday of the following week when Ellen telephoned. So surprised was Dori that she nearly said, "Ellen who?" Not once since the ugly visit about her "terrible mistake" had Ellen called her, not once written, not once sent a message by Gene. Now at nearly midnight here she was.

"Gene isn't with you by any chance?" Ellen asked.

"No. Was he planning to come here?"

"I don't know. Have you heard that they may shut the whole university down?"

"I saw it tonight on the six o'clock news."

"Gene never got home and he never called. I've been trying to reach him or Miss Pulley. She doesn't answer her phone either, so then I thought maybe he had stopped by to see you."

"He's probably in some faculty meeting and perfectly all right."

"I asked the switchboard operator if there were any meetings this late and she said no." Her tone implied that Dori might have taken it for granted she would have thought of a faculty meeting. "Anyway, if he were at a meeting, he

173

would have been able to get to a phone and call me. I keep thinking about their holding the dean prisoner for twenty-four hours."

"But they admire Gene and they know where he stands."

"I'd go up to the campus myself and see if I could locate him, but if he should get to a phone, I'd want to be right here."

Dori wondered briefly if Ellen was waiting for her to volunteer to go up and look. She imagined herself trying to push through the unruly crowds she had seen all week on the news programs, hundreds of students running, shouting, pushing, being pushed, blacks and whites, mostly men, many girls, as well as younger people from the city's high schools, determined to demonstrate too. "Have you tried Jim and Dan?" she asked.

"They're not in, either one. If you do hear anything, you'll call me, won't you?"

"Of course. I'm sure he's all right though."

She turned from the phone, wondering that she was so undisturbed. To Matthew she said dryly, "According to my sister-in-law, my brother Gene is missing." Then not so dryly she added, "Can you imagine even imagining a college professor missing on the campus? Wartime! It's all so unreal. So many things this year seem unreal."

He began to defend the student protesters but she thought, extraneously, One unreal thing is how much of my life happens now by telephone or by turning on a radio or TV set. That's what comes when you're in hiding; you're tied to the world by a thousand electronic umbilicals that you never thought vital before.

"I'm on the students' side too," she said. "You didn't think I'd not be? Except for two things."

"What two?"

"Their taking human hostages and their photographing private letters and documents. That just sticks in my craw."

He nodded but she suddenly grew heated. "Matthew! If you half think it's okay, 'to get the proof they need,' then how can you ever object to the FBI walking in and photographing *your* private letters and documents to get the proof they think they need? Or Jim Benting's letters, or anybody else's?"

"Whoa, hold on," he said, heated too. "I never said it was okay, did I? Even though they weren't private letters and papers, but official ones proving the university's hookup to the Pentagon and the army. I'm no believer in the-end-justifies-the-means crap."

"But a lot of the students are."

"So they're wrong. Lots of them. But lots of them are also right. Who do you think forced Johnson not to run again, Lyndon Johnson, the most ambitious man in all politics?"

"I know who. And I love them."

"You're damn right. The young. The students. All those kids with their placards about Vietnam and the draft and napalm, all those students working day and night for Gene McCarthy, and now all the others backing Bobby Kennedy."

As he went on, staccato, more excited than she had ever heard him, she thought, This is the way he is at his best, when he gets most involved, with the things he believes in, or with Hildy and Johnny. Suddenly she saw that part of this defense of the young, of the rebellious young, was a kind of *a priori* defense for what might lie ahead for his own young rebel at home.

"Let's hear the latest," Matthew said and flipped on the radio.

". . . and an estimated one hundred," a voice was saying, "all wearing white handkerchiefs around their arms as signals that they are faculty, are maintaining their vigil before the five occupied buildings, to resist attempts by the authorities to eject students by force."

"Gene!" she said. "That's where he is."

"Professor," an interviewer asked, "could you tell us the purpose of this action?"

"Why, simply that we feel that with us out here, there's less chance of their getting rough with the students inside."

"Who, sir? There are no police here, are there? We were officially told not."

"But there are hundreds of private guards, plainsclothesmen, detectives."

"Have you proof of that, sir?"

"Plenty. And we hear the university may call in the police officially at any time."

Dori waited no longer; she dialed Ellen. "About a hundred faculty are standing guard in front of Hamilton and Avery and Fayerweather and Low—have you heard that?"

"No. Where did you?"

"No wonder Gene can't get to a phone." She told her what radio station to turn to, and could hear the relief in Ellen's voice. She accepted her thanks for having called back, and heard the grit of restraint enter as Ellen remembered the unresolved hostility between them. It suddenly didn't matter.

"If anything were to happen to one of those professors standing guard—" she said as she turned back to Matthew.

"Not with those armbands. What if any student got killed?"

"It's unbearable to think of."

"They'll probably shut down soon."

"Shut what down?"

"Everything. No classes. No lectures. No seminars."

"God, it's like a siege."

❋   ❋   ❋

They shut down the next morning. It was Gene who told her, having stayed up there all night and arriving home, as he said, "on a few hours' leave."

"They did attack us," he added. "Sometime around twelve or one. They came charging right through us, and the hell with us being faculty."

"Who, the police?"

"University guards mostly. Savage too. A young instructor in the French Department, I don't know him, got a scalp wound five inches long and bled like a dying animal."

"Were you hurt?"

"Shoved a bit. God, something snaps inside you when

they start to straight-arm you. I'll be fine right through, don't worry!"

"Right through? What does that mean?"

"I'll get some sleep and then go back. Twice as many will be out today as before. And if they do call out the regular police, with the nightsticks and tear gas and guns, they'll just galvanize ten times more supporters, students and faculty both."

"Oh Gene, be careful."

In the afternoon Matthew called to say he couldn't be with her until after the weekend. There was an agitation in his voice, despite his obvious will to control it. "Johnny's been hurt," he said, "and I'd better stay close tonight."

"Hurt how?"

"Not too seriously, but he's pretty worked up. Another kid had his nose smashed and was taken to a hospital."

"What happened? Where were they?"

"Up at Columbia. Another big contingent of high school boys, from lots of schools, like the crowd yesterday, to join the demonstrators. Five guys from Johnny's class went, they're all big enough to pass for freshmen. But he's the only one who got hurt."

"Oh Matthew, how awful. Will he be all right?"

"He's back from the doctor now. He had five stitches in his hand, in his palm under the knuckles, and he's a mass of contusions. I'd better stick around. Hildy and Joan are upset too."

"Of course. Oh darling, I'm so sorry. What a gutsy kid he must be."

"He's that, but what a time and place to show it! I thought we'd have at least three years' leeway before we got into this kind of thing."

There was a fatalism in the way he said it, outlawing any *if*'s and *but*'s about Johnny and the next years. Three years more of high school, she thought as she turned away from the phone, and then four at college; it would be 1975 before Johnny could be regarded as educated and independent. But somewhere in there would be the draft and

Johnny's decisions about the draft board and whether to take that step forward or refuse induction and be sentenced to prison—

Her heart sank. In 1975 her own child would be seven, and she would be only three years from being fifty.

*　*　*

It's the way it was during the war, she thought, when every family you knew was affected by it. Gene was in the air force then, Ron in the navy; only Alan, just sixteen, had remained out of it. If anybody with two brothers in action could be said to be out of it. Heaven knows she hadn't been out of it.

Now here was Gene at fifty, haggard with his need for sleep, appointed to the new Senate of the Faculty in a nonfunctioning university and here was Matthew with no connection with campus or faculty, yet caught up in this violence because of Johnny. The stitches across the boy's hand would be removed soon and the contusions were in their final purpling, but for the first time the headmaster of Johnny's school had sent for Matthew and wondered aloud about the need for psychoanalysis for his son. It was Johnny, he said, who had argued the other four into going to Columbia the day the police were there; the others' parents had charged him with being "an organizer" and ringleader. That was probably unjust, but Johnny did have a long history of insubordination, persistent enough perhaps to be termed neurosis.

"I'm not scared off by the word *neurosis*," Matthew assured Dori, "I know better than the headmaster that Johnny isn't exactly a nice normal well-adjusted member of the establishment."

"You'd hate it if he were. A square, aged fourteen?"

He smiled without much amusement. "But the idea of professional therapy carries such an or-else in it, it puts me in a sweat."

"Just the same, it could be a great insurance policy against anything serious later on."

178

"That's what I keep telling myself." He was moody to-night and she did not wonder. He had forbidden Johnny to return to the Columbia campus, but for the first time he knew that that would not keep Johnny from returning, if returning was what Johnny intended to do. To know that control was passing from your hands to your child's must be a good feeling if your child was eighteen or twenty, but when he was fourteen and willful and driven to some endless battle with those in authority—there was nothing gratifying about that.

"Johnny may have had enough excitement by now," she said without conviction, "to make him more amenable to what you tell him. Or enough of a scare." But there was no response from Matthew and she felt a little hypocritical. There was nothing to make a boy like Johnny lose interest in the Columbia revolt. A thousand city police had finally been called in, some of them careful, some vicious, seven hundred students had been arrested, over a hundred had been injured, and the siege was officially over. But that was "officially." Johnny still talked of nothing else.

"It's part of something so much bigger," Matthew said at last. "If it were only Johnny. Or only Columbia."

"Or only ten Columbias." Each day brought an explosion of student revolts, at Cornell, at Duke, at Ohio State and Northwestern and Stanford and fifty other campuses in the land; across the oceans other students were in rebellion in Prague and Rome and Tokyo and at the Sorbonne, especially at the Sorbonne, where people were already beginning to talk of "another French Revolution." Somewhere she had heard the younger generation called the new international underground, and she responded as she would to any other resistance movement. But what lay ahead? Danger, she thought, and worse violence and even war.

She ought to be afraid. She ought to be thinking, What a time to bear a child, what right have I to bring a new human being into such a world? But she could not think it. At a hundred other times in the world's turbulent life there were people who had said it, but birth had gone on un-

deterred by death. During the First World War there had
been women giving birth; during the Second World War,
during the first horror of the atomic bomb, there had always
been those who cried, "What a crime to bring a child into
so vile a world," but steadily, surely, conception went on,
pregnancies went on, birth went on, as if to flout the killing and the death.

"If ever I did get a divorce," Matthew suddenly said, "you
can imagine what it would do to him, therapy or no therapy."

Unexpected, unforeseen, his words caught her, miles from
what they had been talking about, miles from anything to
say in reply. She gazed at him as if she were trying to understand the separate syllables of some unfamiliar tongue.

"Darling, look," he went on, "you know by now that half
of me wants to leave everything behind and start again
with you."

"I don't think of it. I don't let myself."

"But I do. Especially since we've come back together. But
then I immediately think of Johnny and Hildy, and of course
Joan. There's not much left for Joan and me apart from the
kids, but she's not one of these women who would be able
to start again at forty-two and make anything of it."

He looked depressed, sodden with a sadness she had
never seen so plainly. She tried to think of the right thing
to say but found nothing. "Perhaps I'm the one needs the
therapy," he added, and again she said nothing.

"I don't mean just in general," he went on. "I suppose
everybody could use a psychic checkup just in general.
But me—something's been bugging me recently and I can't
shake free of it."

"Do you want to tell me?"

It seemed hard for him to begin. He didn't look at her
when he spoke. "It's something I wrote you once, that's got
into some cross-tangle with when my mother was alive. I
see the connection and that's supposed to rid you of it,
isn't it? Only it doesn't."

He had never said very much about his parents, but
neither had she about hers, beyond sketching in her love

for her mother and distaste for her father. In their first weeks there had been no time for reminiscence and anecdote except about themselves as adults, and in the month since Matthew's return, they were once again too full of their immediate life. She knew that his father had died when he was a boy, but she was not clear about when he had lost his mother, or whether they had been close or distant. He had admired his mother, that she knew, had called her a fine lawyer, a remarkable person to have succeeded some thirty years ago when the law was still regarded as a man's profession.

"Maybe talking it out would help," she said quietly.

"I think it started that first morning I left you in bed," he said almost irritably. "You were half asleep and I wanted to wake you and I didn't, and then I tried all day to get you by phone and couldn't, and I wrote you instead."

"I remember."

He surprised her by switching abruptly to his early life with Joan, to the slow realization that they were never going to have a large easy circle of friends, to the time Hildy was born. He began to hurry his sentences, he slid over their difficulties with his mother, hardly mentioning Joan's shyness or unwillingness, making it his own unwillingness to go through awkward scenes. At last he talked of his mother sitting in silence looking down at the infant Hildy.

"That was fifteen years ago," he said, "and for years I never thought of it, but now it keeps jumping out at me like a flash shot on a movie screen. So okay, I was thoughtless and stupid about family things, but how many young couples get in wrong with in-laws or parents? And why the hell should it start needling me at this late date?"

He broke off, angry, and she waited. At last she asked, "Your letter to me. Where does that come in?"

"My letter? Oh that. It's mixed in somehow. Sometimes the connection is clear and sometimes it goes foggy, and right now the hell with it. I've said too much as it is."

She wanted to cry, It's not too much, Matthew, it's not enough. Why can't you say straight out, how and why your letter comes in? You must feel it or you'd never have mentioned the letter at all. But she thought of his friend Jack forcing his own words back. Jack knew you couldn't give insight to somebody like a gift. She knew it too.

❊   ❊   ❊

The sense of frustration would not go away. Long after he was gone she continued an interior conversation with him, depressed that she had thought it hazardous to hold it openly while he was still there. At the end of his recital they had dealt only in the small banalities that often follow revelation, when, spent with the emotion of telling, he needed only comfort, a kind of retroactive absolution, and she, giving both comfort and absolution, had wondered whether he would regard the matter closed and never return to it, or pursue it the next time they met. To be unwilling or unable to talk things out, even after one had started to talk them out, was no way to reach firmer ground in any close relationship. She should have made it easier perhaps, should have asked the questions that would have helped him dig for the answers that were already his.

"Darling," she prompted him now in her mind. "Don't you see why everything is cross-tangling?"

"No, do you?"

"It's only a theory. It could be so wrong."

"Tell me."

"Why I think it happens whenever you're afraid of hurting somebody again."

"Hurting Joan?"

"Joan or me, either one. I wonder if you don't know that it's better to face things with somebody you love than to avoid a scene just to keep the peace, that if you do avoid scenes about something important, you end up by 'diminishing' the relationship, and feeling diminished yourself too."

She could imagine his wincing at the *diminish*. Though he knew perfectly well about himself as a lover, the sexual association would be there, a major affront. She could see his look become distant, as if he had never mentioned the letter, the only letter he had ever written her, could see his look of distaste, of disbelief, then of a faltering acceptance. Yet it was Matthew who had cross-indexed the two lines of thought, he who had finally seen that he had been rather a weak man in that early crisis in his life and was perhaps uncertain whether he were going to go on repeating that kind of weakness. It was too difficult to say any of this to him; he did not wish to say any of it aloud himself. Not so far. If he were to end his marriage, he would again live with guilt, would again have the same inability to excuse himself for what he had done. And yet he also felt guilt about not ending his marriage, about keeping it "intact" while his real life was here with her. His instinct was to say, Let's marry, but he had to stamp it down; her instinct also said, Let's marry, but he had to stamp her down too.

So he lived with one guilt while fleeing from the other.

I was immobilized, he had told her when he talked about his three months away from her. *Until I understood it, I was immobilized.* Now wasn't he immobilized again?

He would not put it that way. He would not put any of it the way she had just put it; for one thing he would speak not of leaving Joan but of leaving Johnny. Tonight was the exception, the one time he had ever permitted the formation of those words about leaving Joan, and he had negated the idea instantly. Joan was not a woman who could start life anew in the forties. She, Dori, was a woman who could, so she was elected to do it.

He would never have it out with Joan. He could not stand scenes, except in court where conflict was part of the *modus vivendi.* He would live on in silence, old guilt interweaving with new guilt, threading in and out of it, reinforcing it, warp and woof, dependent one on the other, inextricable. Poor Matthew. It was not a good way to feel.

And me? Dori thought. Am I immobilized too?

*   *   *

The summer came suddenly and she walked with a little less than her striding energy. The park was nearly at full bloom; wherever she looked there were flowering trees, cherry, peach, pear, apple, or so she named them in her new status as botanist. She had never known before that there would be so many banks of rhododendrons, so many beds of tulips; the deep pinks, the pale pinks, the shimmering white and newly fresh green delighted her constantly.

It pleasures me, she thought; what a lovely old verb. Around a curve she came upon a girl out walking too, walking toward her slowly, apparently not seeing her. She was a young girl, in her late teens probably, or her earliest twenties, slender, pale even for the lightness of her skin and hair. Her cheeks gleamed wet in the sun, with tears streaming from her reddened eyes and her face ugly in the distortion of grief.

"Are you sick?" Dori asked without thinking. "Can I do anything?"

"No, thanks." She looked up briefly but did not slow down or attempt to hide her face.

"Whatever it is, I'm sorry," Dori heard herself say and they passed each other and the girl moved off behind her, around the curve in the path.

It left her shaken. A husband lost in Vietnam? A boyfriend unfaithful to her? The news that she was pregnant?

She was suddenly convinced—it was that, the news just given her in some doctor's office or at some clinic. The lab report was in and it said "positive." ("Oh no, oh God, what will I do, where will I go?")

The words rang within her as if they were being cried aloud to her and again the extraordinary conviction came that she had guessed correctly. For weeks now she had forgotten that frieze of faces she used to think about; she had been too much immersed in herself, too grateful for the passing days and their ticked-off accomplishment, but now again, stark and vast, a multitude of unwilling frightened girls arose before her, three hundred thousand who were not grateful, who did not have the freedom she had to step aside for a while from jobs and salaries and offices and factories and earnings.

184

Of the two pieces waiting for her return to steady work, this one on the terrified and trapped was the nearest to completion, but she had put aside the final writing of it, afraid that in her continuing mood whatever she wrote might, despite herself, sound patronizing. Like that morning after Martin Luther King, she thought, when I wanted to talk to that woman I passed.

It would be better to set it aside until she began working again, in September or October. She was going to come back here with the baby after the hospital and live right here until she could show herself to the world once more, get to work once more for Tad Jonas and any other editor who needed pieces written. How fortunate that Mrs. Steffani had insisted on a lease for an entire year. She had known all along she could not be going straight from Harkness to her real apartment with a new baby in tow, had known she would have to return from that legendary world cruise as she had left, with the same two suitcases and the borrowed plaid carryall and nothing else. But she had also known that the shorter her total absence, the more acceptable her cruise story.

So, the interim stop would be right here in this blessed ugly familiar place, and as soon as she could show herself again she would have to hire a maid to live here with the baby, while she went home alone and resumed her "normal life." She laughed at the words. Normal life indeed. With her coming over here every single day to spend hours with her own baby, and moving back in every Friday evening to take full charge while the maid took her two days off.

It was all part of her still-evolving plan. She was saving in every way she could and it was still going to be a big chunk out of her nest egg, but if ever there was a palpable nest involved in that phrase, this had to be it!

Two months would go by, three, and she would be seeing friends and colleagues again, magazine editors, newspaper people, and the vagueness of memory about other people's goings and comings would have set in among all of them. Then only would she break the news that she was adopting a baby and arrive at home one fine day, no longer alone, but with the classic blanket enclosing a very new baby.

Classic, except for the lack of the proud husband beside her.

She thought once more of the weeping girl with the distorted face. She should have stopped, not walked on, stopped and said, Look, I'm in a fix too. You don't know me, don't know my name and I don't know yours, so why can't we talk about it? It might help, it gives people a release to tell somebody else, that's why they go to priests, or analysts, or talk to strangers on a train or boat.

Daydreams. Fantasy. Fairy tales for the pregnant. Here she was holding unspoken conversation with Matthew, giving unspoken sympathy to the girl in disgrace, experiencing the outer world largely through radio and television news and the telephone.

But she was lucky. Compared to the weeping girl she had passed, how blessedly lucky. She *could* carve out a year of her lifetime and pay for it. That simple economic fact had made the difference between disgrace and delight.

Not just that, she thought in sharp rebuttal. There you go again, belittling, deprecatory, another way of being defensive. Damn it, you know perfectly well that even if you didn't have a cent in the world you'd still be having this baby.

*   *   *

She opened the door eagerly. "Good morning, Doctor."

"Good morning, Mrs. Gray. Mrs. Grange—I beg your pardon. You see I had no problem with the bell. You look splendid. How do you feel?"

"Splendid too."

He was alone, as she had known he would be. She had made up the bed in its daytime incarnation, and on one end of it she had flung an ostentatious sheet for draping. To get ready would take less than a moment; she was in a loose smock that was like a hospital garment, except that it was strewn with pink carnations.

He did not notice either her garment or the sheet. He was in street clothes, not in the starched white coat, and he looked different, not so remote as he did in the office. From his bag he was drawing out his stethoscope and sphygmometer, taking a swift look about the large room as he did so. He maintained his usual impersonal mien about whatever it was he thought of it and its decor, and already had managed at once to take charge of her the patient, as he did in his own office, signaling her to sit in the armchair while he drew up one of the small straight chairs.

"Good," he said after using the stethoscope, and "good" after its second placing, and "good" at her blood pressure, and "good" once more when she had stepped on her bathroom scale and he had read the dial. Then he had motioned, with one continuing gesture at the waiting sheet and the tidy bed, and said, "I'll have a look at you now," and busied himself returning his instruments to his black bag.

The visit was brevity and authority and reassurance. Without more than his repeated "good" he had told her again that he was satisfied with her progress and that he had again ruled out even the most minor of complications. Therefore she was surprised when he seated himself at her desk, drew out a prescription pad, and began to write.

"Mrs. G-r-a-n-g-e, Grange," he said aloud as he wrote her name. "You see I practice too. When the time comes, I will practice on a birth certificate. These are Nembutal I am giving you, twenty should do it."

"I still don't need them, Dr. Jesskin."

"So much the better. But if you do, they will be here. One at bedtime, the label will read. Now as to your walking. You will probably continue the full three miles as yet, but if you should begin to tire too much, cut away half a mile, even a whole mile."

"So far that's all right too."

"I can see it must be. I am more than pleased with the way it goes." He rose and looked about for the door. She had an absurd impulse to make him pause, to offer him coffee or some problem that would detain him. "Next visit, there will be measurements again and a blood sample, and until then, of course, telephone me at any time."

"I will. Thank you."

He left. The whole visit had taken less than twenty minutes.

* * *

She thought of the Nembutal one night because she was unable to get comfortable, but decided to turn her light on again and read a little longer instead. Over her book she looked down at herself and thought, Soon we won't be able to. Except for the last few weeks, Cele had told her long ago, and it had seemed too far off to consider. But here it was the last week in May and soon it would be June, and after June, as everybody knew, there would come the magic of July.

She slept. In the morning, she walked past the gleaming windows of her bank and idly glanced at herself. She was big. She was startled to see how big, as if in the last week or two, when she wasn't watching, nature had played a trick on her. The pitch of her body had changed; she walked now as if she were canted back, solid on her heels, though she knew she had not altered her posture. It gets going, she thought amiably; it may take a long time but sooner or later the bigness is there. And it's saying, This baby's going to get itself born in a few weeks.

Nine weeks. For the first time she was thinking in weeks, instead of in months. Wrong. At the beginning she had also thought in weeks; the sixth week, the tenth week. But then the reckoning had gone over into the more solid unit of months; she could remember when she had first thought "the third month," and then "the fourth month."

And here was the eighth month already begun, and she was back again to thinking in weeks. An orbit, a circle, perfect and harmonious. Though on the twenty-third of June she would be thinking in months again, since it would be the beginning of the ninth month, the final month, the great month of termination.

The great month. She was at last great with child, for all the world to see. At the corner where she turned east to go home, she paused, then retraced her steps, to pass before the bank's expanse of plate glass once again. She wasn't all *that* big; she would get bigger. But nobody could for a moment doubt that she was pregnant. This was not being overweight, this was being with child, in the lovely archaic phrase she had always thought so remote and unattainable.

It's me, she thought now. Me and my good construction. She grinned at her image in the window and started for home.

That night she shifted about several times in bed; her body had begun to demand a little planning before it was comfortable. Always before, though she had never noticed it until it was gone, there had been a firm hard line of contact as she lay on her side, her rib cage, her hipbone, her knee, her ankle making the points of contact with sheet and mattress. Now, between rib cage and hip there was a rounded extension, as if she had put down a package close to herself, which lay beside her, obedient to her movement but quite definable and apart too. She liked its presence; she felt fond of it. It keeps you company, she thought, and felt completely satisfied.

*   *   *

"You promised," Cele said, "and you're welshing on it. 'When I'm a big hulk' you said, 'then I'll get a maid.' What do you think you are now, hey?"

"A big hulk. But, Cele, it's so pointless. It's nights you're worried about and the maid wouldn't be here then anyhow."

"There's no statutory regulation that things go wrong only at night."

"You know nothing is going to go wrong. You're just getting nervy."

"That could be."

"Well, I'm not and you ought to be ashamed of yourself. Maybe I'm not one of the crinoline types that nobody suspects until the last minute, but I sure seem to be the peasant type that squats down between the furrows."

"Some furrows. Harkness at a hundred a day."

"For only four or five days. Thank the Lord for that or I'd really go broke. It piles up, doesn't it?"

"Are you starting to worry about money?"

"Not 'worry,' no. I'll probably bear down hard for a couple of years to make some of this up, but that's okay."

"Don't talk so lightly about bearing down, Dorr."

They laughed and Dori said, "So stop nagging me about a maid until I simply have to have one, to get working again. Where the devil would she stay in this place anyway?"

"You have a point there." She glanced at an open catalogue of baby carriages and cribs and strollers, lying open on the desk. "Especially after a few of *those* little items arrive."

"Cele, *do* be a goodie and go see them tomorrow and choose. In case there's any snafu or warehouse nonsense or any of the usual. This is the third of June, after all, and we don't want to wait too long."

"July third would be plenty of time. You just want to see a crib and a baby carriage under your own roof."

"That's it. Will you? Tomorrow?"

"Yes, pest, tomorrow. Glory, will I be glad when this is all over and I can ignore you."

Dori laughed. Matthew was again in Boston and she had asked Cele over for the evening. It was oddly pleasant, pleasant in some new way, and she speculated from time to time about what the newness implied. There was something in any good long friendship between women that was calm and solid, she thought, a shared knowledge that needed no mouthing or measuring, and this she had felt often before. She might even have fitted words to it in some piece or other that she had written; certainly this was not what gave her now a sense of discovery.

What was new then in this particular pleasantness of having Cele here this evening? She had told her of the girl in the park, of the vision of herself in the plate-glass window, of Dr. Jesskin's brief visit ("sort of austere, Cele, almost curt. And sans Miss Mack. I'm glad he wasn't that silly.") They had pored over the catalogue's pages of nursery equipment and Cele had been the old pro whose every nay and yea carried weight.

And then suddenly Dori thought, It's a vacation from problems, that's why it's so nice. Ethics, morals, duty to one's children, to one's wife, the opposing duty to the other woman, to me, to my life—poor Matthew, it all does weigh on him and he can't help it, and it also weighs on me and I can't help it either.

"Matthew and I," she said impulsively, "have been talking out some awfully big matters of late."

"That's good." She sounded guarded.

"Probably Johnny will start with a child analyst when they get back from Truro after the summer. They're driving up at the end of the week. School closes for both kids on Friday."

"Does Matthew fly up every weekend?"

"We've never had weekends."

"Suppose you—" She broke off, and Dori finished for her.

"Go to the hospital on a weekend instead of Tuesday the twenty-third? Then Matthew won't even know about it until it's all over."

"Soon enough," Cele said dryly. Then as if to cover up a slip, she swiftly added, "Do you still say you don't know which you'd rather have?"

"A boy or a girl? I still say it."

"Have you chosen the first batch of names?"

"For the falsies?" She laughed. "I'll have to write it all out for poor Dr. Jesskin. If it's a boy, his false birth certificate will be James Victor Grange, and if it's a girl, Dorothy Victoria Grange."

"That damned V in your monogram. Nobody's ever going to see your towels or teaspoons at Harkness."

Dori ignored this. "But on the permanent birth certificate, after the adoption—" she began tentatively.

"You've changed your mind."

191

"No. It's still Eugene or Celia. That's never changed, either of them, since I first told you."

"Eugene Bradford Gray. Celia Varley Gray. I've never let on how that pleased me."

"It's the middle ones I'm thinking of changing," she said uncertainly. "I'm not sure whether I ought to ask permission first or what."

"Whose permission?"

"I got thinking about this, Cele, and it won't go away. Suppose it were Eugene Cornelius Gray? Or Celia Cornelia Gray? I'm not so sure of that one—it sort of rhymes."

"Why, Dorr, it's quite an idea. When did you come up with it?"

"How do you ever tell a doctor thank-you for something like this? I got thinking about it and thinking about it and once the idea came it just wouldn't go away. Ought I to ask him first?"

"I wouldn't dream of asking him. Tell him when you're out of Harkness. Or let your Mr. Cox tell him." With sudden emphasis she added, "You're so right! If it weren't for Dr. Jesskin all those million years back, where would any of this be?" Her wave took in the room at large, the open catalogue and Dori herself in her ample smock of pink carnations.

Dori looked around too. "And not only the million years back," she said. "What about right now, and all along since it happened? Without you and without Dr. Jesskin, it would have been a whole other ball game."

Cele thought of Matthew Poole, but let it pass. In a switch of mood she said, "Apart from all that. I've got a surprise for you. In half an hour or so."

"What surprise?"

"Marshall's coming over. It's all his idea."

"Coming to see me? You're making it up."

"He's bringing you something. A hospital gift, call it. I could have hugged him, it's so right."

Automatically Dori started for the bathroom mirror and brushed her hair. Behind her Cele jeered and called out,

"Don't forget the false eyelashes," but Dori went ahead changing her lipstick, which was all the makeup she used now on her tanned skin. Then she stepped out of the smock and into a brief white skirt with a thigh-length tunic of turquoise. Apart from the heat, the navy silk was now tightly obsolete.

"You do look good," Cele conceded.

"My party clothes." She was amazed at how much an occasion it seemed, to see good old Marshall so unexpectedly. Cele, Gene, Matthew, Cele, Gene, Matthew—for all these months since January, it had been these three and not once had she felt deprived. Yet now the advent of another friend took on importance and excitement as if she had been off in exile.

When he arrived, she let Cele open the door while she stood in the center of the room waiting. She stood motionless, in profile, as if she were assuming a pose for a painter, and watched him look her up and down before she said, "Hi, Marshall," and went over to kiss him. He returned her kiss with a warmth he had never shown before, and said, "This is blackmail night."

He offered her the package he had brought, and she said, "Ooh, a present. I love it already."

There was a solid heft to the oblong and she sat down to open it. As her present came into view, Marshall said, "The one sure thing is, you'll use it; there's something about them when they're new that drives you nuts. It's to take to the hospital."

It was a camera, complete with film pack, flashbulb, automatic light-setting, and almost instantaneous outcome. She was delighted and oddly touched that so practical a man of affairs as Marshall should have visualized her taking pictures of a just-arrived baby. She kissed him again and began asking how to operate it but suddenly interrupted to ask, "What did you mean, 'blackmail night'?"

"Get up and stand the way you did when I came in." He took the camera from her hands. "I may sell you the negative for a hundred thousand and then again I may not."

"I never even thought of a picture of me pregnant," she cried, posing with alacrity. "But do I ever want it! I'll keep it in a safe-deposit box, but then I could always prove it, twenty years from now."

An extraordinary vanity permeated her and she had to restrain an impulse to lean backward and look bigger than she was. How long did you keep a secret like this from the baby you gave birth to? Twenty years? Twenty-five? Forever? She did not know, nor could she know; life itself would teach her the answer to this one. But all at once she felt a desperate need for a photograph for that distant day, proof, evidence that it was not fantasy, if in that distant day no other evidence would still exist.

Marshall was opening the camera and peeling off the picture. He glanced at it, showed it to Cele, and then Cele smiled and handed it over to Dori. "Real good-looking," she said, "except for being straight as a board."

CHAPTER TEN

It was the camera that circuitously started her first flare-up with Matthew. She had taken two pictures of him, showed him the ones Marshall had taken of her the night before, and repeated the jest about blackmail.

"What does *in camera* really mean?" she asked. "No pun. I know the adoption papers will be *in camera* and I thought I might put these pictures *in camera* with them, and all my checks signed 'Grange' and the false birth certificate and the hospital bill and everything."

"You can't use the courts like a safe-deposit box," he said, amused. "If any case is heard in private, in a judge's chambers instead of in open court, then the proceedings are *in camera*, and in your case, your lawyer—"

"Matthew, I should have told you—"

"Your case will be *in camera*," he went on. "So all the documents become secret records for all time, not open to the public at any time, remaining always in the possession of the court." He went on to elaborate. Nobody could ever see the papers, neither friend nor enemy, unless some court of law ordered them to be shown. That could not be done at anybody's simple request, not even at her own. No lawyer could request them, no reporter could stumble on them, not even the adopted person himself could get at them. Only in the event that the adopted person were involved in some criminal trial would the process be set in motion whereby some future judge could rule that the inviolable secrecy of that *in camera* might be breached.

"Not in any civil action," he ended, "no contract litigation, no divorce action, no libel or slander suit, nothing but a criminal prosecution could get at those private papers. See?"

She nodded. "Matthew, there's something else. I should have told you this, but the right moment never seemed to come up. One day while we were apart, I asked Dr. Jesskin if he knew a good lawyer to handle the adoption for me."

"A good lawyer?" he asked stiffly.

"This was while we weren't seeing each other and I sort of panicked and I asked Gene and then Jesskin, and Dr. Jesskin did."

"Did what?"

"Arranged it for me. It's a man named Bob Cox, a friend of his."

"Of Cox, Wheaton, Fair—?"

"Yes. It's a good firm, isn't it?"

"Very."

"Do you know Mr. Cox?"

"I've met him. He's good too."

"Are you annoyed? I could cancel it. I've never met Mr. Cox or even talked to him by phone so far."

"I'm not annoyed."

"It was just that—well, I hadn't heard one word from you and I had decided I never would, this was already April, and you had said you wouldn't be handling it yourself in any case."

"But I assumed you did want my firm to handle it."

"I did. I would have. Only all that time, it was already April—" The old defensive feeling, rising, infuriated her. Here she was explaining, repeating herself, offering extenuating circumstances. "You needn't look like that," she cried angrily.

"Like what?"

"As if I'd done something dreadful."

"I don't exactly enjoy being told off."

"You haven't said one damn word about it since we've been back, either," she said. "Not one word, about courts, or what the proceeding is or when it's done or how long it takes, nothing."

"I didn't think it needed saying. When the time came—"

"You can't really think I could just let it slide happily along forever."

"Now, Dori, I never thought that at all."

"It's not the only thing you never thought at all. If I ever told you all the things you never think—" She turned fast, and slid both hands over her face. She saw again the slippery wet cheeks of the girl in the park and ground her fingertips into her eye sockets so that pain flashed. She felt his arm on her shoulder and angrily shook it free and sat there, huddled in on herself, hugging her bulk with her arms and elbows while her hands remained covering her face.

There was silence. He went to the kitchen and poured a drink of Scotch. She thought of that time in January when he had done that, not bothering with ice or soda, and the memory was sharp. Would he again go to the door and tell her he needed time to get it into some sort of shape? He had no overcoat to walk out with this time, maybe that would make it different.

"I'm sorry," she heard herself saying into her tented hands, "I don't know why I said all that."

"To punish me."

"For what?"

"Does it matter?"

"Don't take that injured tone."

"I didn't mean to." Suddenly he was beside her, telling her it was natural enough that she had been angry, that it was quite true that he had been legal-minded, knowing

197

there was enough time, forgetting her very human need to see ahead, to have everything prepared well in advance.

"I'm glad you blew," he said. "It's not an easy time for you, darling, and you have the right to blow your top once in a while."

"It's better if I don't."

"But you did, so forget it. I'll start lining up the right man for the adoption at the office tomorrow morning."

But the reluctance she had already felt came back. "Please don't do it, Matthew." It sounded regretful, as if she were about to ask something difficult of him. "Maybe since it's all set in motion through Dr. Jesskin's friend, it might be best to let it stay that way."

"You mean not have me in the picture at all?"

"Not your firm." She thought he might be angry but a wild need transfixed her so that if she had wanted to change what she had said, she could not have done it. This was right. This was somehow native to her; if he had delayed so long on this, it revealed a reluctance in him too, one that he wasn't willing to see. It wasn't even very important, unless it indicated vaster reluctances.

Not only in him, but in herself as well. Insight. Nobody could hand it to you all done up in festive papers and gleaming ribbon; you had it or you had to dig for it until you found it. There was something here, some clue, buried, in retreat as yet from reason, deep in her own character, and for the first time she knew that she did not dare to sidestep the search any longer.

* * *

Early next morning she unlocked her suitcase, drew out a sheet of her real stationery and wrote:

DEAR MR. COX,

This is just to thank you in advance for taking on the case Dr. Cornelius Jesskin asked you about. Knowing that you have agreed to do so gives me a peace of mind I'm grateful for.

If all goes according to plan, I should be phoning for an appointment early in August. I can't tell you how much I look forward to it.

Sincerely,
THEODORA V. GRAY.

She addressed and stamped the envelope and went out to mail it from the nearest postbox. This letter needed no San Francisco or London postmark, or Tokyo or Rio either. She stood with her hand on the lid of the postbox, staring at the slot which had taken her letter. Her own name on her own stationery with her own return address, talking of a face-to-face meeting in early August. It was like leaning into the future.

* * *

June was the only bad month. Graceless at best, horror-filled at worst, Dori continuously felt a malaise that had no precise name, that lay somewhere between the heights of euphoria and the depths of depression.

She ascribed it to the newest assassination, she ascribed it to the deepening fears of racism in the election, she ascribed it to the pure physical deprivation of not making love. For the first time, she felt clumsy and plodding; she felt the slowness of time; she felt that none of this was the full sum, and this single certainty intensified everything else.

Matthew was never absent except on the unvarying weekends, eager always to arrive, loath always to leave, openly grateful for her rage at the sentencing of Dr. Spock and the others to two years in a Federal prison, talking to her hungrily about the plans for appeal, about his own appeal for young Benting. She understood for the first time that he rarely spoke of his work to Joan. He was taking on a new case, similar to Benting's but in New York, where he would not need to work through an associate lawyer as he did in Boston, this time without a fee, because this time his client was black and poor instead of white and well-to-do.

The argument about her own lawyer was all but forgotten. Neither of them ever spoke of it. When she did think of it she assured herself she was glad it had happened just that way, because she had been open and honest and free from the artifice that too often made a relationship pulpy and unreal.

And yet she also wished it had never happened. The slow elapsing days seemed to be a piling on and piling on of other things she wished had never happened. It was on the very night of the argument that she had been wakeful and restless after Matthew's departure and listened in the dark to an all-night music station, falling asleep to a Beethoven quartet. Through the music, tearing through the first thin veil of her sleep, had come a sudden voice, the voice not of the music announcer but the voice of crisis. "We interrupt this program to bring you a special news bulletin"—the news that out in California, on a night of triumph, Senator Robert Kennedy had been shot, perhaps fatally.

She was alone with it and stayed alone. It was three thirty in the morning here although half an hour past midnight out there; Matthew, Cele, Gene would all be asleep. That was good. She could not speak now to anyone, not again, not so soon again after April. If Matthew's family had already left for Truro, she would probably have called him anyway, but she was obscurely glad that it was out of the question. She briefly considered waking Gene or Cele, but at once, in a kind of pre-audition, she heard the words that would follow and knew she could not stand hearing them on her own lips and in her own ears. To be mute, to say nothing for a few hours—that was what she needed now, a reversal from that other time when she had wanted so much not to be alone.

It was as if she had suddenly become a sister of silence, a nun in some holy order with vows to remain without speech. She listened to all the stations in turn, her eyes dry, her throat clamped in a collar of steel, unyielding and pitiless, like a collar within the column of her throat pressing outward. It was like a maniacal replay of nightmare, a confusion and yet a sameness.

When at last her night-black windows began to fog into

gray, she dressed and made up the room and then had breakfast. It was too early for the *Times;* that came at seven. Seven would also bring the two-hour news and interview show she sometimes listened to; she would hear only the bulletins and turn off the interpreters, the philosophizers, the assayers and the theorizers. Not again, not this time; there were limits to what you could stand.

But *they* stood it, his mother, his wife, his children, Mrs. King, her children, the people getting the official telegrams from Vietnam, the wives, the mothers, the children—

The life force. Birth going ahead in the midst of horror and death—why had she limited herself to the two world wars and the atom bomb? Why had she not begun with the Civil War, why not with the French Revolution, the Inquisition, why not with Christians thrown to the lions in the arenas of Rome, why not with Jewish children born in the Nazi decades, with Negro children born today?

The paper finally came, the television screen began its special reports and she yielded briefly to both and wanted only to get out to the quiet park and walk. At eight she called Gene and Cele, to say she knew and was going out, and when she came back an hour later she heard the flatted muted ringing of the telephone as she was opening her door and talked to Matthew in the same truncated way. He came in for a little while on his way home from his office and then again after dinner. Both times she seemed numb, unable to explain that she felt huge with it as if it were within her, another pregnancy, all of it, that long-ago November and then that night in April and now this one in June, that she felt filled with all of it and unable to accommodate the pull and drag.

"Take a sleeping pill tonight, darling," Matthew said. "You can't do this, not now, only a couple of hours of sleep the whole twenty-four. Take it now and I'll wait until you're in bed and then I'll go and know that you'll get some rest."

Obediently she went to the medicine cabinet, swallowed a yellow capsule, and in a moment was in bed. The latest bulletins still vacillated: there was a chance, there was little chance, there was the possibility that the body might live on without the functioning mind. She was riven by dilemma as if it were her responsibility, to decide which would be more tolerable, that or the finality.

"Darling," Matthew said, leaning over her from the edge of her bed, "I know this is a terrible time to think of us, but in a way, it's the right time too. There are no easy solutions for us, not ever, but I love you more and more and if you'll let me, I want to be part of your life from now on. And of the baby's life."

"Oh Matthew."

"I don't know that I've rung up any great success as the father of my own children," he went on. "But they keep telling us that a father figure is vital in any child's life, and if a father figure is all that important in this baby's life, and if you'll let me, I'll be that father figure always."

She wept, silently, not hiding her face, letting her cheeks glisten wetly as the girl in the park had done. She held tightly to his fingers, and when she fell asleep, he left her.

*   *   *

The crib arrived and was set in place, the carriage arrived and was given a corner of its own. And still it remained a bad month. Dori shortened her daily walk by half a mile and then lengthened it again whenever the mornings were cool. She resumed her work on her two pieces but then saw, with a slicing clarity, that she could not have these printed soon after her return without shouting to them all, Look, here are my new interests, illegitimate birth and adoption. There would have to be two or three other pieces first, another Martha Litton, another Dr. Spock, and then in a year or two, but no sooner, these two.

This must have been a hidden reason for her delay in finishing either one; she who never blocked up on unfinished work. A brief cheer permeated her at this clarity. Clarity always was an asset, clarity about anything. She remembered the upward leap of her spirits when she had first made a list of majors and minors, when she had fired Nellie and gone forth for her first maternity clothes. From that minute on there had been clarity.

If only she could see what it was that remained unclear about herself and Matthew. That night when Senator Kennedy died he had moved her to tears and yet as the days inched by she knew nothing basic was changed. As long as she was herself alone, Dori Gray alone, Matthew was what she wanted, was what made her happy: his nearness, his presence as often as possible, his love and his making love.

But there would come the time when she could no longer think of herself alone, Dori Gray alone. To give birth was not to restore herself to being "herself alone." Wasn't that a state to which there was, thank God, no returning?

She was changing, but was Matthew? That night when he had finally told her about Jack Henning he had blurted out, "That was the shutout, right there. Nothing's going to change that."

But she would be even happier with a child growing up. Would that be a shutout too? Perhaps he would be close enough to the actual living developing child to feel a part of its life, a part of the future, feel that it was his too, and no shutout at all.

To a point, yes. To a degree, surely. In a partial version, an approximation, better than nothing, lovely up to the limits that their circumstances would permit.

"Why isn't he ever here on Saturday or Sunday?" An unknown little voice, high and unformed like all children's voices, sounded clear in her mind. "Why can't he ever be here on Christmas?"

Cut that, damn it, she ordered herself. Does it have to be all or nothing? Are you going to turn your back on what's there and moon around for what isn't there?

No, she wasn't. Yet she suddenly remembered the night she had gone down Central Park West at one in the morning, remembered the night sky ablaze, remembered her excitement over Cele's news that Matthew had called, and remembered too that on that threshold of their renewed life together she had wondered whether it would be the same Dori Gray that he would find.

* * *

"One more visit," Dr. Jesskin said, "and then I do not see you until the delivery room. Is that welcome news?"

"I can't believe it."

"Of course not." He began to put away his instruments but the austere brevity of his last visit was missing. His "good" and again "good" of last time was replaced this morning by "excellent" or "perfect," and he had asked how many sleeping pills she had left and had she any questions to put to him. "I see by the crib and the carriage that you plan to return here."

"Do you have a few minutes? Could I give you some coffee? I haven't any questions, no, but if I could take a minute and tell you what I'm going to do after Harkness?"

To her astonishment he said coffee would be fine and sat down in the straight chair, leaving the armchair to her. As she told him her "postnatal timetable," she saw him nod and thought how absurd it was that she should want his approval even on practical matters like these.

"That is a fine transition plan," he said, "ingenious and very sound."

"Then after the hospital, when I can start working again, I'll get a maid who likes babies—"

"Nobody under seventy," he said in a tone of sudden warning.

"Under seventy?"

"A reliable geriatric," he said calmly. "That is my plan for your private nurses at the hospital."

"Private nurses? Aren't they awfully expensive?"

"Only for the first night and day while you're coming out from the anesthesia." She looked baffled and he added, "In case you babble."

"Of course!"

"They will be seventy at least, still active, still in good health, but as much over seventy as possible. Eighty would

204

be even better. Then even if you should hand them the whole truth, they wouldn't have too long a time left, poor things, to be indiscreet about it."

This was so deliberately spoken, and with such open self-approval, that she guffawed. He was pleased at her reaction and said slyly, "I would not wish old age on anyone, being already fifty-two myself, but an inescapable fact is that in certain circumstances a lack of longevity can be a great desideratum. Is that not so?"

"You think of everything. Oh, Dr. Jesskin, suppose I had never been sent to you, back in nineteen fifty-five?"

He finished his coffee and stood up. "Then I should have missed knowing a remarkable patient."

＊　＊　＊

Long after he was gone, she heard the phrase sounding. Like his three thinkings, like her good construction, this about a remarkable patient struck for itself at once an indelible outline in her memory.

A remarkable patient. *Then I should have missed knowing a remarkable patient.* But surely he had gone through this entire business before, of the unmarried pregnant woman. He must have; in all his years of practice he must have had other patients who were with child but without wedding ring or husband. She could not, by the law of probabilities, be the only patient he had ever had who was having an illegitimate baby. Had he then turned the others away? Impossible. He had been through it all before.

That was why he was so ready with solutions, his suggestion about Harkness and the two names on her door, his readiness about the false birth certificate, his cleverness about geriatric nurses, all of it. He had not said so, of course; in a doctor's life everything was automatically *in camera.*

The knowledge that there had been others pacified her, mollified her, yet a few moments later she realized that it also robbed her. She did not know of what. Something. Something she valued, something she didn't want to give up.

She suddenly laughed self-consciously. Why, I want to be the only one, she thought, a goddam unique character in his whole medical career. But I'm not, I couldn't be. She could ask him someday, she supposed, ask in the most general terms, whether all gynecologists and obstetricians did not, in the course of a long practice, inevitably have a certain number of illegitimate births to cope with—but he would use the most general terms back at her and not tell her a thing. As for Miss Mack, asking her would be like asking the Great Stone Face.

Good old Miss Mack. Just yesterday she had telephoned to "remind" Dori of Dr. Jesskin's visit this morning, and had added, "And I'm to give you Doctor's telephone number in Huntington too, though the service always hops to it for anybody on the special list."

"What list?" she had wanted to say. "The list of people in the eighth and ninth months?" But all she had said was "Huntington?"

"His summer place. He's in town all week, but from June first on, he's still out there weekends."

"Thanks, I'd love to have it." She had taken it down, read it back to Miss Mack, and then later had thought, What did she mean, 'still out there weekends'? Anybody but Miss Mack would have said, "But from June first on, his family is out there and he goes out weekends." Like Matthew's family. Like all families. But Miss Mack would not commit herself to informing a soul that "Doctor" had a family, despite the photographs on his desk. If Dori herself asked her, Miss Mack would never admit that any Dori Gray had ever begun as a sterility patient and ended up having a baby. Miss Mack must have taken the Hippocratic oath all by herself.

Someday when all this was over, she would send Miss Mack a great big bunch of flowers with a card that told her some patients blessed their lucky stars for a doctor's staff too.

He's still out there weekends. It sounded as if the place in Huntington had been there for a long time. It also sounded as if it were in the past tense except for him. Did the rest of the family not go out there weekends? What about those kids and that pretty woman she was sure was his wife?

Kids? They were about ten or twelve in the photographs, and she had visualized them that way. But when he first told her of Bob Cox, had he not said that his son was finishing Harvard Law this summer with Bob Cox's son and that both of them were joining the firm as junior law clerks?

Then those photographs must be ten or twelve years old. Older. If you got out of any graduate school before twenty-five, you were an exception. A son of twenty-five and a daughter of twenty-three? Perhaps both married, and out at Huntington only for visits. That must be it. The inscrutable Miss Mack would never have mentioned it, any more than Dr. Jesskin himself.

But what about his wife? Why didn't Miss Mack say, "They're out there weekends?" And if that were the case, would she have inserted that enigmatic "still"? Wouldn't any couple keep going out to their summer place? Need one specify that the man went out there still?

She had never wondered about Dr. Jesskin's life, never visualized him as father, husband, brother, as anything but doctor and specialist. No, that wasn't quite so. The day after Martin Luther King's death when she had called him in agitation about lawyers, he had said, "I think many of us couldn't sleep last night," and like a streak of daylight she had had a flash of him as a political being, one who couldn't sleep either because of a hideous murder of someone he admired. She had forgotten that until just now.

She thought, I wish I knew more about him. When this is all over, I'll research the man! She wondered whether there were any medical articles written by him; that would be easy to find out at the Academy of Medicine. She wondered if the great big directory of physicians, which told all about a doctor's or surgeon's degrees and hospital connections, also told about his general life, as *Who's Who* did. In *Who's Who* the names of your children were listed, the name of your wife, the date of your marriage or divorce, and if there had been any death in the family, a lower-case *dec.* appeared.

Did the Medical Directory do the same—and would the lower-case *dec.* be there?

The embarrassment returned. More fantasy, more fairy tales for the pregnant. She really was beginning to show signs of the stress that lay in too much peace and quiet. What had started her on this remarkable train of thought?

Remarkable. The word in the context. *Then I should have missed a remarkable patient.* He had meant something by it. She was positive now that he had treated other unmarried pregnant women, so the "remarkable" did not have that sense. Nor was it another of his odd phrasings that betrayed his birth in Denmark or Sweden or wherever. She didn't even know that much about him. Here was a man who had become as necessary to her as breath and she knew not even the first detail about him as a man.

How absurd we are, she thought, how trapped in good manners. Why had she never been able to sit there at his desk and glance openly at the photographs and openly say, "Is that your family? The children look like you." What would have been intrusive or rude about it if she had? He could sit there above an open folder, and say, The last time you had intercourse was when? The period you skipped should have been when? Could sit there and tell her, You will want to know whether you may continue to have intercourse. Of course, you may. It is natural, normal, indeed, the stimulation of hormones during pregnancy—

But of course that was professional, every syllable was spoken by a professional about professional matters. He knew everything about her that mattered, knew of her having an affair that had produced this baby, knew that she would be wanting to have intercourse and was thus having an affair still.

Had she made it clear to Dr. Jesskin that the pregnancy was antecedent to this affair? She couldn't remember. She thought that she had, at some point, said quite definitely that that affair had been coming to an end, and since he never missed anything, never forgot anything, he must have realized that her interest in whether you were permitted to have intercourse during pregnancy applied to somebody else and not the man who had helped her achieve it.

Quite suddenly it mattered to her that it should be clear in Dr. Jesskin's mind. If she were still involved with the man who had, as they say, sired this baby about to be born, then Dr. Jesskin would know that it was a deep and abiding relationship, reaching backward in time, reaching forward, a relationship of dimension, important and enduring.

But it isn't, she thought, or at least I'm not sure. How could she be sure of that reaching forward? Oh, that was what was troubling, that not being able to be sure of its reaching forward when this summer, this year, next year were done.

Suddenly she was back again at the side of Dr. Jesskin's desk in Dr. Jesskin's office, before Christmas of last year, telling him she had done the three thinkings and was going ahead and would he help her. Again she felt the awkward touch of his fingers on her own, as if he were trying to shake hands. Again she heard his words, "I am proud of you," and all at once they fused with these words today, "I should have missed a remarkable patient."

He liked all this—that's what it meant. He liked her in the context of it. She was not merely a patient but a human being also and he had touched her fingers in a human code. This, today, had been the code still, undiminished all these months later.

Undiminished. That word again, she thought. It keeps at me and I wish it would let me be.

*   *   *

As it neared its end, June stopped being the bad month. Dori grew more adept at managing her bulk, as if there were a technique one could ease into. The discomfort of her recumbent body was there still but somehow she could "sleep around it" as if she could redistribute her entire body in secret ways to get the better of the bulk and awkwardness.

When she woke at night, she took aspirin and slept again. She began to take afternoon naps as well, drowsy with weight and immobility, and for the first time her ankles, which had always been as tight to the bone as skin could be, grew puffy late each day, the thongs of her sandals cutting into the rising flesh. All this she reported to Miss Mack, to add to the record. She did not want to call Dr. Jesskin unless there were some emergency. Miss Mack sent her a prescription for pills for the edematous ankles but week by week there was no emergency.

"What day do you think this is?" she asked Matthew one evening as he came in, and before he could answer, "The first day of the ninth month."

"Hooray. Let's drink the champagne to it."

"You'll have to put another bottle by though."

"I guess I can manage another."

"Look over there," she said, pointing to the smaller of her suitcases, standing in the corner near the crib. "It's all packed for the hospital."

"Jumping the gun, that's known as. Let's drink to the gun too."

He was impatient to have it all over, to have her as she was when he had found her, her body tight and slender and beautiful, swift in movement, swift in response to him, to have her in bed again where all their problems were forgotten, where they either were conquered or appeared to be conquerable.

"I've been packing suitcases too," he said as he began to work on the cork of the bottle he drew from the icebox. "Metaphorical suitcases."

"Such as?"

"I told the family yesterday I wouldn't be up the weekend of the twentieth, that I couldn't make it." The cork popped and he rushed the bottle to the waiting glass. "Here, darling."

She accepted the sparkling glass and waited for him to fill his. "You thought of that," she said. "I'm glad. I had wondered, What if it should be early?"

He looked surprised. "Did you think I'd be off, that close to the official date?"

"I didn't exactly think about it." She raised her glass to him. "But I'm glad you won't be."

He raised his own glass. "Here's to gun-jumping," he said. "It would be most obliging of you not to be a stickler for the twenty-third."

"But I gather it's lots likelier to be late than early."

"Then at least Mrs. Steffani will have the thrill of seeing Mr. Grange here for one weekend anyway."

They laughed. Mrs. Steffani, after seeing him put his key to the door several times, had one evening addressed him as "Mr. Grange," and he had accepted the title without demur. Behind him, in the door that stood ajar, Dori had said, "I meant to introduce you," but Mrs. Steffani had given her a wary look that invited no further effort. They had tried to decide whether she knew he was no Mr. Grange and they had come down on the side of Mrs. Steffani's hidden wisdoms. "Otherwise, why would you show only Monday through Friday?" Dori had demanded.

"Because I have to be in Vietnam the rest of the time."

Now he added, "You mean, suppose you hang on till the following weekend? Then I'd have to say again that I couldn't make it, but my God, Dori, you wouldn't be that ornery, would you?"

"I'll try not."

She looked tranquil again and he became equally tranquil. The early part of the month, he thought, had been their worst time since they had been back together, and he was glad it was over at last. He now felt with Dori a blessed return of ease; she seemed to have resumed her early simplicity with him, the tangles smoothed away again.

"You're never ornery," he said with sudden warmth. "You are my lovely Dori and there's nobody like you."

"Matthew. You are a little drunk already."

"Not drunk at all." He kissed her. "Look, this damn rotten month is over and this is a good time again and there'll be lots of them. There'll be bad ones too, but we're stuck with each other, no matter. If we fight we fight, if we can't make love we can't, if we have to be apart, we have to. But none of that changes *us*, does it?"

To her surprise she asked, "Do you just say 'I can't make it' to Joan? Is that enough? Or 'I won't be in' or something like that?"

He set down his champagne and stared at it. It was the kind of question he resented, the kind any man would resent. It was rare, this sort of thing from Dori, but it struck a bad chord, left him aquiver with dissonance and minor key. She knew every essential about himself and Joan; he had never dissembled to Dori, never glozed over, never indulged in the tinny clichés of the wife-blaming husband. Then why such a question at all?

"I shouldn't have said that," she said as if he had spoken aloud.

"I agree. I don't think you should."

"But why not? I can't help thinking about it."

"Then why did you just say you shouldn't have?"

"I thought that too. I know it's illogical, but people aren't always all full of logic." He stared at the wine and his silence vexed her. "It's impossible not to wonder once in a while what *I* would do, Matthew, if you told me sometime, 'I can't make it' and let it go at that. I'd probably just up and say, 'Why can't you?' before I even thought not to."

"Dori, let's not get into this. There's no sense to it."

"I suppose there's not."

He returned to the champagne but the effervescence was gone. He was angry at her for flatting it out of existence and yet knew she had not done so purposely. She was troubled about many things ahead; he was also. Dori was not one of those mindless optimists who gabbled romantic nonsense about how glorious everything was going to be for them; she saw too intelligently the difficulties and crossed wires and crosscurrents—

Damn it, he thought, as long as it isn't cross-purposes and crossed swords. I'm crossed up and screwed up with too much analyzing, when all I want is to carve the possible out

212

of the impossible. That's all Dori wants too. Then why can't we have it and let everything else alone?

"Darling, listen." He told her what he had been thinking and she kept nodding, phrase for phrase, though he felt that he was losing the point he wanted to make in the delicate task of transmission from mind to words. She had the look he had come to know, half of apology that she should have caused strain or tension, yet with it another half that maintained a point of view, her point of view, as if she were also saying, I'm tabling it for now, but not simply brushing it into the incinerator. It won't burn up. It won't just conveniently disappear in smoke and a nice crisp smell of burning.

"So I think we have to take it as it comes," he ended. "We've solved it all so far. We'll solve the rest of it too."

"I know we will. Of course we will."

CHAPTER ELEVEN

A shaft of steel speared upward and Dori woke with a small cry. She had never felt anything like it.

It was gone almost before she knew it. For a moment she wondered if it had been part of a dream, drug-induced, weight-induced, discomfort-induced. She glanced at the small clock on the table beside her; it was ten after one.

She closed her eyes thinking how it had been. It was like a metal wedge forced upward through the pelvic arch, a chisel driven into two halves of a boulder to break it asunder.

Then she knew. The image told her. It had begun.

She was wild with elation. She was to time the pains. That was the first order: Time the pains. How many dozens of repetitions had the admonition had, not only in the past weeks but all her life before, when the directive was not for her but merely part of the folklore of childbirth. You timed the pains; you didn't call for help until the pains were coming every five minutes. Her instructions were different because she was alone. She was to call Cele the moment she was sure there were pains at regular intervals, no matter how far apart; Cele would come over in a taxi and they would decide when to call Dr. Jesskin. She herself would decide at what point to telephone Matthew.

She looked again at the clock. The minute hand had scarcely left the ten-after position.

Perhaps this was something all by itself, instead of number one in a series. Again she closed her eyes thinking about it, thinking, For once somebody is going to describe it; I'm a writer, or I used to be a writer anyway, and I'm going to remember every bit of it so I can set it down for the record. All anybody ever writes about is the cries and groans and the beads of sweat. She smiled, superior. She was a better reporter than that.

Her thoughts grew hazy with sleep. For the past two weeks, she had meekly obeyed the doctor and taken one of the glistening yellow capsules each night as she went to bed. Since the final process had begun, that final re-positioning within her, her center of gravity was changed. A personal center of gravity was one more thing she had never contemplated before.

The wedge again—the chisel, the boulder. The same, the same splitting apart, the same, no deeper, no worse, the same.

She looked at her watch. One twenty. Ten minutes since the other one. Twice; not what you would call a series. Maybe it was something else, some mishap, the first. She hadn't expected this entering wedge anyway; she had been told she would have cramps, like menstrual cramps, yet deeper, and also toward the back. Something was going wrong, then, for there had been no cramps. But this was Monday, the—

She sat up suddenly, as suddenly as she could do anything. It was no longer Monday. It was Tuesday, the Tuesday she had waited for, the twenty-third of July.

There was no mishap, there was nothing wrong. She would wait for just one more, and if it came when it should, she would call Cele. She lay back, waiting, surprised in some far-off part of her, as if there were an exterior Dori observing her, surprised that she was so calm and so excited at once. She was alive with watchfulness, stirring with expectation, a little crazy with delight. If this should smooth out and go away and not continue, she would be savage with disappointment.

She glanced at the clock. Only a minute? Ridiculous. She closed her eyes. No woolly sleep now. The Nembutal might have flown clear out of her body. In another moment she once more sat up, but this time she left the bed and went to the kitchen. Tea or coffee? Or something cold? She put the kettle on.

She waited for the kettle to whistle, taking an almost clinical checkup on the way she felt. Shaken by anticipation and uncertainty, but otherwise good. If those two were the start, then nothing but good; if they were signs of mishap, then she was alarmed, since mishap had been so totally absent from all these nine months.

She started to glance at her wristwatch and stopped her eyes halfway in their journey. The timing would be reversed for this next one. She would look at her watch only if the third pain arrived, a confirmation after the event, not a possible psychic inducement beforehand. She felt very clever over this decision, poured scalding water over the tea bag in her cup and jeered at her self-approval as fatuous.

She took the tea carefully to her bed table, her eyes averted now from the little clock. She had left the camera for the last minute's packing and as her tea cooled she thought, Just for luck, and placed it next to the suitcase, on the floor beside it. The suitcase itself she did not touch. Everything was already in it but her toilet things and her Grange checkbook.

She went back to bed and sipped her tea. God, ten minutes could be long. If pain number three didn't arrive, ought she to notify Dr. Jesskin's service at least, that something seemed to be wrong? She was to call him at home if labor had begun, but if she were not sure?

Her breath sucked in on itself. The chisel, deeper, rocking her whole skeleton, prying the halves apart. The first sweat

217

spurted from her pores. She looked at the clock. One thirty. She dialed Cele.

"Cele, it's me. It's started."

"How far apart?"

"Ten minutes, and I've had three. Not cramps at all, sort of being gored upward."

"Are you okay? You sound shaky."

"I'm terribly excited, that way shaky."

"I'll start out the minute I phone Dr. Jesskin. I think if it's ten-minute pains, I'd better call him first."

Moving slowly, Dori began to dress. The disappearance of the Nembutal amazed her; she might never have gone near it, so wide-awake was she, whereas her usual experience these past nights was to feel half drugged even the next morning when she awoke. That partly explained her aversion to sleeping pills; never had she taken them regularly except that one time when Tony left.

She dressed quickly, brushed her teeth and hair, and packed her toilet kit into the suitcase, along with the camera and checkbook. Then she looked thoughtfully about the apartment. There were last-minute checkups she had assigned herself to do.

The last page of her desk calendar; she tore it out and took it with her. She tried the lock of her other suitcase and felt for its key in her purse. She signed the note she had already written to leave for Mrs. Steffani, saying she would be back in a few days and would Mrs. Steffani take in her papers and magazines instead of letting them pile up at her door. She paused over her signature to be sure that in her excitement she signed it not Gray but Grange.

Again the shaft of metal, again the burst of sweat, this time an involuntary animal grunt from the back of her throat. She sat rigid, waiting for it to be over. Her wristwatch said one forty. Perhaps a fraction of a minute less.

With a start she realized she had not phoned Matthew.

*　　*　　*

She stared at the telephone, unwilling. The reluctance

again. It was as if a hand had fallen on her shoulder, a light hand, a hint of a hand, accompanied by a voice saying, Stay, this is real, think about that.

She thought, Not tonight, not this one special night. As if someone were whispering on her behalf. Just don't do that tonight.

This dialogue had sprung from nowhere, perhaps from the sedation, still at work in her mind despite its apparent disappearance. Don't call Matthew; having him take you to the hospital is playacting and you know it, while this is real and you know that too. And her plea in reply: Let me alone, Uncertainty, let me alone, not tonight please, not on this one particular night.

She jabbed a finger at the telephone and dialed. "Matthew, it's happening."

"Darling. I'll be there the minute I can."

"Don't shave or anything. I waited to be sure, so now a lot of time has gone by already."

"I'll not shave. How are you so far?"

"Excited."

"Good girl. I'm on my way."

"Cele is too."

Again pain, different this time, like a blow, but still the feeling of cleaving, riving, splitting asunder. She was ordered to yield to it, not fight it, but she forgot the order until her whole body was clenched in resistance, when she suddenly let go, limp and collapsed. It was easier at once. Maybe her pains were harder right from the start because she was forty. *Forty is not old, not medically. Cosmetically perhaps is a different matter, but you are a fine healthy young woman and forty is not regarded as anything but young today.*

The bell rang and Cele's voice sounded outside the door, with Cele's key already in the lock. Absurd delight welled up in her; now it would be all right.

"Having one right now?" Cele asked as she came in.

"It's passing. How did you know?"

"Anybody would know. Sit down again." She crossed to

the bathroom and came back bearing a bath towel which she tossed nonchalantly straight at Dori. "Dry off some of that. We might take it with us in the cab. I told him to wait."

"Are we starting right off?"

"Dr. Jesskin thought it might be wise to get you settled in."

"But Matthew's on his way."

"I told the driver we might be a few minutes. He's willing. He's got four kids and this doesn't faze him."

"What did Dr. Jesskin say?"

"He said, 'Yes' and he said 'Ten minutes?' and he said 'They will be expecting her, I will notify them myself.' Cucumber conversation."

"He's always cool. Did he say when he would be there?"

"Lord, no. He'll probably go back to sleep for a couple of hours. They'll call him in plenty of time. He also said he told the Admissions desk to hold back on filling out blanks until you were installed in your room."

"He didn't want them asking Matthew."

"Matthew? Does he know about Matthew?"

"Only that I'd be going up with you and a man, another close friend."

"Who he assumes is the father."

"He never assumes anything. Anyway I think I told him, way at the start." She waved all that aside. "Oh Cele, I can't believe that by tomorrow morning this will all be over."

"Hush your big mouth, Dorr. Forget about tomorrow, forget about everything, and when they tell you to bear down, you bear down but good. Now let's see: suitcase?" She took it and set it just inside the door. "Air conditioner? Let's leave it on for now; it's hell's own furnace outside. I'll not forget. When will Matthew get here?"

"Any minute. I told him I had already let a lot of time go by."

"Clever girl. Thank God you're not going in for natural childbirth—when it gets too rotten, yell for a shot of something. But for now, you just sit there and think how skinny you'll be next week."

220

When she stiffened with the next pain, Cele merely said, "Hang on, Dorr, I know it's rough." During the jagged clamor of the next moments, Dori thought, She does know; it's one thing women know and now I know too. It's not like *pain, I'm sick* or *pain, I hurt myself;* it's pain *for* something and you're not angry at it. She mopped her arms and throat and face with the towel and the pain ebbed and the bell rang and Cele let Matthew in.

He went straight to Dori, leaning over her, free of self-consciousness despite Cele's presence, kissing her damp face. "Is that our cab out there? I held mine too."

They all laughed, Dori suddenly shrill in a mounting sense of occasion. "Oh, Matthew, I'm glad you're here. You and Cele—" She turned abruptly away. How could she have thought, even for a moment, of not calling him? What madness would that have been, what careless slamming of a door? He was real too and everything they had was real. Limited, bounded on every side, circumscribed but real. Was she to tear it down because it wasn't unlimited, like a frantic angry child?

"Matthew, why don't you pay off your guy?" Cele said. "Mine's all contracted for, big tip promised, I'm committed." He nodded and disappeared to dismiss his cab. Cele said, "Come on, Dorr," and picked up the letter for Mrs. Steffani and turned off the air conditioner. "Here we go."

It was all in somebody else's hands, Dori thought, in Cele's and Matthew's and Dr. Jesskin's and the baby's. The baby knew it was time to end the nine months inside and she was merely obeying, just as Cele was obeying and Matthew. From that first pain on, the baby had been in command. Nature then, but it was nicer to think, The Baby.

"What are you smiling at?" Matthew asked as he returned.

"Nothing. You feel good in between, that's all."

To Cele he said, "What's the schedule now?"

"We're starting right away. This girl is still on a ten-minute rhythm, but they do seem to be blockbusters, and the doctor said to get her up there."

"Right," he said. "Come on, darling." He held both his hands out to Dori and she pulled herself up and forward on their strength.

In the cab she sat between them, silent, listening to their spurts of talk, aware of their bodies close to her own. There was a core of detachment, though, a high pure knowledge that she was almost, nearly, not quite but almost at the culmination. She felt steady with the knowledge, steady within it, as if it were a frame built close around her within which she was tight and safe.

The pain came again, slicing through, sharper, more purposeful. It was no ten-minute lapse since the last one; she knew it without trying to see her watch. It was speeding up, it was fiercer, it was under way and nothing could roll it back now.

＊　＊　＊

At the Admissions desk Matthew said, "It's Mrs. Grange, Dr. Jesskin's patient."

"Oh yes, Mr. Grange."

"I am not Mr. Grange."

The clerk glanced at Dori and then at a card. "Yes, that's right. 'Two friends.' You can go up with her for a while." She rang a bell sharply. "Chair, please."

"I can walk," Dori said, but the chair was arriving and obediently she let herself be put into it. Flanked by Cele and Matthew, pushed swiftly by an orderly, she did not speak. The huge empty elevator stopped at the eighth floor, and again the swift silent progress began, down a dimmed corridor. At the door of her room, she looked eagerly for the two names she had so often visualized. They were not there.

Inside Cele said, "I'll unpack," and Matthew gave her the suitcase, saying, "Here's where the useless feeling gets going." Dori said, "Oh no, if you and Cele weren't here . . ." and let her voice float away. In her ears it sounded strange, light and half muted. A nurse entered, young, smiling, saying, "I needn't ask who's the patient, need I?" and then a moment later, to Cele as much as to Matthew, "Would you wait outside for a while?"

This was no geriatric; Dr. Jesskin must know that the routine part did not matter; in a sudden flash of understanding Dori knew there would be many nurses tonight, many orderlies, the anesthesiologist, the people in the delivery room, to all of whom she would be just one more woman in parturition, faceless, nameless, except for the strip around her wrist saying "Grange" and bearing a number, her Harkness number which she would never use again.

She went rigid to another labor pain, deeper, more savage; this time her breath caught hard and the nurse turned at her gasp, nodding as if to give due recognition to pain, otherwise unimpressed, except to note the time. "We'll get you to bed," she said, "and prepare you. With first deliveries you never can be sure."

The pain did not stop. For the first time Dori screamed.

*　　*　　*

She could remember begging somebody for more anesthesia and she could remember being wheeled on a table and she could remember a brilliant light in the ceiling and she could remember voices but she could not separate anything from anything and she did not know whether it was still happening or whether it was over and she tried to open her eyes and could not and she went off again into a swarm of warmth and heavy softness. . . .

Somebody spoke and she could not answer. She knew it was a boy but she did not know how she knew, and when the voice came again it was Cele, calling to her, "Dorr, Dorr, it's Cele," and she tried to answer and nothing sounded and then she heard Matthew saying, "Dori, it's over," and she said, "Has he all his fingers and toes?" and fell back into the heavy dark softness again.

Quiet and darkness and a spurting upward like a fountain somewhere and it was happiness, the fountain, and she opened her eyes, and there was Cele bending over her and saying, "It's all over, Dorr, it's a boy," and she saw Cele and then Matthew and suddenly she knew them and her eyes opened wide and she said, "Is he all right?"

"Yes, darling," Matthew said, "and you're wonderful, and you can sleep if you want to—we'll be right here."

The spurting fountain again, and a rushing of warmth and she sighed and went away from them again but somehow knowing they were there, and wanting to be back with them, and being unable to do it as if she were sliding away into something thick and clinging and marvelously comfortable.

A door opened and she heard Gene's voice and everything went clear and she half sat up as he put his arm under her shoulder and said, "Congratulations, you," and she said, "Oh, Gene, you know Cele and this is Matthew," and she watched them shaking hands.

"Can I see the baby?" she asked. "What does he look like?"

"I'll go tell them you're out of it," Cele said. "He's huge and he doesn't look like anybody."

"How do you feel now?" Matthew asked. "Do you know what time it is?"

"What time?"

"Three in the afternoon." To Gene he said, "Cele called you when she went into the recovery room, around twelve."

"Did it take all that time?" Dori asked.

"Ten hours."

"When can I see him?" She half closed her eyes and when she opened them again the room was empty. The light had changed at the window; it was yellower and deeper, as if the sun were way down toward the rim of the sky. There was a rustle of newspaper and she turned her head. Rising from the chair in the corner of the room was a thin little woman, smiling, white-haired, pink-skinned, with a starched cap on her head.

"Hello," Dori said.

"I'm your four-to-midnight nurse, my name is Schulz. You've had a fine sleep and your baby is fine too."

"Can I see him now? I thought I was awake but then I went off again."

"That's not only postnatal but post-surgical."

"Surgical?"

"You needed some surgery at the end. Dr. Jesskin will tell you about it, but you're to rest in bed." She reached for her wrist. "No walking yet."

"Could I see my baby first?"

"Of course. I'll take your pulse later."

For the first time Dori was aware of her bound and tender breasts. She knew about the tenderness and the binding as she "knew" about everything; Dr. Jesskin had told her that since breast-feeding was out of the question, she would be wearing a tight bandage-bra arrangement to support her milk-filled breasts until the production of milk stopped. She had agreed without discussion; if she was to live apart from the baby for most of the first two or three months, what discussion could there be? Yet now, in one swift longing, she wished it might have been different. It was over as swiftly as it had come. You cut out all the *if-onlys* and *ah-buts;* she had accepted that from the start. Tender breasts were part of the bargain, useless milk part of the bargain. How little a price. She watched the door.

Matthew and his stubbled face—she suddenly remembered his bending over her and saying she could sleep, they'd be right there. Ten hours, he had said, and then hours more in the recovery room, and he and Cele had stayed right there, waiting for her, watching her sleep after she came back to her room, wanting her not to wake to an empty room.

The door opened. Mrs. Schulz entered backward, her thin spare back pushing the door inward. Then she turned carefully, her left arm a cradle, which she brought close to Dori, saying, "Eight pounds and five ounces, this young man. I'll go back for his bottle. It's not full milk yet."

Instinctively Dori's hands cupped together but the nurse said, "This way's safer," and placed the baby within the crook of her entire arm. Dori looked down.

Her tears burned her eyes, impossible, but there they were, a shimmer of distortion as she looked down at the red little face, the eyes closed, the skin shining, the wisps of hair faint against the red skull. She heard the door close and was glad.

In a moment she peeled aside the crossed corners of the encasing blanket and saw the tiny clenched fists. She raised one, and saw the bracelet around the wrist. *Grange*, and a number, the same number her wrist bore.

She stared at the tiny breathing morsel, the shimmer slowly passing, the grip at her throat slowly easing, a burst upward in her heart. She did not think in words, her whole response was an intuiting, not strung out in time like the beat of a pulse, but as simultaneous as a chord of music. This, this sleeping being warm on her arm, this new life, this continuing of her life—

Simultaneously she remembered herself before the long mirror at home, toweling herself dry after that bath, catching again the first unbelieving glimpse that said her breasts were a little fuller, looking down again to see between the jut of her hipbones a most tentative orbing.

Let it be true, she had thought, let it be true. And now there was this new morsel of humanity living the first hours of its own separate life. If she were to die this minute, he would not die, he would go on, he would live.

A new human being, she thought, her heart filling. Nothing else matters.

*   *   *

Sometime in the night, Dori felt pain and half woke, fuzzily thinking that she was still in labor. Then she remembered the tiny red face in the circling blanket and she knew she had already given birth and that it was over. She stirred and saw a dim light, reached out to her bedside lamp and saw that her wristwatch had not been returned. A voice spoke to her in a heavy accent.

"I'm Mrs. Czennick, your midnight-to-eight nurse. How do you feel?"

Dori sat up. She saw a plump old woman, massive compared to the spare little Mrs. Schulz, her hair a roaring henna above a face crosshatched with wrinkles and grooves. But she seemed pleasant enough, even glad to have her awake.

"I think I was dreaming, but I feel fine. What time is it?"

"Three, and you've been sleeping like a baby—like your own baby."

"Is he all right?"

"Wonderful."

"I don't suppose I could see him?"

"You better let the little thing get his rest, Mrs. Grange. He needs it too."

Dori nodded. She had been reading as much as she could lay her hands on about the care of infants and she gathered that nothing and nobody could possibly rob a healthy baby of twenty hours of sleep a day. But she was acquiescent, willing to wait until daylight. She accepted the pulse-taking and other attentions Mrs. Czennick offered, understood that the discomfort she had dreamed about had been real—I'll never use the word *pain* again, she thought, for anything less than *that* pain—and dismissed it since she knew it was a normal aftermath of the surgery, still unexplained but one of the matters Dr. Jesskin would tell her about when he came in the morning.

"You had several phone calls before I came on," Mrs. Czennick said, consulting a slip of paper she drew from her pocket. "Your friend Mrs. Duke, just to check in, she said she'd be back in the morning, and a Mr. Poole, also calling in the evening, to see if he could drop in for a few minutes, and also your brother."

"I can see people tomorrow, can't I?"

"Oh yes. Your early nurse told them all you were resting easily and that the baby was fine and that tomorrow you could have visitors whenever you liked."

"Any special visiting hours?"

"Here at Harkness, anytime unless the doctor says not, but he didn't. He also called in for reports of course."

"Did he say when he'd be here?"

"Early; that's his usual way." She offered Dori a glass of ginger ale and said, "You'll sleep again now; you'll be surprised." She turned the light out without asking and went back to whatever soft rustling pages she had in her shaded corner of the room.

Dori closed her eyes and waited for sleep. A silky comfort came over her, gentling, soothing. The surgery could not have been too serious; she could feel a tenderness, but it was part of the slightly battered aftermath feeling, and she accepted it along with everything else. She did not care whether she slept or not. It was marvelous to lie here knowing that it was over, that the great ninth month—

But this was Wednesday morning; it was no longer the ninth month. That was over and gone, as gone as the eighth month, as the seventh, as all of it. This was the tenth month.

Hazily she repeated the words. They had a new sound, unexpected, unexplored. The tenth month.

There was an appeal in that: the future. Once she had wondered whether the change in herself—not in her enlarging body but in her essential self, that change she kept catching glimpses of—whether it would prove delusive and transitory, would vanish when July twenty-third had come and gone. Now she knew it was still there; July twenty-third was not a finis but a beginning, not an ending but a becoming, a process—she had almost thought "a promise"—a process that would go on and on if she herself did not stifle it. The life process. Her own life.

In the darkness she thought of a phrase that kept repeating itself in her mind. You give birth, you get born. She was not sure what the words meant, yet she responded to the unseen equation with them. Cause and effect, the systole and diastole again. You give birth, you get born.

The tenth month. The first month?

*　*　*

The morning was a waiting for Dr. Jesskin's visit. She had awakened at first light and lay tranquil and silent, remembering. She was at last fully awake, her mind clear, her spinal cord and blood and brain no longer host to the blessed anodynes and opiates. The nurse had heard her move and at once Dori had asked, "Can I see my baby now?"

"The moment we take care of you, Mrs. Grange. Your medication and making you comfortable."

"Oh of course."

This time the baby came in crying, his face contorted with his energy, his skin damp with exertion, and as she took him, she felt a sudden admiration for the ferocity of communication from this mite. Eighteen hours old he was, not yet one day of life behind him, and yet a million years of instinct were guiding him in this demand for sustenance and survival.

She offered him the bottle and he kept yelling. She experimented, tentatively poking the nipple at his mouth until suddenly his lips closed about it and he began to pull, his ferocity draining away into gratification.

I think of him as he, or it, she thought as he was again taken away from her. Or just the baby. I can't think of him by his name yet. Maybe that's good. I certainly don't want to get used to calling him James or Jimmy while I'm here, just for the nurses' benefit.

The private nurses. She had seen only two, but she was sure the third would give off the same faint aura of polite concern that she should be without her husband at this time. They had been briefed, she knew, by Dr. Jesskin, and the floor nurses would also be briefed, about the husband off in Vietnam, had been told that his absence upset her very much, that it would be wise to make no reference whatever to it, nor to her wish that he could be here.

Did any of them believe it—the private ones or the floor nurses to come? She glanced at the large woman and Mrs. Czennick instantly smiled back. Despite the garish hair and the raddled flesh, she looked like a friend and ally. Perhaps when you were generally considered too old to be employable you were thankful at being summoned back into the world of the needed, and showed your gratitude by pampering your patients.

Or perhaps it was simply that this was Harkness at a hundred a day. A cynical thought for so felicitous a time, but there it was.

At eight a Mrs. Smith entered and took charge. She looked older than either of the others, grayer, even a little shaky, but she exuded competence and greeted Dori by saying crisply, "Your doctor is down the hall. He seems good and chipper."

A moment later he was there, a tap on the door to announce him and a simultaneous entry. As she looked up from her bed, he looked taller than usual in the long white coat, smiling at her, nodding dismissal to the nurse, with no sign of his usual detachment. He said nothing at all until the nurse left the room.

"May I offer my congratulations?"

"Oh thank you. Have you seen the baby?"

"Long before you did."

They laughed together and then he became again all physician. "You will want to know how it went, when I got here, all that."

"Do all your patients ask that?"

"All. It was about seven yesterday morning, and it went as it should go until I became concerned—after about nine hours of labor, quite within the normal range of labor—but I became somewhat concerned, not for you but for the baby, nothing drastic you understand, but concern."

"Was he in any danger?"

"Not to say 'danger,' but signs to concern one, heartbeat and such. We avoid forceps deliveries of course and so I performed an episiotomy."

"Which means?"

He explained and a swift imagined slash of the scalpel knifed through her. But he was continuing his explanation and her attention was riveted on it. "That is why you are not to get up for a day or so, and you may have to remain two or three days longer than I expected."

"It's nothing."

"I am sorry at the miscalculation. Once again a miscalculation."

230

"How can you be sorry about *anything?* Without you and the help you've given me all through—"

There was silence. She wished he would say something, move, change his position, but he did nothing and said nothing. She made herself glance back at him. He was simply looking at her. At the same time he seemed not to be seeing her, to be lost in some reflective gazing that focused nowhere except on thought. Soon he would say his usual "Now I'll have a look at you" and this visit, this single time when he seemed to be friend as well as doctor, would be over.

But he did not say it. Instead he said, "I have a colleague, a Dr. Earl Wingate, who assisted in the delivery. He will look in on you later this morning—I have asked him to."

She nodded and he began to move toward the door. Suddenly he smiled as if at some private joke. "I will hold the door wide, Mrs. Grange, so you can see that they are there."

He swung the door far back on its hinges and though she could not read the typed names she saw the two cards affixed, one over the other, and a larger sign which she could read. NO VISITORS, it said, and as she glanced once more at him, he murmured, "Except for the select few," and disappeared. She could hear his steps recede down the long corridor.

* * *

It was not only that morning that Dr. Wingate looked in on her, but every morning. Apparently, once the delivery was over, Dr. Jesskin assigned to others whatever postnatal and postoperative care was indicated, and remembering his crowded waiting room every morning she was not surprised. Dr. Jesskin, who had another patient on the floor already, still dropped by at about eight each morning to see her, reading the chart, asking how she felt, inquiring after the baby, giving an order to the nurse, but in five minutes or less he was once more on his way.

It puzzled her that he had not told her beforehand how

it would be, he who had been so punctilious and so patient about preparing her for everything else. Dr. Wingate clearly stood high on his roster of colleagues; nevertheless a small feeling persisted that Dr. Jesskin was firmly moving her off center stage. She saw the folly of this but she could not quite dispose of it.

The baby was now center stage; center stage in the world of doctors would soon be occupied by the pediatrician, Dr. Baum, who had taken care of all three of the Duke children. She would probably have one final check by Dr. Jesskin after she left the hospital, but apart from that visit and the routine annual checkups, he too would be off center stage.

God, I'd like to start all over again this minute, she thought after one of his fleeting appearances. If only I never had to work again, if only I could stay in hiding for six years instead of six months! But, poor man, I'd never have the nerve to go to him for help a second time.

The door opened and there he was again, looking uncommonly pleased. He waited only for the nurse to leave once more and then demanded, "Do you not know a playwright named Martha Litton?"

"I wrote a piece about her, yes, and interviewed her for it."

"You see why I ordered no walks in the corridor?"

"*She's* not here having a baby?"

"But her daughter is, and the mother is here every day, and out at the desk giving orders and finding fault. I just heard the mother's name out there."

"But who told you that I know her?"

"The daughter is my patient, married to that young man who plays the lead in the mother's newest play, I forget the name."

"*Time and a Half.* But I still don't—"

"Miss Mack put it all together. She reads many magazines and newspapers and if anything involves a patient, she does not forget. She read what you wrote of Martha Litton, and put it on my desk."

"Good old Miss Mack." It came out spontaneously, and

he said, "Yes, indeed," and laughed. Then, his mood changing, he added, "She also put on my desk the piece you wrote about Dr. Spock. That one, I'm afraid, she disapproved of. Which is where Miss Mack and I differed."

Her heart jumped at the compliment. Center stage or off-stage, Dr. Jesskin would always hold his special place in her life. If she were young she would have wondered before this whether she were being romantic about him; as it was, she knew that her feeling was an admixture of gratitude and a kind of personal dependence she had never before felt toward anybody, not in her adult years. That would fade now, slide back into the past tense, recede as his footsteps receded down the corridor while the heavy door to her room was making its stately close.

*　*　*

Matthew motioned the cab away and turned toward the river. There wouldn't be any air there either, but he was restless and somehow dissatisfied with the way the hour had gone. Dori was allowed out of bed now, and the floor nurses never came in unless she rang, but there was no real privacy and tonight something stilted seemed to attack him, as if he were seeing her off at an airport, one eye on the clock.

But then it's always this way at the start, he thought heavily. Even with Johnny, I really didn't feel much of anything until he was beginning to walk and talk. It was different with Hildy because she was my first, and there was that damn ego involvement of knowing you had reproduced yourself out of your own genes and DNA and all the rest of the biological hereditary miracle.

Of course I can't feel it now, with a baby that's only a week old. Even if it were Dori and me together, instead of Dori and whoever the hell it was, I still would be feeling this void where emotion about the baby is supposed to be. I can't fake it, I'd better not try to fake it, not with Dori, she always knows what is put on and what is really there.

She's the one I'm in love with anyway, not her baby. I'm not letting her down if I do have this uninvolved whatever-it-is toward the baby. Interest in it, affection for it, love for it, all of that will come later; it must come. It comes to people who adopt children; after a while they love them as much as any parents ever loved their own child. You hear that over and over, you read it over and over. Even though you're sure it could never be more than an approximation, you have to admit that what evolves in these happy adoptive parents is apparently a mighty close second, so close that nobody in the world could tell you definitely whether it is the same or not.

He had no worry about a year from now, but right now, when he was at the hospital and the baby was mentioned, he had to force himself. Not that Dori gurgled or crooned over the baby; actually she rarely spoke of it herself. Perhaps it was he, Matthew, who brought the baby into their conversation. Self-consciousness, that was. She had shown him the several pictures she had taken, and others of the baby and her, but that was about it.

She didn't even talk very much about the birth itself, nowhere near as much as Joan had done. She had reported Dr. Jesskin's explanation of the surgery and had been rather funny and bawdy about it.

"I gather," she had ended, "that it was one swift zip of the scalpel in the right places, and if you won't think me vulgar, I gather also that the patient is stitched up tighter than ever, afterwards, so not to worry."

That was when he had said, "God, Dori, I ought to be arrested." Crassly, ignominiously, desire had roared upward through him. "I ought to go home before I rape you."

"In Harkness? Lovely."

Now it was almost time for her to leave the hospital, but it would be another mouth or so before they could make love again—he couldn't remember what the prescribed time for abstinence was. Too damn long. Dori would be impatient too. He saw again the gesture she had made the first day they were alone there; apart from patting her stomach and crowing over its flatness, she had suddenly said, "And look, all nice and skinny and no puff-up," and from under the sheet at the end of the bed she had extended one slender foot, the anklebones sharp under the taut skin. She must have known that this was a kind of sex shorthand telling him that she would be slim and firm and tight again soon, with the distension gone and the need for care gone and all the nay-sayings and prohibitions gone.

Dori, Dori. If the baby made her happy, then the baby made him happy. If it fulfilled the denied part of her, then he welcomed it. If he were to resist it, he would be a more selfish man than he was. He did not resist it. He would not let himself resist it.

* * *

"Better let me carry the baby," Cele said. "Then if we run into anybody, they'll think *I* just had him. Come on."

Something like outraged possessiveness streaked through Dori as Cele picked him up and started down the corridor ahead of her, but she followed, docile enough, carrying only her suitcase and a small shopping bag with a bottle of formula and some of his things.

"You're thinner than I am right now," Cele grumbled as they waited for the elevator.

"Still bosomy though." The arithmetic of it tickled her: the baby had accounted for over eight pounds of her eighteen-pound gain, and the amniotic fluid and placenta and all the rest for another four or five, so thirteen pounds had gone, whoosh, in that one night, and she herself had remained accountable for only five. Ten days of three-mile walks and then a new dress and let any doorman examine her all day long.

It was still too early for visitors and outside there was no taxi in sight. Already it was hot in the blaze of the July morning and they stood on the pavement, side by side, two women and a newborn infant. Momentarily Dori felt forlorn, thinking wryly, What's wrong with this picture? At last a cab drove up, discharging, first, a young man, and then slowly, carefully, a very young woman, her face tense, her shoulders constricted. Dori stared at her, as Cele hailed the

235

cab, stepped inside, and gave the address on West Ninety-fifth. Automatically Dori followed, and there at last Cele transferred the baby to her arms.

Dori gazed down at him but she was thinking of the young woman just now beginning labor, being wheeled down to the elevator, being wheeled down the long corridor of the eighth floor. Was she afraid? Did she have that wedge of steel cleaving her apart? Don't be afraid, she thought. It's not pain-I'm-sick or pain-I'm-hurt, it's pain *for* something. You won't even know what to call the something. You'll call it the baby and think that's what you mean, but it's something else too, something bigger than any baby, even your own baby. Much bigger, vague, all-the-world-big, the-whole-human-race big, and maybe you'll be smarter than I am and not even try to find words for it.

CHAPTER TWELVE

There was an eerie excitement in being all alone with the baby. When Cele left in the late afternoon, Dori stood for a moment looking across the linoleum shine to the crib in the corner, to the small swathed creature within it, and she suddenly felt tense.

It was just the baby and herself now, alone for the first time behind a closed door. No friend to help, no nurse to advise or correct her or show her how, just that eight-day-old being and herself and whatever stumbling new knowledge she had about how to take care of him.

Suddenly she grinned. She was forgetting the baby's help, forgetting that he would let her know when to feed him, let her know when to change him, let her know whether he was uncomfortable in any way at all. Advise and consent, she thought, like the Senate. She started the record player and crossed to the crib to look down once more. This time she did not have to seem matter-of-fact about it; she could just stand there and stare for as long as she wanted. How little time it took to regard this one baby as the only baby.

The hum of the air conditioner, the faint noise above it from the street, the muted music in the room, the week's piled-up newspapers awaiting her, all combined to make a pleasing easy evening. Matthew was up at Truro early this week, something about a changeover in their house from the collapsing old furnace to a new oil heating system, though why that should be scheduled for the last day of July she didn't remember. In any case, she was half glad that he was away for several days, or at least half pleased at being quite alone for a few nights. One needed interims.

He knew already that they were under orders not to make love until September. Dr. Wingate's orders they were, on his last examination at the hospital. "You should not resume relations for another five weeks, especially if there is any discomfort." The discomfort was negligible, though she still had a faint surgical tenderness, but medical orders were to be followed, despite Matthew's quick protest. "Five weeks more? Good God, that's not until after Labor Day."

It was already two months since they had last made love, but for herself, she was not impatient at the dictum. Perhaps after the heavy final weeks of pregnancy and after the actual act of giving birth, it was instinctive for women to draw back for a while from any form of sex.

The trouble is, she thought ruefully, when there's no sex, you can think. The body's prohibitions of sex permitted problems to remain problems instead of letting them dissolve in the hot chemistry of passion. The word *passion* aroused her a little, but there was a tentative quality in her feeling, too, a willingness to evade it for a while longer.

I have to get used to everything first, she thought. It's like starting all over, with a new set of rules to learn. Once I get back to my own place, get working again, seeing people again, the whole special new feeling will merge with everything else but for now it's like being handed a whole new life.

Whatever had gone before was of course life, but now it seemed a half life, a partial life, full enough of love and pain and work and all the other ingredients of living, but it had always been her own life and now it was more than that. Now it was "our life," a family's life, a child's life interwoven with hers for the next twenty or more years, and there was nothing partial or halfway about that. In the hospital she had thought about the future, and here it was lying quietly, entirely in her care.

* * *

Before the weekend was over she felt as if she'd been in sole charge of a newborn baby a hundred times before and when Matthew arrived for dinner Monday evening, she was actually impatient for the baby to wake, cry, and need changing so she could display her effortless prowess in her new tasks.

But when he finally woke, she was so wary of being the effusive new mother that she stiffened into an impersonal efficiency, a nurse in a maternity ward performing the duty she was trained to perform. It was an idiocy of shyness, but she was caught in it. She changed the baby in silence. Matthew watched in silence.

"I don't think men react to them," he said, "until they start to walk and talk."

"I've always heard that. When I'm alone, I do react but I feel sort of funny in front of anybody, even Cele or you."

"It'll all shake down in a few days." He moved away and stood waiting for her. "Don't lose weight too fast, Dori, will you? You look the way you always did already."

"It's this new dress." She paraded up to and then back from him, like a mannequin modeling at a fashion show, delighted with the dress and herself. It was a bright wild print, short and full-skirted, swinging easily about her as she moved. She had bought it just that morning while Cele stayed with the baby. "If you were Bill the doorman welcoming me home, would you guess I'd had a baby?"

He shook his head and swiftly took her into his arms. "God knows how I'm going to get through until the third of September." She moved back and he at once changed his tone. "No doorman alive. Do you know when you can go home?"

"That's what I meant when I said I had a surprise. I'm going tomorrow afternoon."

239

"You got a maid!"

"I interviewed three on Sunday, and this one seems just right. She's no geriatric but she's not anybody I'm likely to meet in any friend's house later. She's not very good at English and she's sort of fat and sloppy, but she looks kind and the agency that sent her says she's reliable and good with children."

"Great. So tomorrow night I don't come here."

"I'll see how she is with the baby tomorrow and if she really is good, then I'll leave around five. I'm suddenly so impatient to get back there again."

"It will be damn good for me too." He moved toward her and again she stepped back. "I won't keep pestering you, Dorr, don't look so watchful."

"It's just . . . it'll be easier if we don't sort of inch toward things."

"No inching. It's a deal. But you have a date for September third, right?"

"Right."

He left after the eleven o'clock news and she was impatient for the morning and the arrival of Maria; she suddenly wondered whether she had chosen wisely, whether the woman, with her faulty English, had really understood what the arrangements were to be.

"I'm signed up for a two-bedroom apartment in that new building at the corner of Columbus Avenue," Dori had lied easily, "but that won't be ready for occupancy until around Christmas. And since there's no second room here, I'm turning the whole place over to the baby and you for now, and I'm moving in with a friend of mine, Mrs. Duke. She has a spare room."

Perhaps Maria hadn't believed a word of it, but she had accepted it without expression. Dori had explained too that she would be in to stay with the baby for part of every afternoon and Maria could do her marketing then and whatever else she wanted to do, because she, Dori, would be working (she had waved vaguely at the typewriter on the desk) and would probably be spending three or four hours right there every day.

In the morning Maria arrived an hour early, looking pleased to be there, apologizing in her mixture of English and Spanish for the huge suitcase she had brought, which turned out to be only a quarter full of her things. They were her regular clothes, with no sign of a maid's uniform, and Dori was oddly reassured. She was a workingwoman, not a proper maid, certainly not a baby nurse. Her own children were grown and married, and she was alone and needed the money, and that was why she worked.

The baby cried and it was Maria who attended to him, Dori watching, reassured again. Maria liked him. She was not constrained about showing it, either, but made little sounds and murmured over him and had an offhand way of turning him and diapering him that bespoke years of practice. Dori smiled. It was going to be all right.

Soon she went out for a walk. She was not yet up to any hard three miles, but she was on the way. She walked eastward through the park this time, nearing Fifth Avenue before she turned and began to go back. It was hard to believe that at last she was going home, back to the locked-up apartment where it had all begun. A sudden longing possessed her, to be there this very moment. She thought of her impatience to look up at the eighth floor of Harkness, of the bus ride uptown, of the way she had stood there on the street, counting the floors upward. And now she had the same impatience again, but this time for her own four rooms, the rooms that had been home for a decade.

If only she didn't have to leave the baby behind. Now he would be the one in the hideout, one small baby hiding out in a vast city! But you won't be in hiding from me, she thought swiftly, and it's only for a couple of months. I've just got to go back to the world the way I left it—just me alone.

She was apologizing to herself, she realized, not to her baby. She was making obeisances to the necessities as she saw them; she was in the final stages of the long plan now and she was not going to balk and undo everything. It was crucial to get the next part right or the whole thing would collapse. She walked more purposefully.

By four in the afternoon she was satisfied with Maria in every way, even with her slightly shuffling movement about the room. She seemed to be without nerves; she seemed calm to the point of being lackadaisical. Fine, better than hustle and bustle around the baby, she thought as she finished packing her suitcases and the carryall. At her desk she wrote out, in clear large calligraphy, Cele's telephone number, Dr. Baum's telephone number, and finally a number unattached to a name, her own. "Some evenings I will be at this number," she explained. "Just ask for Mrs. Grange."

In the taxi crossing the park she stirred to a high excitement. After all these months, after all that had happened, she was going home. As the cab drew to a stop, she watched the doorman spot her, and her pulse raced.

"Welcome home, Mrs. Gray. Good trip?"

"Wonderful, Bill, but it's grand to be home."

"Your friend said to expect you, when she was here with the cleaning people." He took her luggage, replete with airplane tags from Marshall's and Cele's bags, and as she followed him to the elevator, she felt the eagerness of a child.

But once upstairs silence greeted her. The place had been cleaned by a professional service, flowers stood on the low coffee table, sent by Matthew and arranged by Cele, but there was no voice to speak, no family or friend to greet her.

I want my baby, she thought, and I want Matthew.

She moved around each room of the apartment, seeing each picture as if she had just acquired it, sitting briefly at her desk, stretching out on the red sofa listening to one of the many recordings left behind. It was an old favorite; she might play it when Matthew came this evening. Tonight would be their first time here since that day in January.

No, she wouldn't play a record; it would be wrong to create moods when there were rules and schedules and prohibitions hemming them in. It would be better to go out for dinner, much better, much less provocative and also rather fun. She suddenly had a vision of a delightful restaurant, any delightful restaurant, with large luxurious menus, gleaming silver, candles and flowers. A young eagerness bubbled up. It was a hundred years since she had gone out anywhere. Going out to dinner would be a symbol that her days in the hideout were over.

*　*　*

"Oh yes, Mrs. Gray, Mr. Cox is expecting you. Would you come with me?"

It was absurd to be seeing him so soon but the desire had been overwhelming and Dori had yielded to it and telephoned for an appointment. Only with this legal step under way would she be really ready to face the dozens of appointments she was making with everybody else.

The reception clerk led her past several heavy doors of paneled walnut. Unlike most offices, there was little of the slide and clack of typewriters, and she had a whimsical vision of all those law partners and junior clerks writing their briefs and letters longhand as they must have done whenever this venerable set of offices was first established. It pleased her, this lack of modernity at Cox, Wheaton, Fairchild, Tulliver, though she could not have said why. She even liked its being way down here in this old building near Trinity Church in the oldest part of the city, where, some eighty years before, the original Cox, Wheaton, Fairchild and Tulliver had begun their practice of law. She half expected her Mr. Cox to appear in appropriate nineteenth-century raiment though she knew perfectly well that he and Dr. Jesskin had taken their advanced degrees at Harvard together.

When he rose to greet her she was surprised. Far from being antiquated, he was amazingly young, seemingly in his forties, a little stocky and bald but tan, fit, smiling not with formality but with an outgoing warmth. "So you're Mrs. Gray," he said. "Congratulations."

"How nice of you. Thank you."

He indicated a leather armchair and moved around behind it to close the door before he resumed his seat on his side of the large table which served as his desk. "I suppose you know from Neil that I'm delighted to be your attorney. From Dr. Jesskin, I should say."

"He said you felt a vested interest because it was his case."

"That too. But I was also interested because it's interesting in itself."

"Is it going to be difficult?" She was opening her purse and now handed him an oblong of heavy paper, bearing a seal and official printing. "There's the certificate."

"Department of Health, City of New York," he read aloud as if for her benefit. "This is to certify . . . yes, yes . . . James Victor Grange . . . sex, male . . . date of Birth, July twenty-third, nineteen sixty-eight . . . place of Birth, Sloane Hospital." He looked up at her. "Neil told me he was going to fake the hospital too, since he was faking a few other things."

"He's on the staff there also, isn't he?"

He seemed not to have heard the question. He was folding the certificate lengthwise; he then reached for a long envelope into which he inserted it, sealed the envelope, and in ink wrote across the sealed flap on the back, *"Private. Not to be opened."* Below this he wrote the date and his signature, and then handed the envelope back for her inspection. When she had glanced at it, he offered her his pen.

"I don't need to," she objected.

"Just to be legalistic." He grinned. "Lawyers like to be legalistic, and new clients should pamper them, don't you think?"

"Without a doubt." As she signed her name under his across the sealed flap, she suddenly thought, But they were at Harvard together, they must be the same age.

"Now let's get some details straight," he said. "Your baby is not living at home with you as yet?"

She gave him the address on West Ninety-fifth and told him of her daily visits. "By the first of October," she ended, "when everybody's forgotten I've ever been away, I'll take him home for good."

"Ostensibly, then, he'll have been in a foster home since birth, with people on West Ninety-fifth. Then he comes to you on a trial basis of six months. When we appear before the judge, of course, he will know that this is your natural child, that you are going through these several steps to protect that child."

"I understand perfectly."

He went on to tell her about the routine of the social worker's calls, and the private documents, and she listened as if she had never before heard of any of it. "When the adoption is over," he ended, "you'll have a new birth certificate made out in the name of your legally adopted son."

"Will there be any connection, any provable connection at all," she asked, suddenly sitting forward, "between that new permanent certificate and this first one?"

He sensed her heightened concern. He ripped open the envelope they had each just signed and leaned toward her with the certificate in his hand. "See that big long number there?"

"Yes." She read the digits out loud.

"That same big long number will show up on his permanent birth certificate," he said slowly. "And nobody in this or any world could ever link the two together without going through some very stiff judicial procedures."

He talked about the procedures and again she listened as if she had never before heard any of it. When he had ended he repeated the ritual of the countersigned envelope and then picked up his pencil once more.

"And now, what are you naming your adopted son? That's the only name that will appear in your files here."

"Eugene Gray." She hesitated for a moment. "Eugene Cornelius Gray."

For a fraction of a second his pencil paused and she said, "It's a private way to say thank-you. You won't have to mention it, will you?"

"I will mention nothing of what either of us says in this

office." He looked at her with a steady attentiveness that seemed new. "I wish it were not private, though, this one point. It would please him."

"But it is private." She sounded ill at ease. "I'm sorry, but otherwise I just couldn't—"

"Of course, then it's private," he said briskly, again writing. "Eugene Cornelius Gray—that's the permanent birth certificate you will receive and James Victor Grange disappears from the history books forever."

"And that will be—let's see, six months from October. That's November, December, January—" She burst out laughing. "There I go, counting on my fingers again."

He grinned at her as he had done before. "Better watch that habit—it can get you."

*　*　*

On her way to the subway she stopped and called Tad Jonas at the paper. "Okay, be mad at me," she began, "for not coming around before this. Can I drop by and say hello? It's Dori. I'm down on Wall Street."

"Who'd you think I thought it was? Sure, come on."

She made for the subway and once inside glanced at the list of names she had scrawled on a slip of paper in her purse. For today, three more after Cox and Jonas. So it was going, day by day. "Can I drop by?" "How about lunch?" "Come on in for a drink on your way home." The process of getting back into the stream of things with the peripheral people of a life was always easy, she was certain, because peripheral people did not care deeply about anybody but themselves; when she said she'd enjoyed her cruise, they asked a perfunctory question or two about where she had been and moved on to their own news, their own jobs, their own worries or triumphs or projects. Not one asked how long she'd been away. Not one, she noted a bit ruefully, had actively missed her.

With this visit to Tad Jonas she was very nearly through with the process. Earlier in the week she had even said to Gene, "I think Ellen and I might as well make it up now—

how would you like to ask me over one night and *not* talk about having children?"

"What about a night when Dan and Amy are here too, or Jim and Ruth?"

"Do they know?"

"Not a damn thing. Ellen wouldn't go that far. She's not mean, Dori, just orthodox."

"An orthodox family evening suits me to the ground."

It had taken place just last night and she had enjoyed it. She had never faltered once over Dan's and Jim's queries about where she had been, shrugged off their "Long time no see," and even found herself smug because Ellen was uncomfortable when they met while she herself was nothing of the sort.

There would be nothing uncomfortable now, she thought, as she opened the door to the newspaper office, waving hello to a reporter she knew. Across the city room Tad Jonas shouted, "Hi, just let me get this off," and she went to his desk and watched until he finished marking copy for the boy waiting for it.

"Do you want to come back on the staff?" Tad finally greeted her.

"Thanks for asking, but no."

"Still the free lance. Well, I've an assignment looking for a writer."

"Election stuff? Mrs. Nixon or Mrs. Humphrey?"

He bridled. "There you go, charging me with the old crime! What I meant was a follow-up on Spock's conviction. The appeal will take a year or more. While it's hanging, what happens to kids resisting the draft? What are Spock's long-range plans? Like that."

"When would you want it?"

"Fast."

The word was a stimulant. A specific task with a specific deadline or an implied deadline, that was a stimulant too. She wanted to get back to work, to earning money. "If you don't crowd me, Tad," she said.

"Could two weeks do it?"

"Just about."

"And the price tag? Let's say three weeks of your old salary."

"Let's."

*   *   *

We all live at so furious a pace, she thought as her cab turned into West Ninety-fifth. She had forgotten such rush and hurry. She was exhilarated by the day, but tired too, and the stop here with the baby invited and beckoned as the promise of respite. As she saw the white stone houses leading away from the corner of Central Park West, geraniums in their green window boxes, their brass trimmings glinting in the afternoon sun, their stone still managing to look newly sandblasted and free of city grime, she felt nostalgic. There had been repose while she had her daily life here; there had been time to reflect, to think, to evaluate. Already the memory of it was slipping away; already she was looking back upon it with the faint poignancy of regret.

After leaving Tad Jonas, she had kept her engagement for lunch, put off her other two until next week and gone instead to the main library to begin work on her new piece on Dr. Spock. Two hours had fled, her eyes had finally wearied under the spotlight of the microfilm machine, her notetaking had edged off into the mechanical, a sign always to quit, and she had for the first time found herself wishing she were not seeing Matthew that evening, not seeing anybody, just going to the baby and then on home to a long cool tub and hours of just reading or hearing music while she remembered every word of Bob Cox's once more. And that involuntary pause of his pencil over "Cornelius." And why she had not said, Tell him if you like.

Maria opened the door at the touch of her key. "He's asleep," she said, "such a good baby," and at once Dori became Mrs. Grange again, the not fully explained woman who arrived every day without exception but who lived there only during Maria's two days off.

"You can go out for quite a while, Maria. I'll be here till about six. I'm dead-tired and it's so cool here."

Left alone, she took off her street clothes and put on the old loose smock with its pink carnations. It swung from her shoulders now, as free as a painter's smock in an old-time Paris studio, and she loved to wear it and be aware of non-bulk as she had once loved to be aware of bulk. She put a record on, fixed herself a "water on the rocks" and moved toward her typewriter. She might try a fast draft of an outline.

Midway she paused and returned to the crib. The way they slept! How short they looked, even long ones like hers, with their legs still folded up in the fetal position. Gene Gray indeed. She still thought of him as the baby, or he, or when she looked directly at him, as "you." Are you going to like the name Gene? Maybe you'll want to use all of it, Eugene, so you won't get teased as poor Gene always was about having a girl's name, Jean. You could use your middle name if you feel like it. But that would be shortened too. Neil, Bob Cox had said.

Neil. She would have guessed Nils as the Scandinavian nickname, or something like Nelius, to rhyme with Delius. Her knowledge of Scandinavian nomenclature was a bit sparse, and she could at least have asked Bob Cox that much. She had gone rigid at the notion of asking anything about Dr. Jesskin.

The baby stirred. Everybody said how handsome he was, but she never thought the word "handsome"; she could get no further than "marvelous," a kind of all-meaning word she needed. He still didn't look like anybody; he was no unmistakable image of herself or of Dick Towson. The baby stirred again. Perhaps he would wake and give her a few minutes—no, he was already back in the depths of sleep.

She looked around vaguely, as if she had forgotten the typewriter and were searching for some pleasing activity to help her wait out the baby's sleep. Then she crossed the room and called Matthew at his office. He answered himself and at her voice he said, "Telepathy. I've been trying to reach you."

"I've been out since nine. Has something come up?"

"Not come up, but I'm a lunkhead and forgot. Jack and Alma Henning are in town for the evening, and it's been a date for a couple of weeks, so I can't ditch them. Is it okay if I'm fairly late?"

"Well, not so okay. That's why I called you."

"You haven't a date *you* forgot?"

"No, silly, I haven't." The good old one-way street; the enlightened Matthew preferred it the way all males did. "What I have, though, is a headachy lot of fatigue from this frantic pace I've been in, and I thought I might go home and sleep from about eight P.M. to eight A.M."

At once he was concerned. "You do sound tired, darling. You really have been pushing it too fast too soon."

"So maybe it's lucky you're tied up with the Hennings—some benevolent genie taking care of me."

"Then tomorrow night?"

"Tomorrow."

She hung up, suddenly aware that the air conditioner was very loud. Illogically she remembered that tomorrow she was to see Dr. Jesskin and that the day after tomorrow the baby would be one month old. Another milestone, a different sort, shared, existing not only in her life but in her son's.

*   *   *

Just after nine in the morning Miss Mack telephoned to say there had been a change in her appointment. "Doctor will be away until after Labor Day," she said, "and he set up an appointment for you instead with Dr. Wingate. Will that be satisfactory to you?"

She was taken aback. A broken appointment, broken by Dr. Jesskin? "He's not ill, is he?"

"No, nothing wrong. We've already cleared this with Dr. Wingate, but if you prefer somebody else—"

250

"Of course not. But I—that is, will you give me Dr. Wingate's address?"

"He's right near here." She gave her the address and said that eleven was still the time unless there was some reason to change it. "He expects you as Mrs. Grange, of course."

"Of course. Thanks."

"And your address on Ninety-fifth Street."

"Yes, I'll remember."

"Doctor said he would suggest an appointment here sometime after his return in September."

"If it's a vacation, give him a 'bon voyage' from me, would you?"

"I'll do that."

Unpredictable disappointment invaded her as she hung up. Off center stage, of course, she had expected it, and this was merely the routine postnatal checkup, but she must have been looking forward to it as a chance to report on the baby, on her visit to Bob Cox, on being at work again.

Well, all right, sometime after Labor Day. Cele and Marshall were going away for the weekend, Gene would be away, Matthew of course. Suddenly the weekend loomed long and empty ahead of her. Labor Day was early this year, the weekend after this one, but she hoped to be finishing her piece for Tad Jonas before it ended, and then the day after would be the third of September.

She felt unsure suddenly, a throwback to her old self, not the new Dori she had been feeling recently, but the old Dori, aware of an empty weekend, lonely, aware of the need to get through time. Perhaps she too needed a vacation, a week or two away from everything and everybody, even the baby.

Another world cruise? She laughed aloud and felt better. Work was what she needed, and a nice tangible check in payment, something you could deposit in your bank and use to buy things with. No more transfer of money from savings, no more cheerful watching as the sum grew smaller. She had used about three thousand and that was enough. From now on she paid her way again. The money left in the bank would now become Gene Gray's college fund.

College fund! Instantly she saw him as a tall young man crossing some campus, hair tousled—would it be shaggy and long? would he have sideburns and wild clothes?—a member of the class of, let's see, Good Lord, of 1990, boys usually were twenty-two when they were graduated. Would he be a rebel like Johnny? Or by that time would there be new ways to register convictions, new mores for disillusioned youth? Probably. Techniques kept changing though protests there would always be. And Gene Gray, class of 1990, would never be a smugly satisfied member of the establishment.

She worked uninterruptedly for an hour, and welcomed the first cry from the crib. In the morning she went back to the library and time began to speed by again and she lost track of days, racing to finish her piece a day or two before her deadline.

Gradually August dwindled away in its own implacable heat, and on a Sunday morning September began. As she bathed and changed the baby she said aloud to him, "One more month and you quit hiding out and you come home with me for good."

*   *   *

It was the night after Labor Day and Matthew had phoned to say he would arrive early. His family was staying for another two weeks at Truro, and they were still able to start their evenings by having dinner together. This time she prepared the things he liked best, a sense of occasion tingling along her nerves. It's so damn girlish, she scolded herself, but the scolding changed nothing.

He brought flowers and a record, and talked of her piece for Tad Jonas and asked if he might read it.

"Of course, later."

"Later? I'd better read it now."

"We're going to have dinner now." She began to serve it, and told him that she had asked for, and received, Mrs. Steffani's permission to sublet the apartment from October first. "'Mr. Grange is coming home from Vietnam,'" she had said, "'but he's to be stationed in California, so of course I'm taking the baby there.'"

"Does Maria know?"

"I asked Mrs. Steffani not to say anything. I'll give Maria plenty of notice or pay her instead. I'd keep her on if it weren't for her knowing about Mrs. Grange."

"Did Steffani promise?"

"She just gave me one of those shrugs, and reminded me that the deposit of the last month's rent was all hers if I tried to walk out."

"Nice."

"Fine, as long as she won't stop a sublease. Four weeks to go and he'll be living here for good. I can't wait."

They lingered over dinner and then he said, "Darling, let's go to your room."

Moments later she was standing naked, letting him look at her, hearing him say, "You're more beautiful than ever," letting him kiss her, letting him take her to bed.

They made love, carefully at first, tentatively, then more freely. They were greedy for each other and responsive and quick, each creative for the other, neither of them a selfish lover. Then came the silence they always permitted themselves, a communication in its own style.

"You're Dori again, the same Dori as before," he said at last and looked down at her. At once he added, "Does it hurt now? Is anything wrong?"

"Nothing, why?"

"You look a little, I don't know, sad maybe."

"I'm not sad."

"Thoughtful then."

"I suppose so." It's the first time, she was thinking, that it's plain and simple being in bed and making love. It's two people having an affair and that's all it is. It's not his fault that it's only that; it's mine. Nothing has changed for him, only for me. "Don't worry about it," she said lightly, "or I'll never look thoughtful again."

She closed her eyes and he lay beside her, silent. When he began again to kiss her, she said, "Please not."

"Something *is* wrong."

"Nothing, but please not again." I've caught up to him in a way, she thought; now he's not the only one with something else at the core of his life, coming ahead of us, coming ahead of everything. "Matthew, don't be mad at me," she said. "It's just—"

"I'm not mad at you. It'll be different next time."

When he left, she lay against her pillows, still thoughtful. She was not restless; she lay there pleasantly, willing and permissive as to the direction her thoughts took. They had come full cycle, she and Matthew, back to this same bed where they had made love at the start. They were still perfect as lovers, each for the other, attuned to the other, responsive, creative, still right together. She was the same Dori as before, he had said.

But I'm not, she thought. I seem the same, but I'm not. You give birth, you get born. You get to be surer about what is first-rate and what is a little less than that. An affair was not necessarily second-rate, but what was thoroughly first-rate was honesty, and an affair was anything but honesty. It could not be; by its nature it had to be hidden, laden with subterfuge, managed by lies and silences and absences unexplained.

She was not going to moralize about it; she could accept it, as Matthew himself accepted his own affairs, those others he had had, the ones that he had always brought to a close when the gears began to grind. Here at least she could be the emancipated woman, with as much ability as he to have an affair minus blindness, and enjoy what there was to be enjoyed. And now she could have the ability, as he did, to keep intact those other parts of life that needed to be kept intact.

* * *

Ten days after Labor Day Miss Mack telephoned to suggest an appointment. "I did see Dr. Wingate," Dori said automatically, "didn't he tell you?" and then quickly added, "I'm sure he did, and of course I'll come in whenever you say."

"Tomorrow at eleven then. Same time, same station."

Another of Miss Mack's locutions. It would be nice to see her again. It was months since she had done anything but talk to her by phone. Last April had been her last office visit, and here it was nearly fall, with the first crispness of autumn in the air.

In the morning Miss Mack greeted her as always, and Miss Stein also, but neither of them spent so much as two seconds gazing at her. She was not surprised; what did surprise her was that when Miss Mack signaled her turn, she barred the door to the dressing room.

"No need for getting ready," Miss Mack said. "Doctor says he will see you in his office."

He was standing as she entered. He was not wearing his long white coat; he was again in street clothes, and with a start she thought, he *is* as young as Bob Cox; I was making the family doctor out of him in my own mind, because the first time I ever came here I was in my twenties. She said, "Good morning," and he answered without smiling. This was one of the times when he held the chair for her, asking how she felt, how the baby was.

"I had a good report on you from Earl Wingate," he added, "and I gather that your visit to Bob Cox also went well."

"Oh very." She was about to go on, but he had picked up his pen, though her folder was nowhere in sight. He seemed more preoccupied than usual, and she decided this was not the time to talk either of Cox or of Wingate. He seemed to discover the pen in his fingers and hastily laid it down again.

"I have something I must say to you now," he said gravely. He looked at her carefully, and a prescience stirred in her. This was not merely a reversal of the usual routine; this was not to be a regular visit at all and that was why she had not had to change to the plastic toga.

"I have thought this out most carefully," he went on, glancing at her and then pausing once more. "I hope you will believe that."

"I do already. Whatever it is."

"I canceled our appointment and suggested Dr. Wingate as a temporary expedient because I was still not through thinking."

"I see." She had never heard him speak in this somber way. She sat immovable, waiting.

"It is not a simple matter, but now that your confinement is accomplished, I shall have to ask you, after all, to choose permanently another doctor."

"Permanently? But why?"

He seemed not to hear the question. "Once I poked fun at you, I recall, and asked you, 'Did you imagine I would refer you to another doctor?' Do you remember when I did that?"

"Of course I do."

"But now I do have to refer you to somebody else. Perhaps Dr. Wingate—but permanently, under your own name, now that Mrs. Grange is about to leave us."

"But why? How could I ever go to any other—?"

"It is not now a question only of wishes," he said slowly, his finger raised in that cautionary inch of his, asking her to consider, to avoid rashness. "It is now also a question of possibilities. My possibilities, perhaps I should say." He looked at her again, and then away. "Have you ever been analyzed?" he asked unexpectedly.

"No."

"Do you know anything about the relationship between analyst and analysand?"

"Only what I have read."

He picked up the pen again, but then he sat silent, staring down at the tip of it. She instantly was back at that concert so long ago, staring at the conductor's baton, staring at it as if it were the one point of solidity in a light swarm of fever.

"It is an unwritten rule of analytical ethics," Dr. Jesskin

256

went on slowly, "that if an analyst should find himself beginning to be emotionally preoccupied with a patient, he should send that patient to another physician for further treatment. He could no longer maintain the necessary objectivity, could not maintain that professional distance which is so fundamental to any analysis."

"Oh."

"Each branch of medicine has its own unwritten rules—" He broke off and stood up, facing her in silence. She stood up also. She did not look at him. She swallowed and she heard the dry tight noise of the swallow and thought he must have heard it too.

"Fools and vulgarians," he went on, so carefully that it seemed it must be physically painful for him to speak, "think that a gynecologist takes some personal interest in his patients. Of course he does not."

She shook her head for no.

"But if he finds, in the course of circumstances, if he finds that he builds up an admiration for a patient, that over a period of time this admiration grows and even becomes tinged with—it is hard to say it clearly. I have probably said it all anyway."

"Oh, Dr. Jesskin." She turned sharply and went to the door. There she stopped, her hand on the knob, unwilling to open it. "When did you—could I ask when you decided this, about sending me to Wingate or another doctor for good?"

He did not answer at once. He was still at his desk, standing as if at attention; she had a moment to think his color had risen.

"I am not entirely certain," he said, choosing the precise words he needed. "It was after the baby was born, sometime during the next hours perhaps, perhaps during the next evening, surely before I returned to the hospital the following morning. As to the necessity that led to my decision—" He threw open his hands, palms up. "That is what I cannot be certain about, whether it was all at once there or whether

257

it had been a long time developing. That I remain uncertain about, only that. Everything else is clear."

She nodded and quickly opened the door.

* * *

She could not go home. She had expected to put in several hours of work before going to the baby, but work was impossible. Orderly thought was impossible. Her mind was like a starburst, in all directions at once, bright with light of some kind, bedazzled with it so that comprehension was shattered.

She crossed Madison and then Fifth and went into the park, dear and familiar over on the West Side, but still strange over here on the East Side. The morning coolness was already conquered, but she did not care. She had to walk, move, go from here to there, no matter where, just to give herself the illusion of direction.

What was he telling her? Probably nothing, except that he had become involved with her as a human being through all the long secret story of the pregnancy and the actual birth. He looked on her as a special patient, not just one more woman in his waiting room. "A remarkable patient," he had said that morning on one of his last visits, and it had sent her spirits on a rollicking spin. Now he was reiterating that and adding that it was improper to have patients one regarded as special in any way.

That's not what he was telling me. I know what he meant. Why am I running from it?

But I don't know anything about him and he knows everything about me. He knows about Matthew, but he can't possibly know whether I am totally happy with Matthew or partly happy or not happy at all.

And I am still happy with Matthew. I know the limitations on us, I've always known them from the first minute we met. There are always limitations, there are no simple solutions—

Limitations. God, there I go again, like the time I wrote

"wretched." I am forty-one and this may be my last chance at finding something more than a love with limitations.

It would indeed be the final chance if she fell into a comfortable year or two or three with Matthew, with the sex drive satisfied, so that she would have no instinctive dynamo impelling her on to continue searching. A long affair, replete with those limitations, she had always accepted. That was the name of the game: my family comes first, you must accept that.

Why must I always accept? Isn't that being defensive too? Unsure, accepting what there is because you never really believe you can reach out the way other women do, to a life where you do not have to be willing to do without?

Suddenly she was crying. Where did these wild angry rushing tears come from? What longing and deprivation came with them, shattering her self-control?

All three thinkings. How long ago Dr. Jesskin had told her to take time, to think with her mind, with her feelings, with her instincts.

She thought, Oh, God, why did I never see it before?

CHAPTER THIRTEEN

She needed time. She couldn't see Matthew tonight either; she would have to tell him so. Tomorrow was Friday and he'd be going straight to the airport from his office, so again it would be nearly five days before she saw him Monday evening. She needed that much time. Then she wouldn't be blurting things out. Then she could say that she was troubled, that perhaps they should not see each other at all for a month or two while she thought about everything that was still strange in her new status as a woman with a child.

"While I get things into some sort of shape." That's what she ought to say, with a fierce justice behind the words. She would not say it; it would be a spiteful echo of his own words, but if she did say it, if she could say it, it would be an avowal that it was not so simple to remain sweet and tranquil with an affair that could never grow to anything, an affair in whose limitation lay its own mortality.

Just an affair, just two people making love. Suddenly she shrank back from the vision of them in bed together, suddenly she felt that lovemaking was over between them, that she no longer could respond and share in a sexuality that held in it no conceivable seed of any future life. At the beginning, there had been a reaching, unexpressed, unexamined, toward something they said in words could never be, but which each kept wondering about nonetheless. Now in the last weeks she at least had come to accept the reality.

She walked on and on in the park, heading north, past the reservoir, toward the pond that in winter turned into a shining skating rink. The wind rose and once she sat down to rest. At her right, through the fringing trees, were the buildings of Mount Sinai Hospital, of Flower, of the Academy of Medicine. She kept looking toward them. Then she rose again, found the nearest exit from the park and emerged on upper Fifth Avenue. To her left was the handsome building that was the Academy. She moved toward it and went inside.

* * *

Late Sunday afternoon, driving back from the country in their station wagon with three children and two dogs, Cele said to Marshall, "You might drop me at Ninety-sixth and the park."

"What for?" the children all demanded but Cele only said, "To visit somebody I know. I'll be home in half an hour."

"Who is it?"

"Do I always ask who you kids see or where you're going?"

That silenced them and as they neared the transverse that cut through the park, she left them and walked around to Dori's. Within minutes of her arrival, Dori was telling of the dismissal by Dr. Jesskin, careful to draw no conclusions for her, but telling. How long it had taken her to offer a word about Matthew! How natural it was now to tell of the broken appointment with Dr. Jesskin, of the subsequent one, of his careful choice of words, of her burst of feeling in the park, even of her trip to the Academy of Medicine and the directory that had yielded nothing of what she had gone to find out.

"So I still don't know and I can't be sure what he really meant, Cele, but I've just got to call everything off for a while."

"Meaning Matthew?"

"Meaning Matthew."

In an impatient non sequitur Cele demanded, "But when you were with Cox that time, couldn't you have brought up the damn photographs on Jesskin's desk? Maybe during the bit about the baby's middle name?"

"'Oh, by the way, Mr. Cox, is Dr. Jesskin's wife conveniently dead?' Like that?"

"Jeer all you like. You know what I mean."

"I just couldn't make myself; I'd have stood there with my mouth open and not a word coming out. And if I could, Cox would have told me nothing, not one solitary thing. They're all the same, every doctor, every lawyer, their basic training is *Confidential, Top Secret, In Camera.*"

"And who are we to complain?"

"Exactly."

"But suppose you were doing a story on Jesskin, you'd find out if he was married or a widower or whatever."

"Not unless he tossed it at me. His work would be the story, any papers he'd written—the directory did say he's published several, and I also found out in a couple of other places about various honors and degrees, even that he was born a Dane and came here when he was ten."

"But if it were a personal story, including family, you'd manage somehow. You'd never let yourself be stopped cold."

"I'd probably try bribing Miss Mack or Miss Stein and get thrown out on my ear. Or I'd go out to Huntington and ask his grocer and the gas-station attendant and the local post office if there was a Mrs. Jesskin around. Can you just see me?"

"Okay, okay. I was just speculating."

"And don't think I wasn't."

* * *

On Monday, Dori felt apprehensive as evening approached, and when the elevator stopped at her floor, she went to the door, opening it before Matthew put his finger to the bell. She was melancholy too, with a sense of impending change, perhaps impending loss and farewell.

Matthew didn't notice. He seemed troubled too, telling her quickly of "a rotten kickup with Johnny."

"He wants to change schools," he said. "And now that the analysis is only three weeks off, he's refusing to go."

Something unwilling rose in her, the reluctance again. She had never felt it before about his children. At once she felt herself a traitor, but immediately thought, I am not a traitor. But if I ever needed him at the same time Johnny needed him—oh, God, do I resent being second to a man's child?

That wasn't it. If there ever came a time when her child needed him at the same time his child did—

That wasn't it either. These were fragments of it, but no more. It was deeper, the something that had been growing within her for months, the willingness to say, This is playacting too. I have never seen Johnny, never had a meal with him, never heard you talk to him, never heard him talk to you—how then can he be real? And in all the years ahead, I won't ever know Johnny or Hildy either, then how can they ever be real to me? And if they are unreal, sort of half-people I hear about but never see, then you and I can never be real at the core, where our children live too.

"Matthew," she said when he ended about the kickup, "I want to talk to you about us."

"Us?"

"About me." She looked at him without speaking, as if she were searching for the precise words she needed, and she remembered Dr. Jesskin, as he had stood there by his desk, doing the same thing.

"I've been searching something out," she said, "and it's become awfully important. I'm not sure when it started, except that it was toward the end, before I had the baby."

"What sort of searching out?"

264

"It was about being big and pregnant, a good feeling, that *this is for something*. There it was, the opposite of aimlessness, the opposite of what's-the-use-ness, the feeling of intention."

Very slightly she stressed the word *intention* and then she glanced at him; his face was somber, reminding her of the many times she had found in it a look that said he wasn't often happy. For a moment she faltered, as if to discontinue, but this time a small shock of power, like a spark, prodded her to go on.

"Pregnancy, God knows, is intention, is promise, is the future tense, and if you think of a relationship between two people, you can carry over the concept. I got to feeling that without intention between two people in love, there's only the present and the repeating of the present."

"But there is intention, there is a future—"

"I couldn't get hold of any of this for a long time, and I kept turning away from it and telling myself to be happy in the present and not even look ahead at a lot of impossibles. I labeled those daydreams and sentimentality, and shoved them out."

"You know that half of me wants us to marry—"

"But the other half says Johnny and Hildy and Joan, and I am accepting that and always have, from the beginning."

"Accepting? You don't sound as if you were accepting it."

"All along I did accept it as the only premise we could go on. You know I did, we both did. But there was another premise for me, that accepting the limitations was better than losing you, better than going back to a year of nothing that used to follow the ending of any affair. That's where the change began to happen."

"Are you telling me you don't want us to go on?"

"I'm trying to tell you that I don't want to go on without any future tense."

"There is a future tense. There's always a future tense. Do any of us know what may happen tomorrow, next month, next year?"

"You mean I can pin my hopes to some taxi accident,

some awful disease, hoping that Joan will be conveniently dead?" She used the phrase purposely and he flinched and she saw it and knew she had meant him to flinch. She wanted him to see it now, not three months from now; it was nothing to stay immobilized about for week after week. "You moved me terribly that night," she went on, "when you said if a father figure was so essential in a child's life, you'd be the father figure in my child's life. But Matthew, that's playacting, isn't it? If he can't have a father, he'd better grow up with only a mother, like a million other kids in this world, but a real solid mother, not a combination of mother and make-believe father."

He was angry and she saw it, but there was no way to soften what she had said and keep it said. She felt an elation at not having faltered, an elation at managing words for this that she had been so slowly arriving at.

"Are you breaking with me?" he said. "Is that what it comes down to?"

"I think that's what it comes down to. I was going to suggest staying apart for a month or two, seeing what that did, but it would just be more difficult, that way, in installments."

He said abruptly, "Is there another man?"

"I don't like your asking it in that tone."

"Are you to call all the turns?" he demanded. "Haven't I the right to ask if you're having an affair with anybody?"

"I'm not having an affair. I won't be having an affair. I don't want any more affairs. I'm sick of affairs, even good ones like—like—the way ours was to start with."

He made a rough gesture as if to brush all that aside. "But I asked if there was another man and you don't answer that."

"I'm not sure," she said. "It may be that there is. I can't think about it too clearly, not yet, not right away."

"What does that mean? Have you met somebody new or haven't you? You must know one way or the other."

"Please, not that tone."

"What tone? Am I supposed to ask not even a simple question?"

"But not to cross-examine. You once said—"

"Right. I did say that. God, that was long ago."

"It isn't anybody new, it's somebody I've known for years and years but still don't know too much about."

"And you're in love all of a sudden?"

"I didn't say I was in love."

"Did he say it?"

"It's so vague. You're trying to box it, but it's still so vague." She turned and left him, going to her bedroom, going to the window, looking down to the street. She could hear him move about and she waited, to give him time to compose himself. After a while she went back and said, "This isn't easy for me either, and I'm sorry."

He put his drink down and stood up. "I suppose there's no point in talking it out anymore now."

She shook her head and they looked at each other. He moved toward the front door and she stood quiet, watching him go. Rue, she thought, what a lovely sad perfect word.

"Good night," she said. "It's true that I'm sorry."

⁂

She worked. Tad had praised her piece on Dr. Spock and immediately given her a second, easier to do, with less research. She wrote a first draft, cut it hard, rewrote it, and set it aside for a day and then attacked it for its final version. Work was part of life, a big part, a good part. She had been in hiding from work too, all those months of pregnancy, but now she had regained full citizenship in an open world, a world where intention was part of life, where the old satisfaction could be had, of starting from nothing and trying to make it over into something.

She thought of Matthew often, wondering about what she had done. She told Cele about it, and Cele merely shrugged. "One thing's sure, Dorr. If you wanted to prod him into some sort of definitive action, that's the way to prod."

"I didn't want to prod him into anything."

"Probably you haven't."

She turned her second article in; again Tad Jonas liked it and offered her a third.

"Am I pushing you too hard?" he asked. "You're going great guns, but you said not to crowd you."

"It's good for me, I'm waiting for something and getting uptight about it."

"Anything I can help with?"

"I might ask for a letter of reference."

"For what, in God's name?"

"Next month," she said, "a baby's going to get born and I'm supposed to be the one to adopt it. They might want references about stability and such."

"You're kidding."

"No, just waiting."

"Through who? Which agency?"

"None. A private adoption, through a doctor I asked to help me."

"God, Dori, way back on the *Trib,* when we first met, you were talking about adoption. You were still married. Remember?"

"Did I really? Well, it's taken me this long, so wish me luck, will you?"

"I'll be damned. Do you want a boy or a girl?"

"Either. I didn't specify."

"Well, good luck next month. I hope nothing slips up."

"So do I. Look." She held out two fingers, crossed hard against each other, and then left. It was the first time she had tried announcing it and it had gone easily, and with Tad of all people, tough and knowing Tad. She felt triumphant, the euphoria of certainty. She could do it and do it with conviction. One small final lie, a matter of three months off a baby's age. She wouldn't need to try it with anybody who'd be likely to see him close to, just with the world at large. And in a year or six or ten who would remember a little boy's exact birthday?

She went home and again started on the new assignment, pleased that it had nothing to do with the election campaign, which she could scarcely stomach. She had to force herself to look at the evening news programs, laden as they were with inanities and lies about peace, but one night she saw that four specialists in foreign news were to discuss last month's invasion of Czechoslovakia, and one of the four was Dick Towson.

Alone in her living room she watched him and listened to him. How long since she had thought seriously about him, yet how calm and fond her feelings were whenever she did. This was the Dick Towson who had made her pregnant; this was the man who was the father of her child, though he was not the father in any sense except the physical sense of being the donor. A sudden impulse burned in her to let him know, to thank him, to tell him if only "for the record" of his own life. But long ago the decision had been made about that, and she could not heed any sudden impulse. Warnings sounded like bells: Careful, this is a test, this is a time for control, for silence.

She studied the face on the screen, trying to see in its features any resemblance to the small face that looked up at her from that crib or from her arms. Nothing definitive; perhaps something in the eye socket, perhaps something in the chin, nothing more. She had done the same thing when her brother Gene had dropped in one evening to see the baby. Gene had held him, bent over him, examining, studying, and all the time she was comparing the tiny head and face with Gene's, but again she had found nothing definitive, only now and then a glancing recognition that came into being and was as quickly gone.

"He's his own man," her brother had finally said. "I'll be damned if I can see you in him at all. Does he look like whoever the—?"

"He looks like Gene Gray and nobody else in the whole world."

*   *   *

Dori was like all the rest, Matthew thought, starting with one need, the need for love, for companionship, for sex, and then ending with another, the need for marriage. She

269

didn't plan it, she hadn't it in her to set snares, but it had worked out the same way.

That's right, buddy, blame the other fellow, there you go again. Always the other, never yourself.

He had called her twice more; each time she had said, "Of course, if you want to talk," and he had gone there and she had let him do just that, talk. She had not given him any of the good old stuff about remaining friends, but she had already changed from his Dori into being just Dori, anybody's Dori. She hadn't put on any big madonna act about the baby; he was grateful for that. She scarcely mentioned it at all, except to say she was already telling people she was adopting a baby. She was bringing him home for good next Tuesday.

"Cele's moving his crib and carriage over in the station wagon," she had said. "What I ever would have done without Cele!"

Damn Cele and damn everything. There was no use denying it, at times he even felt, damn the baby, or rather, damn the timing of it, damn the patterns life had followed, damn the schedules and calendars. If it had happened a year later, if it had happened between them, if he had made it happen, the whole story would have been different. Then he would have had to get a divorce; he would never want a child of his brought up without his name and he would have had to get a divorce. By now he would already have had it.

He imagined Joan, listening unbelieving, as he told her he wanted it, and the reason for it. He could see her face, could see Hildy's direct young stare when he told her, see the disbelief and disapproval in her eyes: love and sex at *his* age? Johnny would be the only one on his side. "Wow, Dad, wild." Or would he be?

He was bitter. They were all self-centered, seeing everything their own way, and the hell with putting out any effort to feel what he must be feeling. Even Dori was following her own God-given set of rules; she was through with affairs, she was sick of affairs, she was throwing him out because what they had been having was just an affair and there was no sign from him that it would ever be converted into something more than an affair.

Damn it, the insistence of women. October was coming up; that meant less than a year had passed since they met, and already she had run out of trust, out of patience. She'd rather sit there alone holding the baby—

The split-second image flashed, a woman sitting alone on a sofa, holding a new baby, looking down in silence.

Christ, again! He had been free of it since he had had it out with Dori; now here it was again, a new life for it, a new vitality.

He jumped up, outraged. It was long after midnight and everyone was asleep. Dori was asleep too, or he would call and try once more to make her see that since whatever else she was thinking of was still vague, it might yet prove to be nothing, might fizzle out, might remain vague forever. This time he needed no long period to get things sorted out in his mind; this time he knew at once what was roweling his gut: she had thrown him out, that was it, in the nicest gentlest sort of way, thrown him out. Usually it was he who got out of a relationship when the gears began to grind. Gears had been grinding for months, from the night she had told him about Bob Cox, but he'd had no ear for them.

He should never have let Cox take over on the adoption proceedings, true, but was that anything to hold against him? He should probably never have told her about feeling shut out, or about the damnable world *diminish* and how it crossed half a dozen other lines in his life. He should never have let her hear him phoning Joan to say he wouldn't be home, probably should never even have told her about clearing it with the family that he couldn't make it to Truro over the weekend of the twentieth.

But she had loved him anyway. Nobody was ever better than they were in bed together. Nobody was ever happier than she was when he had come back after the bad time that had strapped him into immobility. And at the end? Had he not been right there to the end, taking her to the hospital, staying up all night and all the next day? If he'd been her own husband out in the hospital corridor—

Playacting. If she called anything playacting that would finish it for her, but there were situations where a little playacting was the only civilized way to manage. Another name for it was tact, diplomacy, even kindness. Dori knew all that, practiced it herself most of the time as any real woman did. But then at other times—God, in the last few months honesty had become an obsession with her. Maybe because she had been living a huge lie and was preparing to live it for the rest of her life.

He felt perceptive to have realized that. It comforted him. There were matters here Dori did not yet comprehend. He could make her see them. Damn it, he would have to make her see them, for he could not bear the idea of giving in to defeat when he wanted her so much.

Behind him a door opened and Joan asked, "Are you okay? Is anything wrong?"

"I'm just reading. I couldn't get to sleep."

"You've been upset lately. I can always tell."

"Nothing special."

"You've been in every night since we got home from Truro."

"I told you, they're painting our offices."

He ought to face her now, ought to stop this playacting now, ought to say, Yes, something is damn wrong, and the only thing that can make it right is to start over and that means leaving all this here and getting a divorce and saying goodbye to this half-dead marriage. He could imagine her face at the words, imagine the scene that would follow.

"I'm going to make some tea," Joan said. "Do you want some?"

He shook his head and watched her go to the kitchen in her nightgown. The words unspoken too long, the words unspoken forever. He put his head down on his arms.

*　　*　　*

The station wagon pulled up at the side entrance to the building and Dori said, "You take him, Cele, and I'll get the back elevator man."

Inside she said, "Joe, could you help me with a couple of pieces of furniture I borrowed for the baby's room?"

"Sure, sure."

She had told Bill the doorman a few days ago, leaving it to him to tend the grapevine, and apparently he had done so, for Joe showed no surprise at seeing the crib, the baby carriage, various small cartons and the lady at the wheel holding a well-wrapped-up baby.

Cele handed the baby back to her and they went up the back elevator with the furniture. In the elevator Joe said, "How old is it?" and Dori said, "Ten days, no, eleven," in a voice that held no smallest quaver.

"Boy or girl?"

"Boy. Oh here we are. Cele, have you a dollar?"

Once inside and alone Cele said, "I wouldn't trust you around the corner, madam," and Dori said, "Thank you for the compliment. I hope the room won't seem too small with the crib in it."

The fourth room in her apartment must originally have been intended as a maid's room since it was an old building, erected in the thirties when nearly all good East Side apartments had built-in maids' rooms, but by a quirk in the architecture, caused by the setback and terrace on the floor below, it was about two feet wider than the usual cell-like space and Dori had always used it as a "guest room for one." A narrow bed, narrower than twin-size but well made and prettily covered, a small dresser and a single chair were all the furniture it contained, but a plaid rug and plaid curtains made it bright and appealing. The miniature bathroom with a tub one could not stretch out in was pretty too, and Dori had measured off the space for the crib with minute care, finding that it would fit easily if one did not mind a bathroom door that would swing open only half its normal arc.

"It goes in my room for now, Joe," she said as he came in

273

with the crib. "He's going in with me until I can get a maid. And better leave the carriage in my front hall."

"There's a carriage room downstairs, alongside the package room."

"Is there? Good, I'll have to find out about things, won't I?"

Joe said, "Sure, sure," pocketed his dollar tip and left.

"Not around the corner," Cele repeated and this time Dori laughed. For the first time she freed the baby from the shielding blanket, held him high up, not forgetting to prop the small head with her entire left hand, but holding him at eye level so that they were face to face. "We're home," she said. "Did you ever think we'd make it?"

* * *

Two days later the phone rang, and without preamble Cele said, "Dr. Jesskin isn't a widower, and she's not 'conveniently dead.' She's remarried and her name is Summerfield and she lives in Washington—state of, not D.C."

"How do you know?"

"I did what you were too decent to do—I up and asked, and kept on asking."

"Asked whom?"

"Asked everybody, everywhere I went, until I got me an answer."

"From whom?"

"Dr. Baum. Ben Baum, your pediatrician and mine. I should have tried him right off. Every pediatrician in New York knows Dr. Jesskin, or has Jesskin babies for patients. And Ben Baum's been our friend for most of the sixteen years he's been the kids' doctor, so finally I just asked him as gossip, and he told me, as gossip. It's no secret anyway."

"Oh Cele—"

"They were divorced eight or ten years ago. She couldn't stand his hours, the night calls, all that. So they got a divorce." Dori started to speak but Cele interrupted. "Remember what I told you, that time you got sore? Decent men get divorces too, not just rats."

274

"Oh Cele."

"His children were teen-agers then," she went on dryly, "but they seem to have survived. They each got married about a year ago."

"Did Dr. Baum know how they feel toward their father?"

"Like any young marrieds, I gathered. But Ben did know one more piece of family stuff. Long ago, Dr. Jesskin's sister met his friend Bob Cox at some Harvard regatta and they married a year later. So maybe it's her picture on his desk.

"Oh Cele—"

"You're not being too bright today, Dorr. Your conversation isn't, anyway. Suppose you call me back when you can produce more than 'Oh Cele.'"

"All right."

She stood there clutching the phone after Cele had clicked off. Some tactile memory, apparently in her palm, told her that once, a long time ago, she had kept on gripping the crossbar of this very telephone receiver, gripping it after she had put it back into its cradle, as if at a lever to propel herself into action. She had wanted to just stay there, silent, commanding her mind not to leap ahead, but she had failed and had remained there yielding to her mind's rebellion until the clock had reminded her she had to dress for a concert.

It was that first call she had made to Miss Mack, asking for a special appointment, that's what it was, and she had held on and on, not wanting to break the thread that might connect the glimpse in the mirror to something more than an illusion.

Now again she was holding a thread that might connect a first glimpse to something more. Not that there had been any illusion. He had said all those carefully selected words, and she had heard them, and, when she had finally let herself, had understood them. She had tried not to think too much of them since then, but they had kept speaking to her at odd times, always with the picture of their speaker, standing there at his desk, tall, too thin, his color rising.

275

"Emotionally preoccupied," he had said. He had remained silent since then, as she had known he would. He was no man of sudden compulsions, he knew life took time to grow and develop, he was giving it time. He was giving her time.

He would wait until she managed some sort of signal. There would be no flowers from him, no note under the door, no telephone calls. He would wait. And she had to wait too. Wait through the fall, perhaps through the winter. She had to get through the guilt that sometimes took her when she thought about Matthew. Guilt? Guilt that she finally had come to ask more of living than she used to ask?

Emotionally preoccupied. If Dr. Jesskin loved anybody with a baby, she thought half angrily, he would marry her and adopt that baby, not just be a father figure to it.

Eugene Cornelius Jesskin—oh God, more daydreaming. But sometimes daydreaming was *for* something. To show the way, to get you ready, to see if you were certain.

The one thing he couldn't be certain about, he had said, was "whether it was all at once there or whether it had been a long time developing." Everything else was clear but not that.

A long time developing? Probably for her it had been a long time developing too, long before the *remarkable patient.* Long long before had she not sat in his office and thought, He is so good and kind I really love him? She had meant it as a patient means it, a synonym for gratitude, a recognition of kindness and human response to a problem. But she had felt it and now, suddenly, was remembering it.

The fall, perhaps the winter. In January the baby would be six months old. Another milestone, a major not a minor. A half year since that night he was born.

Dear Dr. Jesskin, My baby is half a year old—As if she were already writing them, the words took tangible shape on some tablet in her mind, clear and warm, as if there were a sun shining upon them. *And since you haven't seen him since his first week, I wonder if you'd like to come and see him now that he has reached this immense age. He would*

276

welcome you and so would I. Always gratefully, Dori Gray.
She ought to write it down; she liked the tone of it. But she did not move toward her desk. She saw that she was still gripping the crossbar of the telephone receiver and slowly moved her hand away, stretching her fingers, opening out her palm. She didn't have to write anything down. When the time finally came, words wouldn't really matter.